P9-CED-074

Wes couldn't fall asleep.

He kept seeing Taylor's eyes, and the firelight on her face. And lying there alone, in the dark, his thoughts turned from hearts and flowers and—God, help him—babies, to things of a more earthy nature. His mind wandered where it damned well shouldn't, so that every time he came close to drifting off to sleep, he started to dream of what she would look like with all that hair hanging loose over her shoulders instead of bundled up in back the way she wore it. He started to wonder what she would feel like naked and twined around him, and what kinds of sounds she would make, and what her mouth might taste like, and...

And then he would be wide-awake again, and aching. And wondering just when any man had been hit as hard and as fast as she'd hit him....

Dear Reader,

With the coming of fall, the days—and nights—are getting cooler, but you can heat them up again with this month's selections from Silhouette Intimate Moments. Award winner Justine Davis is back with the latest installment in her popular TRINITY STREET WEST miniseries, *A Man To Trust*. Hero Cruz Gregerson proves himself to be just that—though it takes heroine Kelsey Hall a little time to see it. Add a pregnant runaway, a mighty cute kid and an opportunely appearing snake (yes, I said "snake"!), and you have a book to cherish forever.

With *Baby by Design,* award-winning Paula Detmer Riggs concludes her MATERNITY ROW trilogy. Pregnant-with-twins Raine Paxton certainly isn't expecting a visit from her ex-husband, Morgan—and neither one of them is expecting the sensuous fireworks that come next! Miniseries madness continues with *Roarke's Wife,* the latest in Beverly Barton's THE PROTECTORS, and Maggie Shayne's *Badlands Bad Boy,* the newest in THE TEXAS BRAND. Both of these miniseries will be going on for a while—and if you haven't discovered them already, you'll certainly want to come along for the ride. Then turn to Marie Ferrarella's *Serena McKee's Back in Town* for a reunion romance with heart-stopping impact. Finally there's Cheryl St.John's second book for the line, *The Truth About Toby,* a moving story about how dreams can literally come true.

Here at Intimate Moments, we pride ourselves on bringing you books that represent the best in romance fiction, so I hope you'll enjoy every one of this month's selections, then join us again next month, when the excitement—and the passion—continue.

Yours,

Leslie J. Wainger
Senior Editor and Editorial Coordinator

Please address questions and book requests to:
Silhouette Reader Service
U.S.: 3010 Walden Ave., P.O. Box 1325, Buffalo, NY 14269
Canadian: P.O. Box 609, Fort Erie, Ont. L2A 5X3

BADLANDS
BAD BOY

MAGGIE SHAYNE

INTIMATE™MOMENTS®

Published by Silhouette Books

America's Publisher of Contemporary Romance

If you purchased this book without a cover you should be aware
that this book is stolen property. It was reported as "unsold and
destroyed" to the publisher, and neither the author nor the
publisher has received any payment for this "stripped book."

 SILHOUETTE BOOKS

ISBN 0-373-07809-9

BADLANDS BAD BOY

Copyright © 1997 by Margaret Benson

All rights reserved. Except for use in any review, the reproduction
or utilization of this work in whole or in part in any form by any
electronic, mechanical or other means, now known or hereafter
invented, including xerography, photocopying and recording, or in
any information storage or retrieval system, is forbidden without
the written permission of the editorial office, Silhouette Books,
300 East 42nd Street, New York, NY 10017 U.S.A.

All characters in this book have no existence outside the imagination of
the author and have no relation whatsoever to anyone bearing the same
name or names. They are not even distantly inspired by any individual
known or unknown to the author, and all incidents are pure invention.

This edition published by arrangement with Harlequin Books S.A.

® and TM are trademarks of Harlequin Books S.A., used under license.
Trademarks indicated with ® are registered in the United States Patent
and Trademark Office, the Canadian Trade Marks Office and in other
countries.

Printed in U.S.A.

Books by Maggie Shayne

Silhouette Intimate Moments

Reckless Angel #522
Miranda's Viking #568
Forgotten Vows...? #598
Out-of-This-World Marriage #633
Forever, Dad #694
*The Littlest Cowboy #716
*The Baddest Virgin in Texas #788
*Badlands Bad Boy #809

Silhouette Shadows

†*Twilight Phantasies* #18
†*Twilight Memories* #30
Kiss of the Shadow Man #38
†*Twilight Illusions* #47

*The Texas Brand
†Wings in the Night

Silhouette Books

Strangers in the Night
†"Beyond Twilight"

Silhouette Single Title

†*Born in Twilight*

Fortune's Children

A Husband in Time #7

MAGGIE SHAYNE,

a national bestselling author whom *Romantic Times* magazine calls "brilliantly inventive," has written fourteen novels for Silhouette. Her Silhouette single-title release, *Born in Twilight* (3/97), was based on her popular vampire series for Shadows, Wings in the Night.

Maggie has won numerous awards, including a *Romantic Times* magazine Career Achievement Award. A three-time finalist for the Romance Writers of America's prestigious RITA Award, Maggie also writes mainstream contemporary fantasy.

In her spare time, Maggie enjoys collecting gemstones, reading tarot cards, hanging out on the Genie computer network and spending time outdoors. She lives in a rural town in central New York with her husband, Rick, five beautiful daughters and a bulldog named Wrinkles.

Chapter 1

Not so long ago Emerald Flat, this very spot, had been littered with painted tepees. On a clear, hot night like tonight, there probably would have been a huge fire in the center of the village. And men and women...even children, decked out in beaded ceremonial garb, would have been dancing in time with the steady throb of deep-voiced drums.

The vision was so vivid that for a second Taylor thought she could hear them. A drumbeat so faint it might have been imaginary. Or perhaps not. A flash of color in the distance, where the edges of this haven reached their green fingers out into the desert. And then another flicker, barely visible in the night. Animals? Birds?

Dancers?

Taylor McCoy rubbed her eyes, admitting it was probably nothing more than too many sleepless nights and a vivid imagination. Those things, and a little help from that old man who kept showing up. Turtle, he called himself. Said he was a Comanche shaman, and that it was his duty to observe her progress on the dig.

Funny that none of the tribal elders she'd spoken to had mentioned him. And neither had Dennis Hawthorne, the money behind the project. And the old fellow seemed more interested in telling stories late at night than in the progress—or lack of it—on the dig. Stories she'd rather not hear, and avoided listening to whenever possible.

No, none of her ancestors' ghosts were dancing in the desert tonight. And there were no beaded loincloths or painted tepees on the site. Tonight, and for the past two weeks, the oblong piece of Texas wildland that seemed to sit as a divider between the desert and the rest of the world was littered not with tepees, but with three modern dome tents. Instead of a central fire, there were a handful of portable cookstoves and Coleman lanterns. Sleeping bags instead of tanned hides. Boilable bags of dehydrated food instead of freshly killed game. ATVs instead of painted ponies.

Still it didn't seem to Taylor as if it had really been all that long.

Taylor sat down in the scraggly grass in front of her tent. A gas lantern hanging from a nearby tree bathed the area in white light nearly as bright as that back in her apartment in Dallas. Her temporary apartment. All her homes were temporary ones.

She picked a triangular piece of pottery from the box-ful of bits the team had recovered today, and reached for the soft-bristled brush. Team. She grimaced at the word. Some team. Two grad students and one out-of-work archaeologist. The local big shot funding this dig wasn't exactly generous with his money. Or with time. But since she'd been between jobs when the offer came in, she'd had little practical choice but to accept.

As she gently, reverently whisked the dirt away from the clay, she wondered about the hands that had formed it. She wondered about the person attached to those hands. A woman, more than likely. Had she been old, or young? A mother? A grandmother? A young girl in love?

Taylor drew the piece closer to examine the design, absently humming, and then singing very softly. Barely aware of the words she was using. Comanche words, from an age-old Comanche love song. Kelly and Scourge had retired into the haven of their dome tents, zipper doors sealed up for the night. She sat all alone as she studied the bits of the past dug up today. It was her favorite time here. The silence, broken only by the occasional hum or chirp of an insect or the sudden flutter of a night bird's wings. There had never been enough time for silence in her life. And sitting here surrounded by it, she thought this was exactly how it must have been in this spot centuries ago.

She hadn't wanted to come here. In her career she'd excavated countless Native American sites, but never one belonging to the Comanches. And she wasn't even fully certain why. Fear, maybe. Fear of discovering a people and a past she'd been isolated from for all her life. Of connecting to it...of connecting to anything, really.

During her last dig she'd been working for a university—last semester in Dallas, that had been. No tenure. Temporary position—her students had referred to her as Solitary McCoy. Behind her back, of course. She supposed she'd earned the nickname. It had made her wonder why she'd become as isolated—as lonely—as she had.

The nicker of a horse brought Taylor back to herself with a jolt. Her head shot up, her eyes narrowing as she tried to make out the form in the distance, there on the barren ground just beyond the place where the grass gradually ended.

Her fingers went stiff, and the pottery piece fell into the brittle grass as Taylor slowly rose to her feet. A magnificent horse danced and pawed where the desert began. A dark horse, with a dark rider.

The unnaturally bright light of the gas lantern hanging beside her made it impossible to see details of the man and his horse in the darkness. She could only see that the rider was bare chested, and that long tendrils of dark hair snapped like flags when the wind lifted them. The horse reared on its hind legs, and she realized the man was bare legged, as well. And wore…perhaps…a loincloth and little else.

A chill crept up her nape, and a whisper of the ghosts she'd been thinking about—and the one she'd thought she'd seen just before making the decision to come here—danced through her mind. She stood a little straighter, fought her own silly imagination. This was no ghost.

"Who is that?" she called, nervously brushing the loose grass and twigs from the seat of her pants. "What do you want?"

He sat exactly as he'd been, his hair dancing in the breeze. And she realized with a small shiver that there had been no breeze a moment ago. None that she could feel, anyway. She reached for the lamp to turn it off.

And then he spoke, and her hand froze in midair. The depth and power of his voice made her shiver. "You desecrate sacred ground, Taylor McCoy."

She was trembling now, for no good reason. Who in the name of God was the man? "You're mistaken," she shouted. She forced herself to move, reached for the lamp, but instead of shutting it off she lifted it, held it high and out in front of her as if she could see his face by doing so. Naturally she couldn't. "I don't work that way. Look, I was hired to determine whether there is a sacred site here—at the request of the Comanches who own this land."

"Do you not hear them?" he said very softly, so softly she was surprised his words reached her ears from where he was.

"Hear...who?"

"The great shamans of the past! They scream in outrage."

"But—"

"There *is* sacred ground here, woman, but not for your prying eyes to find." Again the horse reared up.

She shivered, fought it. Heard the rustling coming from the other two tents, knew she wasn't alone. No reason to be afraid. Besides, she didn't believe in ghosts.

Then why have I seen two in one week?

"Why don't you stop behaving like a lunatic and talk to me about your concerns? You can start by telling me who you—"

"Wolf Shadow explains himself to no one!"

"But—"

"Aiieeeeeeee!" His war cry split the night, and as he uttered it, he lifted a war lance high above his head, holding it tight in his clenched fist, the feathers dancing in that breeze she couldn't feel. "Leave here, woman, while you can!"

The rustling sounds from the other tents changed to more-urgent noises as her assistants jolted to life. But by the time Scourge and Kelly came shooting out of their tents, he was gone. The horse had galloped off at the speed of light, and she belatedly realized she couldn't even hear the hoofbeats.

Taylor blinked and shook her head slowly. "What the hell was that?"

Scourge shook his head, scanning the horizon while Kelly rubbed an apparent chill away from her arms and came closer.

A gnarled hand fell on Taylor's shoulder, and she nearly jumped out of her skin as she whirled. Turtle. She hadn't even known he was still here. "God, you scared me half to death!"

He only smiled. "Your young helpers want to hear the tales of your people, Sky Dancer. Even if you do not."

Sky Dancer. He'd been calling her that since the first day he showed up here, uninvited. Said a Comanche woman needed a Comanche name, even if she did deny her heritage.

She bristled at his insistence on addressing her that way, but there were more-important things to do here than argue with an old man.

"What happened, Ms. McCoy?" Kelly asked. "We heard—"

"Are you all right?" Scourge came closer, twelve years her junior and nursing a bad crush, she suspected. She shook herself and tried not to look quite so terrified. Even if he cut that neon yellow dust mop and dumped the nose ring, she wouldn't want him playing hero to her damsel in distress. She was quite capable of being her own savior, thanks.

More calmly she asked, "Did you see him?" And she couldn't help looking toward where the horse and rider had been.

All three of her companions turned to follow her gaze.

"No," Turtle said softly.

"Did anyone else see him?" She faced Kelly, then Scourge, hoping against hope. But it was silly to doubt herself like this, silly to need confirmation of what she'd seen with her two perfectly good eyes. Just because she'd awakened to soft sobbing one morning, opened hazy eyes to see a beautiful young Comanche woman silhouetted in morning sunlight near her bedroom window—a woman who'd faded as soon as Taylor rubbed her eyes—that was no reason to think she was suddenly prone to hallucinations.

And just because the phone had rung seconds later with this particular job offer didn't mean one event had a thing to do with the other.

Or with this latest…apparition.

Turtle's gnarled hand returned gently to Taylor's shoulder. "You did not imagine him, Sky Dancer. We all heard his cry." It was as if he could read her thoughts.

"You heard him?" she asked, searching Turtle's crinkled face, probing the faded eyes that resembled worn black denim.

He nodded hard, so hard his steel gray hair fell forward, so he had to push it away from his face. "Wolf Shadow. Legend says he appears still, to keep the sacred grounds of The People from desecration. To keep the place where his lover lies beneath the earth from the touch of any outsider."

Taylor grabbed his arm, remembered his age and gentled her grip. "Turtle, your tribal elders assured me they believe this site was an ordinary Comanche village. Even if it is older than anything excavated to date, it shouldn't be considered sacred ground."

"The legend tells you otherwise," Turtle said slowly.

Taylor sighed hard. "But that's why they brought me here. To find out which is true."

And again he nodded. His movements were always slow, so deliberate they were almost graceful, so that when he nodded, his head bobbed like a rubber ball floating in gentle waves.

"If you find no evidence that the legend is true, they will sell this land to Hawthorne."

"Because they desperately need the money that sale will bring," she said quickly, and then wondered why she sounded defensive. Why should she? It wasn't her decision. She had nothing to do with it.

"But if you find the evidence, if you dig the past from the earth, it will no longer *be* sacred ground."

She shook her head, exasperated. "You're making this thing sound like some kind of Zen riddle."

He shrugged and got that look on his face. The thoughtful one he got sometimes just before blurting something deep. "The legend says that if this place is preserved, treated with honor, its magic will ensure the prosperity of The People."

"Yeah, well it hasn't done that so far, has it? I saw the community where your people—"

"Correction, Sky Dancer," he interrupted. "*Our* people."

"Fine. Whatever. I've seen where they're living. The school isn't even safe, let alone conducive to learning. The houses are in disrepair. I don't blame the elders a bit for wanting to take Hawthorne's offer on this land. And if I don't find anything to indicate it's some kind of sacred place to them, they'll be free to do it."

"And if you do, Sky Dancer? You have your clearance from the state. You are within your rights under the law to be here. You have the permission of the tribe. Hawthorne is paying you to dig up this ground. He hopes you'll find nothing here, because he wishes to own it. And the elders hope you'll find nothing here, because they wish to sell it. These motives are selfish. But what if it *is* sacred ground? Would it even matter to you, a woman who has turned her back on her—?''

"Don't you dare say that to me." She faced him suddenly, ignoring the two young people who stared as if transfixed by this exchange. But Turtle's solemn eyes held no malice. And they practically dared her to deny what he'd said. And of course, she couldn't. But she hadn't turned her back on anyone or anything. She'd simply been raised white, by loving parents who'd lied to her with nearly every breath. She'd had no connection to her heritage, and now that she was grown she didn't want or need one.

"Would it matter?" he asked her again.

"Of course it would matter," she snapped. And then he smiled serenely at her, closed his eyes, gave a single, slow nod that made her think he looked remarkably like his namesake.

"It would matter, Turtle, but only *if* I found legitimate evidence of it. I'm *not* going to be scared off by some jerk in full costume trying to make me believe he's a ghost.''

Turtle's eyes opened again, looking worried. "Then...you don't believe in Wolf Shadow?"

She blinked, and tried to soften her expression. She'd been filled in about this local legend, even before Turtle had told it to her. Wolf Shadow was a Comanche shaman of incredible power. He'd fallen in love with Little Sparrow, daughter of a chief, and—in Turtle's version at least—a woman of such beauty it weakened a man's heart to look upon her. But before the two became one according to tribal custom, there was a raid on the village. Horse soldiers attacked in retaliation for some wrong they blamed on whatever Indian village was handy and nearby. And Little Sparrow was killed in that raid.

The legend went that Wolf Shadow carried her body to the spot where he had first kissed her. Where he'd given her a pendant he'd made with his own hands, and where he'd asked her to be his woman. He'd buried her there. It was said Wolf Shadow blessed the earth in which she rested, and called on the shamans of his village to protect that spot. He promised that if they did this, prosperity would rain down on their descendants. And then he shed his ceremonial garb and put on the clothes of a warrior. He left the village to avenge Little Sparrow's death, and spent the rest of his days seeking out the soldiers who had raided the village that day, and killing them, one by one. The whites put a price on Wolf Shadow's head, and he was killed a few years later, though no one knew what had been done with his remains.

Turtle claimed the spirits of Little Sparrow and Wolf Shadow were still not at peace. That because she was taken before the two became one, their spirits wandered endlessly, each searching for the other. And that only when one of Wolf Shadow's descendants found true love with one of Little Sparrow's would the two ancient lovers be reunited and know peace.

Taylor had heard the tale from the elders, as well as from Turtle—him giving the more romantically embellished version. Believing it, of course, was another matter. But Turtle was asking her again.

"Do you, Sky Dancer? Do you believe in Wolf Shadow? In the legend?"

She drew a breath. Looked sideways at Kelly, who seemed to have set Taylor up as some kind of role model, a position Taylor didn't ask for or feel comfortable in. And at Scourge, ready to jump should she crook a finger. It wouldn't do either of them any good to hear her put some silly legend ahead of the important work she was doing. Nor would it help them much to hear her, a scientist, admit she believed in ghosts.

She didn't.

"I didn't say that I *don't* believe in the legend, Turtle. I said I don't believe *that* was Wolf Shadow." She narrowed her eyes, searched Turtle's face. "Have you ever seen this ghostly rider, Turtle? Would you know what he looks like?"

Turtle shook his head slowly, then tilted it and studied her face as he spoke. Watching her a little too intently. "I am told he is a man so beautiful that the mere sight of him has weakened the hearts of many a woman. That his eyes are piercing and sharp, and his body as strong as that of his spirit brother, the wolf." He slanted her a sideways glance. "Was that how he looked to you?"

Kelly's soft sigh drew Taylor's gaze. The young woman lifted her brows and breathed, "Was it?"

Taylor thought of the powerful form she'd glimpsed, the black hair waving in the breeze. She licked her lips. "It seems a bit of an exaggerated description to me."

"He *wasn't* attractive to you, then?" Turtle asked.

"Well, I wouldn't say he was *un*attractive."

"Hmm." Turtle rubbed his chin. "It is said that Wolf Shadow appears only to the person in need of his warnings, Sky Dancer. He appeared tonight, only to you."

"Yeah, well, he'll think twice about pulling any more of this nonsense when I talk to the sheriff tomorrow."

"Good idea," Scourge said a little too quickly. "And I'll start keeping watch at night, outside your tent, if you—"

Kelly's elbow jabbed him in the rib cage. Scourge grunted, then shot her a confused glance. "What?"

"Subtle, Scourge," she said. "Real subtle."

His face reddened, and he averted his gaze.

Turtle smiled very slowly. "Talking to the sheriff is a good idea," he said. "Garrett Brand is a good man. He will help you if he can."

Taylor frowned. "If he can? What's that supposed to mean?"

"I must go, Sky Dancer. Sleep now. Perhaps your dreams know the answers."

Turtle turned and loped off into the darkness, in the opposite direction from the one the alleged Wolf Shadow had taken. And not for the first time, Taylor marveled at his agility and grace.

Then she brought her attention back to the matter at hand. Someone didn't want her completing this dig. Someone with an incredible chest and a pair of muscled thighs that looked pretty good clenched tight around a horse. At least...as far as she could tell, it being so dark and all.

The question was, why?

"Never again," Wes growled as he kicked the horse into a gentle lope. "Never, *ever* again!" He rode away from that little camp out into the desert, then slowed the horse to a walk and turned to head back—the long way around. He skirted the site unseen, and reentered it on the lower side where he was shielded from sight by a small copse of trees. Once he got to the water hole he dismounted, and let his horse—scratch that, his *brother's* horse—take his fill of water. Lord help him if Garrett ever found out he'd "borrowed" Duke, much less *why*.

Wes sighed hard, hunkered down and scooped handfuls of chilled water onto his face, rubbing hard to scrub the ridiculous makeup off. It took some doing, and every few minutes a bird would flit from a tree, making enough noise to jolt him right to his toes thinking someone was coming up on him, about to catch him red-handed.

Eventually his face felt clean, and Wes felt a little less like a kid on Halloween. He tied his hair back in its usual style, with a thong. He hadn't cut it since he'd got out of prison. Probably never would. One more way of thumbing his nose at the conventions of society, he figured.

He changed clothes next. And when he was finally rid of the entire getup, he rolled up the loincloth and stuffed it into the duffel bag he'd left hidden here.

Finished, he tucked the war lance and the duffel bag full of makeup and his skimpy costume into their hiding place—the small cave near the east end of the pond. Then he mounted up and rode around the lower side of the dig area, giving it a wide berth, and heading down toward the dirt road below and his friend's place. He had every intention of strangling the old coot.

This was a bad idea. Worst idea he'd ever let himself get talked into. Worse even than going out drinking with that band of rowdies who'd pulled a holdup after he'd left them, and then let him take the rap along with them.

Well, he'd tried it. It hadn't worked. That Dr. McCoy woman hadn't seemed the least bit afraid of his Wolf Shadow routine. The dig was going to go on, and there wasn't a damned thing Wes could do to stop it. And just because over the past year he'd let himself get closer to that old man than he'd ever been to anyone, didn't mean he had to go painting himself up and parading around half-naked for him. It was damned humiliating.

He emerged onto the deserted dirt lane and rode along its edge, the horse's hooves kicking up a slight dust in his wake. And as they rode, he remembered the first time he'd met the old Indian who claimed to be a Comanche shaman. The fellow had been sitting along the roadside in a battered pickup that looked to be rustier and less dependable than Wes's baby sister's was. And that was saying something. Just sitting there. As Wes had driven past, he'd seen the flat tire, and glanced again at the leathery face of the man inside. A twinge of conscience, and he'd stopped to offer a hand changing the tire.

That had been the beginning. Just a coincidence, Wes had said. But the old nut—Turtle, he called himself—had said there was no such thing as coincidence. That he'd been waiting for Wes for quite some time. And since he seemed so in need of a friend, Wes had visited with him for a while. And then he'd gone back.

That was probably the mistake, right there. He never should have gone back.

The mobile home came into sight, looking old and shabby. Pickup truck drooping in the driveway as if it might shed a part or two if they got much heavier. The circular area in the middle of the lawn was blackened and littered with cinders and partially burned lumps of wood. Nearby, a metal barrel with the top cut out of it brimmed with beer cans, the cumulative results of all their nights together around a campfire, sipping a cold one while Turtle told those stories. All told, the beer cans were the only things in sight that weren't rusted.

Wes tied the horse up out back and walked inside without knocking.

But his anger faded when he caught sight of Turtle lying on the sagging couch, his face flushed and tiny beads of perspiration clinging to his brow. Wes frowned and leaned forward to press a hand to Turtle's face. He felt heat there.

"You're feverish, pal. What is it? Are you getting worse?"

Turtle closed his serene eyes, shook his head. "Tell me about your mission, Raven Eyes. Were you successful?"

Wes sighed, rolling his eyes heavenward. "Yeah, I was successful, all right. Successful in making a complete fool outta myself. Dammit, Turtle, I told you this would never work. I must've been nuts to let you talk me into prancing around half-naked and whooping it up like a goldern coyote! That professor woman wasn't any more scared of me than a grizzly bear would've been. And I can tell you right now, there is no way in hell I'm ever going to do anything so stupid again. No way in—"

"You saw her, then?"

Wes bit off his words, and recalled her sitting there on the ground in the lamplight. Jet hair pulled back in a tight little knot, except for the few strands that had escaped. Huge dark eyes glowing. He'd had a good look at her, there in that pool of white light. "Yeah. I saw her."

"And?"

"And what? I was surprised, I suppose. I didn't expect someone named McCoy to look…"

"Like us?" Turtle asked.

Wes nodded and searched Turtle's face. "How'd you know that?"

Turtle only shrugged. "I'm a shaman. I know things. She is Comanche, though not raised as one. Is she beautiful?"

Wes thought about her eyes, flashing like onyx in the glow of the lamplight. Her stance straightening and her small chin lifting as she challenged him. "Yeah, I suppose you could call her beautiful. Though what that has to do with any of this, I don't—"

Turtle groaned softly, and Wes's words came to a stop.

"This is crazy," he said, but his voice was softer now.

"Dammit, Turtle, you're not going to die just because somebody digs up some old dirt. It's ridiculous!"

But he was worried. The old man was obviously slipping. And maybe the fact that he *believed* this would kill him could make it actually happen. For crying out loud, he was as hot and sticky right now as if he'd just run a footrace.

"Look, there has to be another way."

Turtle shook his head. "I have told you, Raven Eyes, I am the last shaman of my clan. A small bit of that land was sacred to the shamans of my line. We were sworn to protect it. If it is violated, I will die."

Wes shook his head. "The McCoy woman doesn't seem to believe any of that. And the state of Texas must not, either, or they'd have at least objected. Hell, Turtle, even the Comanche people haven't raised a stink about this dig—"

"The sacred place is there," Turtle insisted. "She must believe it is there, and convince The People not to sell to this Hawthorne. But she must believe it without finding it, without violating it, or its magic will be lost."

"But why don't the tribal elders know more about it, if it's so damned important? Why don't they know—?"

"The secret of that place was handed down through the shamans of my clan. And of those, Raven Eyes, I am the only one left. I alone know where Little Sparrow lies. You must stop the woman from disturbing that ground, or…"

"Or?"

Turtle closed his eyes and shook his head slowly. "It is good that we found one another when we did," he said. "All the time we had, to sit beside the fire outside while I told you the stories of your people and your heritage. It was good. We had a good year together, didn't we, my friend?''

Wes closed his eyes and thought, Here we go again.

"When my time comes, I will gather all I need and go out into the desert. And there I'll wait for the Great Spirit to take me...."

"No. Dammit, Turtle, no, you're not gonna do that. You do, and I promise I'll ride out there and find you, and I'll haul your butt right back here. You understand?"

Turtle met Wes's eyes. "If the sacred ground of my people is violated, then—"

Wes yanked his hat off the rack and slammed it down on his head. "Your sacred ground isn't gonna be violated, all right? I'll see to it."

"But you said..."

"I said I'd see to it and I will. And while I'm at it, I'm gonna see about having you looked at by a doctor. And I don't want any damned arguments about that, either, you stubborn goat."

Turtle sighed in misery, but nodded. "You are a good friend to me, Wes Brand."

"Yeah, and you're a pain in the backside." He looked back and sighed. "Anything I can get for you before I go? Maybe you should eat something. Or..."

"Go. Your brothers need you at the ranch. Go on. I will sleep. I'm very tired, you know."

Grimacing, Wes reached for the blanket on the back of the couch, and tried to feign carelessness as he draped it over Turtle's old body and tucked it around him. He was worried. Damn, he'd never seen Turtle looking this fragile and weak. Was the old man really going to will himself to die just because of this dig?

Wes took a long look at the man who had become

more than a friend to him. Then he shook his head and left for the night.

When Turtle heard the receding hoofbeats and knew Wes had gone, he flung the blanket back and pulled the remote control out from under the couch cushion. He could still catch the last quarter of the football game. As the screen lit up, he headed into the small kitchen, opened the fridge and pulled out a can of beer and a slice of cold pizza. Then he strode back to the couch, whistling the "Monday Night Football" theme song.

His plan was unorthodox, to say the least. But he had promises to keep. One promise in particular, made to a wonderful woman as she lay dying a very long time ago. Beyond that, he had an ancient mission to fulfill. Keep the sacred spot safe, and yet keep The People from selling it. And make sure the rest of Wolf Shadow's legend came full circle. As the last shaman of his clan, it was all up to him. He'd lived for 107 years. And he knew full well why he'd been allowed such a long life. For this. All for this.

He took a big bite of cold pizza, leaned back on the couch and watched the Dallas Cowboys begin one of their famous fourth-quarter comebacks.

Chapter 2

"Hey, Wes. You're up early."

Wes was halfway out the screen door onto the front porch of the Texas Brand when his baby sister's voice put an automatic smile on his face. She was sitting all alone on the porch swing, looking kinda somber, he thought as he looked her over. And he felt his smile die slowly as he moved toward her. She got up to greet him with a bear hug.

He squeezed her tight, then stood back a little so he could see her. "What're you doing here this early in the morning, Jessi?"

"Gee, I thought you'd be glad to see me." She thrust her lower lip out and gave him her best puppy-dog eyes.

"Well, I am. Hell, we miss you like crazy around here since you moved out. Only see you—what—two, three times a day?"

She punched him in the shoulder. "Just 'cause we have

our own place doesn't mean I gave this one up, you big lug.''

"It had better not," he told her. But he got serious again in a hurry. "So, what's going on? You usually wait till we're at least awake and at the breakfast table to visit. Is little Maria okay?''

"The baby's fine, Wes. And—''

"So it's Lash, then. If he's giving you grief, little sister, just say the word and I'll—''

"Wes, for crying out loud, you won't do anything! Lash is fabulous, the best husband I could even imagine. Gosh, you've seen the way he spoils Maria-Michele, and he's almost as bad with me.''

Wes searched her eyes, decided she was telling the truth and shrugged. "So, then what're you doing here so early?''

She turned toward the horizon and smiled very gently. "I just had a hankerin' to see the sunrise from this porch swing like I used to, is all. It's silly, me being only a few miles away and still getting so darned homesick.''

"Yeah," he said, and he followed her gaze to where the red-orange sun painted the sky with fire so it looked like an abstract painting of yellows and golds and reds instead of the blue it would be later on. "I guess I understand that. This place…it gets into your blood.'' And for just a moment he thought maybe he knew why Turtle might be reacting so badly to having the land of his forebears invaded by outsiders. "I'm gonna miss it, too.''

She looked at him sharply. "You goin' somewhere, Wes?''

He smiled at her. "Not far, kiddo. Not far. I hadn't mentioned this to anyone yet, but I'm thinking about buying the old Cumberland place.''

"Over near where those scientists are digging up the

Comanche village?'' Her brows rose high, eyes wide but interested. "But, Wes, that place is falling down. It's not even livable.''

"Not now. But it's smack in the middle of some of the finest grazing pastures north of the Rio Grande, kid. The land is perfect. The house and barn...well, they can be fixed up. And the price is gonna be low, I can almost guarantee it.''

"You mean you don't know what they want for it?''

"State took possession for back taxes," he said. "The place was abandoned for years even before that. The suits just got around to making their minds up to auction it off and cut their losses. I already talked to the bank. I'm putting a bid in today.''

"Oh.'' She tilted her head to one side. "You gonna run cattle?''

"Nope," he said, and he pushed his Stetson back a little. "Horses. Appaloosas. Gonna start out with a few head, and breed the best horses to be found.''

She grinned up at him suddenly. "You'll do it, too.''

"Damned straight I will," he said. And he didn't tell her that part of the reason he wanted this particular place was that he knew his ancestors had once lived on its lands. Hunted there. Fought and even died there. Funny how his Comanche blood had never mattered much to him before. Not until he'd met Turtle. The old man had a way of making the stories come alive, and of relating them to Wes personally.

"So, you gonna tell me why you're up so early?''

He shrugged, not telling her he was eager to check in on his aging friend this morning. He hadn't confided to his family about Turtle. Not yet. He didn't know why, except that it was a little too personal right now, the things he was learning, the things he was feeling. "Just wanted to get an early start on the chores, kid. You wanna give me a hand?''

"Just like old times?'' she said with a grin. "Sure. That husband of mine can handle the baby just fine for a while.''

Wes searched her eyes and gave a slow nod. His sister looked happy. Really happy.

She'd better be, or her husband would have him to answer to.

They headed out to the barns together, but stopped short when a khaki-colored Jeep bounced into sight, rolling under the arching Texas Brand over the driveway and raising a heck of a dust cloud.

He and Jessi turned as one when the Jeep came to a stop and its driver's door opened. And then *she* got out, and Wes almost choked on his next breath. Taylor McCoy. What the hell was she doing here? Had she somehow recognized him underneath all that paint and the protective cover of darkness last night? But how could she? She'd never even met him before.

She wore pleated khaki trousers and a matching short-sleeved shirt. But the loose-fitting clothes couldn't hide the long, slender lines of her. She was tall, willowy. And her ebony hair was twisted into a tight knot again, only this morning there were no loose tendrils framing her regal face. Instead a pair of black-rimmed glasses, round ones, tried to hide her almond eyes.

Wes swallowed hard, recalling the other reason he hadn't slept well last night. He'd kept picturing her the way he'd first seen her. Sitting outside the dome tent caressing a broken piece of pottery as if it were the Hope diamond. And when he'd seen her face, he'd wondered if she knew all the things he'd never known about his own people. But Turtle had answered that question for him. She knew as little as Wes had known a year ago. She'd been raised away from that world. And maybe this dig of hers was her way of searching for it. Just as Wes's nights around the fire with Turtle were his.

"Hello," she said. "Mr. Brand?"

He just kept staring. Wondering if she knew about his foolish attempt to frighten her last night. Wondering what she was going to say. Her black eyes met his, held them. And he felt something...something he couldn't define.

Jessi elbowed him in the rib cage. He started out of his stupor, blinked and managed to say, "Yeah. What can I do for you?"

"I'm Dr. Taylor McCoy," she said, extending a long and elegant hand. "I'm supervising the archaeological dig over at Emerald Flat."

"Yeah, I know." He took her hand in his. Warm, firm. There were a few calluses. A woman who knew about hard work and wasn't a bit afraid of it, he thought.

She glanced down at their clasped hands, and he realized he was still holding hers and abruptly let go. Damn. Since when did he get all flabbergasted around women? Usually they were the ones tripping over themselves at a glance from him. He *hated* that.

No danger of it with this one, though.

"I have to apologize for bothering you at home, Sheriff Brand, but I just couldn't wait for office hours. This is important and I—"

"Whoa, wait a minute, Doc," Jessi cut in. "This isn't—"

"That's okay, Jessi," Wes said quickly. "Let the lady talk. Meanwhile, didn't you say you had something to do in the house?"

Jessi's eyes bulged so widely Wes wondered if they wouldn't pop their sockets. When she finished gaping at him, she turned toward the woman, and her gaze got narrower as she gave her the once-over. "You sure you're up to this?" she asked the woman.

"Excuse me?" Taylor McCoy frowned in confusion.

Jessi shook her head. "Nothing. Never mind. I'll be inside, Wes." Then Jessi headed back to the house. Wes figured he had about five minutes to figure out what it was the good doc had to say to his brother the sheriff. By then Jessi would have blabbed and Garrett would be out here giving it all away.

"So," he began, and then he met her eyes and forgot what he was saying again. She stared into his eyes for a long moment. As if she couldn't look away. And then she blinked and shook herself a little.

"I...um...don't think your wife liked me bothering you at home."

"My wife?" He blinked. "Oh, you mean Jessi? That's my baby sister. I don't have a wife."

She frowned and took a step backward. "That's funny..."

"What is?"

"The guy at the gas station over in town told me I could find the sheriff out here, where he lived with his wife and little boy." She narrowed her eyes until she was almost squinting at him. "Have I met you before? You look—"

"Nope. No chance of that. Listen, I didn't mean to mislead you. Garrett is the lawman, not me. But he's probably not even up yet, and I...sometimes help him out with things."

"Oh. Then you're *not* the sheriff."

He shook his head. "I'm his brother. Wes Brand, ma'am."

She studied his face, tilted her head. "You're Native American, aren't you?"

"Half," he told her.

"Comanche?" she asked, and he nodded. "Maybe you *can* help me, then. Look, what do you know about the site of that village I'm excavating?"

He shook his head. "Next to nothing." He lowered his eyes, and felt a twinge of guilt that made little sense. "I'm not as knowledgeable about my heritage as I should be, I suppose. But I'm trying to change that."

When he looked up again, there was a solemn understanding in her dark eyes, and they held his in a grip that wouldn't let go. A warm breeze stirred the dust in little whorls around his feet, and her hair danced in slow motion. "I'm...not, either," she said, very softly. "Very knowledgeable about...them."

"But you're an archaeologist."

She nodded and looked away.

Wes frowned. "I kinda figured you'd be an expert on the subject."

She shrugged, still not meeting his eyes. "I'm an expert on Native American cultures," she said, picking her words carefully, he thought. "Every one *except* the Comanches." She looked a little guilty when she said it.

"Why is that, Taylor?"

She looked up, met his eyes squarely. And he felt something...some kind of connection to her, as if he knew her...or should know her...or something.

The screen door creaked, then banged, and heavy-booted feet tramped down the steps. She turned to look at Garrett loping across the lawn with a stride that ate up the distance. Wes glimpsed his brother once, but his gaze was drawn right back to Taylor again. The definition of her cheekbones. Her small, proud chin, and strong jawline. The way the sun painted her black hair with glimmering light as it climbed higher in the sky.

"Dr. McCoy," Garrett said when he reached her and clasped her hand in greeting.

"You must be Sheriff Brand," she said with an easy smile. Broad and white and stunning. Her eyes glowed when she smiled. If she'd felt anything just now, she was hiding it well. Either that or it had all been in Wes's mind. But he didn't think so.

Garrett sent a quick glance toward Wes, and Wes nodded. Garrett returned his attention to the doc. "Call me Garrett. I see you've already met Wes. Why don't you come on inside and join us for some breakfast, ma'am, and you can tell me what it is I can help you with."

She shook her head quickly. "Thanks, but I don't have time for all that. We had an incident out at the site on Emerald Flat last night, Sheriff, and I'm not sure what to do about it."

"An incident?" Garrett frowned worriedly.

Wes tried real hard to look innocent.

The doc opened her mouth, closed it again and shook her head. "It's going to sound a little crazy."

Garrett smiled at her, that big, gentle smile he used when he was trying to make smaller creatures feel comfortable around him, and not intimidated by his size. "I've heard crazy before," he said.

"Okay." She took off her glasses and polished the lenses with a tissue she pulled from her pocket. A way, Wes thought, of avoiding their eyes while she told them her crazy story. "You ever hear the legend the local Comanches have about a man they call Wolf Shadow?"

Garrett nodded. "Sure. We've all heard that one. No one really believes it anymore, but—"

"Well, last night Wolf Shadow was at the site."

Garrett's brows went up. "Come again?"

"He—or someone trying to impersonate him—rode up to the edge of the site on a black horse the size of…of that one over there." She pointed and nodded toward the horse grazing now in the paddock. Wes's heart fell to his feet, and he choked noisily.

Garrett frowned at the horse, then at his brother. He slammed Wes on the back, and nodded at Taylor to go on.

"He said we were desecrating sacred ground and that we should leave while we still could," she said.

"And?" Garrett asked. Wes had stopped choking, but he really didn't want to be here for this. He should have skinned out the minute he'd seen her coming.

"And nothing," she said. "He rode off. I was hoping you could come out to the site with me, see if you can make any sense out of this."

Garrett nodded. "I have a ton on my schedule today, Taylor," he said, calling her by her first name as easily and naturally as if she were an old friend. "And with my deputy off caring for his new baby half the time…" Garrett grinned a little lopsidedly when he mentioned his brand-new niece, then seemed to shake himself. "I'll get out there later on today and have a look around."

Taylor lowered her head. "I don't want you to just take a look around." She raised her head, met Garrett's eyes and slipped her glasses into her shirt pocket with deliberate motions. "Look, this scared me. I want someone up there with me in case this lunatic comes back."

Garrett frowned, and Wes felt more guilty by the minute.

"Did this guy threaten you in any way?" Garrett asked.

She shifted her stance and looked irritated. "I sort of took that 'leave while you still can' part as a threat."

"I don't blame you," Garrett said. "I just don't know that I can pack up and move onto the site to watch out for you. I've got a wife and a boy and a ranch to run, and right now I'm the only law in this town." He shook his head. "I'm sure you're not in any danger. I'll investigate today and—"

"Look, this might not seem very important to you, Sheriff Brand, but this dig represents a lot of hard prep work and research for me, and I'm not going to let some lunatic in a loincloth screw it up." She turned fast to face Wes. "What about you?"

He blinked. "What *about* me?"

"You said you help your brother out from time to time."

"You did?" Garrett blurted, but Taylor rushed right on.

"So how about camping at the site for a few nights to check this out?"

"Well, I...I mean, what I meant was—it's just that—"

"I want someone out there. I want some kind of investigation started and I want some form of protection."

"Now, ma'am, I'm not sure you're in need of any *protection*," Garrett said.

"Insane people are dangerous, Sheriff. And sane people do not paint their faces and play ghostly avenger in the middle of the night. Now, you can help me out with this, or...or I'll just go back into town, buy myself a rifle and the next time someone rides up to my site in the dark—"

"Now, hold on a minute!" Garrett lifted both hands defensively.

Taylor stopped talking and nodded. "I thought that

might get your attention," she said in a calmer voice. Then she sighed hard, shook her head. "Look, I'm not going to go shooting at shadows, gentlemen, but I really am concerned. This shook me. Sheriff Brand, what if it was your wife or your little sister up there in a tent with no protection, and some lunatic was showing up at midnight with war whoops and veiled threats? Would you take this more seriously then?"

Garrett nodded. "You're right, and I'm sorry."

"I have two students with me up there," she told him. "I can't risk anything happening to them. And frankly...I doubt they'd be much help to me if this guy decided to get violent."

"I'll take care of it," Garrett began.

"No." Wes cleared his throat as they both looked his way. "No, I'll take care of it. In fact, I think you had the best idea, Doc."

Wes looked from one to the other. Taylor seemed relieved. Garrett...suspicious. But he couldn't risk Garrett going up there and uncovering his ploy. And besides, what better way to make sure Turtle's precious sacred ground didn't get violated than to be right there at the dig?

"I'll pack up some gear and head out to the site," Wes said, instantly wondering if he would live to regret it. "Hang out there for a few days. Garrett, with Elliot and Ben here, you can get by without me for a short while."

"I don't know," Garrett said. Then he frowned. "Chelsea *is* always saying how she thinks you oughtta get in touch with your Comanche heritage, though. This might be something you ought to do."

"Chelsea's taking her psychology classes way too serious,'' Wes muttered, not bothering to tell his brother he'd been doing just that for the past year.

Garrett glanced at Taylor. ''You realize, my brother isn't a lawman. But I'd trust him with my life. Have, a time or two, in fact, and I'm still here to tell about it.''

''That's good enough for me,'' Taylor said.

Garrett finally nodded. ''Good, then. It's settled.'' He slapped Wes's shoulder. ''Thanks for jumping in like this, Wes. Little Bubba's toddling around into everything, and Chelsea's busy with the women's crisis center and her psych classes. We got cows ready to freshen and fence to repair. Those damned rustlers we caught in Mexico last year are coming to trial, and I have to testify. Jessi's busy with the new baby, and Lash is up nights so much with her that he's not worth much in the daylight these days, even if I can convince him to come into the office.'' He nodded, as if reassuring himself. ''Yup, this is the perfect solution.''

Wes glanced once again at Taylor McCoy, who stood looking at him with her big dark eyes. ''All right, then,'' he said. ''But don't be thinking you're gonna pin any badge on me, big brother, 'cause it's not gonna happen.''

''Wouldn't dream of it,'' Garrett said. ''This will be unofficial. Okay?''

Wes nodded. Garrett tipped his hat to the lady, and then headed out to the barns, leaving Wes alone with the woman once more. He faced her, suddenly uncomfortable, not sure what to say.

''I...appreciate this,'' she said. ''I know it's a lot to ask, but—''

''It's the least I can do,'' Wes said. And it was. He was the one who'd scared the woman so badly, after all.

''I'll come on out to the site later on. I need time to

pack up some gear and I got a...an errand to run in town.''

"All right," she said. But she didn't turn to go. He gave her a questioning glance, and she lowered her eyes. "Will you...be there before dark?"

Hell, she really was scared. He hadn't thought Wolf Shadow's appearance had shaken her in the least, but he'd been wrong. "Yeah," he said. "Well before dark. Promise.''

She nodded. "Good," she said. "That's good."

Wes Brand had eyes that could burn holes right through her, she thought as she bounded over the rutted roads in her Jeep. He'd seemed a little unnerved by her presence. Or maybe it was her story that bothered him.

So what was it about *him* that bothered *her?*

There was something about him. Something that made her feel warm and jittery. But he also wore this aura like a glowing sign that flashed Stay Away to anyone who got too close. She pegged him as a loner.

And then she realized that she had been pegged that way, too. Most of her life. All through college and graduate studies, she'd immersed herself in her work to the exclusion of a social life, much less any romantic attachments. She'd attributed that to the need for focusing on her career. But she knew there was more to it. She knew what lay beneath her detachment. She just hadn't taken the time to examine it closely, or to try to work through it. Old hurts didn't matter. They had nothing to do with the present.

What made Wes Brand a loner? she wondered idly.

He was one beautiful man. Strikingly so. Made her think twice about having him come up to the site instead of his big but safe-looking brother. He could very easily become a distraction, which was utterly hilarious when she thought about it, because she'd never once met a man who could compete with her work for her attention.

Well, there was a first time for everything. But she could handle it. She'd just put on her professor face, and keep a cool, clinical distance between the two of them.

If only she could do the same with the mysterious Wolf Shadow. But it was harder with him, because he was a phantom. A ghost. And last night after he'd gone, he'd returned to her in dreams no cool, clinical scientist ought to be having.

Pretty strange, she thought. Good ol' Solitary McCoy feeling…oddly drawn to two different men in the space of twenty-four hours, when she usually didn't even notice men.

Very strange. She felt a little worried about that as she headed back to the site.

"Well, well, well," Jessi chirped when Wes went back inside. She was sitting at the table, but he had no doubt she'd been watching him with Taylor McCoy the whole time.

"She's got to be the most stunningly beautiful woman I've ever seen," Chelsea said. Garrett's wife gave Wes a mischievous grin and a wink. "Not that you probably noticed."

"She looks like Pocahontas did in the Disney movie," Jessi said.

"Since when do you watch Disney movies?" was the only safe comeback he could think of.

Little Bubba came running across the floor, arms flailing as if he were a little bird trying to fly, and when he reached Chelsea's legs, he hugged them hard, laughing out loud.

Chelsea scooped him up in her arms and kissed his face. "You little speed demon," she said. "You just learned to walk and now all you do is run!"

"Wun!" Bubba said.

"So, Wes," Jessi said, "you gonna tell me what's goin' on with you and the pretty professor?"

"Nothing," he told his little sister. "And that's the last time I want to hear about it." He gave them a warning look, shook his head. "I gotta pack." He tromped through the house, heading for the stairs. Jessi followed. So did Chelsea, with Bubba anchored on her hip.

"So where you going, then?" Jessi asked.

"Garrett wants me to camp out at the site for a few days. They've had some trouble. He'll fill you in. God knows you won't leave him alone until he does."

Jessi laughed. "So you're going camping with a drop-dead gorgeous woman who looks at you like you're a rare steak and she's coming off a hunger strike—and nothing's going to happen between you two?"

He pointed his finger at her like a gun and cocked his thumb. "Bull's-eye," he told her. "And she didn't look at me like anything."

Jessi turned to Chelsea with a huge grin. "Isn't it great, Chelsea? He's in denial."

"Yeah, and he couldn't even *see* the way *he* was looking at *her*," Chelsea said. "Like a sailor lost at sea looks at a distant island."

"Ooh, that's a good one," Jessi said. "Or like a drowning man looks at a life preserver."

"Or like a brown bear looks at a honeycomb."

The two women laughed out loud. Wes just groaned and went into his room to pack.

Chapter 3

Taylor glanced up from the screen through which she'd been sifting dirt, her gaze drawn by something she couldn't have named. She half expected to see Wolf Shadow looming above her, closer and more real than before. But instead she saw Wes Brand with a duffel bag in his hand and a pack slung over one sturdy shoulder. In his tight jeans and Western shirt, that black Stetson shadowing his face, he looked more cowboy than Indian, and for some reason that thought made her hackles rise slightly in resentment.

She shook the feeling away with a puzzled frown, handed the screen to the nearest pair of hands and nearly dropped it when the student didn't react.

Swinging her head around sharply, Taylor saw the girl beside her staring at Wes Brand as if he were the second coming or something. Her brown eyes swam, and her lips curved in a dreamy smile.

"Kelly? Do you mind?"

Kelly snapped out of it long enough to focus briefly on Taylor, take the screen from her hands and go right back to staring at the man. Taylor shook her head in frustration, brushed the dirt from her hands and climbed out of the square, roped-off area where she'd been digging. "Thanks for coming," she told him, and she was extremely careful to keep her voice cool and her expression professional. She didn't want to look the way Kelly did. Not in this lifetime.

"No problem." He shifted the pack on his shoulder a little. It looked heavy. Her gaze lingered on his face— bronzed skin, hard features, that hands-off look he wore. His eyes gleamed. And they kept dipping to focus on her mouth, then jerking up again.

She cleared her throat. "This is Kelly, by the way."

"Kelly Mallone," her assistant said, dropping the screen too hard, and reaching a dirty hand out to shake Wes's.

"Wes Brand," he replied.

"Mr. Brand will be camping with us for a few days," Taylor explained. "In case our...visitor shows up again."

Kelly's lashes fluttered. "I'll feel so much safer now," she breathed.

Wes's jaw went a little tighter, and he averted his gaze from Kelly's blatantly interested one. So his way with the ladies bothered him, did it?

Then he looked at Taylor, and she schooled her features to cool professionalism again. "I'll...uh...show you where to put that stuff." He said nothing, so she set off up the slight incline to the flat area where three dome tents dotted the ground. The sticky heat seemed worse somehow than it had been only moments before, and she wiped the damp hairs from her cheeks, and shrugged. "Just pick a spot, I guess."

"Which tent is yours?"

She whirled to face him, eyes going wide.

He smiled slightly, almost as if he knew what sort of thoughts had jolted through her head just for an instant. "I want to pitch mine close to it, Doc."

"W-why?" Okay, so while she was at it, why didn't she ask herself why her stomach was clenching and relaxing like an overstimulated heart muscle?

"The kid I saw when I got here told me you were the only one who saw this...*ghost*. I want to be sure I'm within shoutin' distance if you see it again."

"Oh." She pushed another loose tendril of hair behind her ear. "What kid?" Did it matter? No, but she hated awkward silences.

"Didn't get his name," he said. "Scrawny. Hairball. Earring in his nose like some kinda damned fruitcake."

Her chin came up fast, and she gave him her best glare, while trying not to laugh at his description. "I'd never have guessed you were the judgmental type," she said. "Scourge happens to be one of the most gifted students I've ever worked with."

"Scourge?" He looked at her as if she were crazy.

Taylor almost smiled at his reaction. She bit her lip instead. "It's a nickname. His real name's Stanley, and he hates it."

Wes grinned at her, shook his head. "And *Scourge* is such an attractive alternative."

She did smile this time. She couldn't help it. She'd been razzing Scourge about his choice in nicknames since she'd met him.

After a moment of sharing that smile, Wes said, "So you're a teacher?"

His rapid change of subjects took her off guard. She didn't answer. Instead she turned to lead him to her tent. "This one's mine," she said.

He dropped his duffel, slung the pack from his shoulder to the ground, then hunkered down to pull the neatly rolled tent from inside it. And when he hunkered that way, his jeans got a whole lot tighter around his backside. He glanced up at her, over his shoulder, caught her looking before she managed to steer her gaze back where it belonged and pretended not to notice. "Then you're *not* a teacher," he said.

"I teach. But I'm not a teacher."

"Sounds deep," he said, and when she looked at him, he paused in unrolling the tent and stared at her. "I'll take a stab, though. You teach to pay the bills. But what you love is digging for bones and broken dishes."

She couldn't seem to take her eyes from his. "You're not even close."

"I didn't think so." And still he held her gaze.

To break the tension, she got up and went to the opposite end of the nylon circle, gripping the edges and pulling it out flat. Wes reached back into his pack for the flexible poles, and quickly inserted them through the fabric.

"A woman of mystery," he quipped as he worked.

She helped him raise the tent, a perfect black dome standing neatly beside her gray one. So close she imagined if she poked her hand into the side of her tent, and he did the same from within his own, they could touch through the fabric.

It was a silly thought. A silly thought that made her tingle somewhere deep. He was looking at her, waiting. "I wasn't trying to be mysterious," she said. "Truth is,

I still don't know what I am." She lowered her head, knowing it probably sounded lame.

"And this digging up the past is your way of trying to find out."

She brought her head up fast, because his words were so accurate. It startled her. "It never was," she said softly. And silently she added, *Until now.* Then she scratched that idea. She wasn't here to learn about herself, her past, her so-called heritage. She was here to do a job. Period.

Besides, she didn't need to look very far to find herself. Her heart was being boarded on a beautiful ranch in Oklahoma. Someday she'd have a home—a real home, not one of these temporary apartments. And she'd bring Jasper there. Feed her carrots and ride her at sunrise, instead of spending the odd weekend with her, between jobs. That was what she wanted out of life. All she wanted, really. Enough money to have that place, for her and her horse. She didn't need anyone else.

"I study the past because I'm good at it," she said finally. "And I learn enough along the way to make me qualified to teach it to others."

"But not enough to let you stop looking."

She blinked and looked away to avoid his eyes. "I dig, I teach, I write now and then. Whatever pays the rent." She glanced past him to see Kelly and Scourge watching the two of them intently, although when she looked, they both got back to work.

Wes unzipped the arched doorway of his tent, slung his duffel bag inside. Then zipped it closed again. "For what it's worth, Doc, I don't think you're gonna find yourself in that dirt you've been sifting."

She met his black eyes, and they made her burn. Because it was as if he knew. As if he knew exactly the lost kind of feeling she'd never really been without. The sense that he could see things she'd rather not share made her uncomfortable. She gave her head a shake. "I'm looking for artifacts, Mr. Brand, nothing more." She lowered her eyes. "And since we're swapping unasked-for advice, I don't think *you're* going to find this trespassing ghostly warrior by standing around talking to me."

"Good point," he said, and he touched the brim of his hat in a mock salute. "So why don't you show me where you saw him?"

She nodded, turned and walked. And Wes followed. She took him to the slight rise in the ground where the warrior had appeared. "He was right here."

"On a horse, right?" Wes asked.

"Yes. A big black. A stallion, I think. Probably four years old, or more."

The man frowned at her. "How can you possibly—?"

"Well, it was dark, but I could see some," she told him. "That horse was no colt. Didn't have that lean, sleek line to him. In fact, he looked a bit overweight."

"I'll be damned." He stared at her, shoved his hat back a bit, stared some more. "So you know horses as well as history?"

She smiled, thinking of Jasper. "Yeah, I know horses."

Shaking his head, Wes knelt, and she saw him examining the ground. Then he shrugged and got up. "No hoofprints."

She frowned. "Well, the ground is hard here. He might not have left any."

"Okay," he said. She got the feeling he was humoring her.

"You are aware that skilled warriors, when they wanted to employ the element of surprise, would wrap their horses' hooves in cloth to muffle the sound. When they did that, there were seldom any clear tracks.''

Wes straightened up, searching her face. "You get that from a history book, Doc?"

"No," she said softly. "I got that from a Louis L'Amour book."

"I'll be damned."

"That's the second time you've said that," she told him, but he was looking at her in some kind of mingling of surprise and...she wasn't sure, but it looked like a hint of panic.

"Is something wrong, Mr.—?"

"Wes," he said. Then he shook himself. "Er, how well did you see him?"

"The horse?"

"The rider."

She tapped a forefinger against her chin and thought back, lowering her lashes to conceal her eyes. "Well enough." Well enough so that she'd seen him again, in her dreams.

"Can you describe him to me?" Wes asked.

He was going through the motions, she thought. He didn't believe she'd seen a thing, probably thought it was all in her imagination. And it made her angry, but she nodded anyway.

"He was wearing paint on his face. His hair was long and dark, and he wore it loose." She tipped her head sideways, examining the hair tied behind Wes's head. "As long as yours is, I think," she said. Then she frowned. "You know, with hair like that, I don't know how you could call Scourge a hairball."

"Scourge looks like he's wearing a lemon yellow dust mop on his head."

She almost choked on her laugh, because she'd thought the same thing about Scourge's hair so often.

"Go on," Wes said, while she swallowed her mirth. "What was this ghost wearing?"

"Not a hell of a lot." She smiled a little. "Then again, I figure any man who looked like he did would probably prefer going naked." He glanced at her sharply, and she lowered her head. "That was stupid. Sorry." She peered up at him again, but he seemed totally at a loss for words.

She cleared her throat and reminded herself this was serious. Good as the rider looked, the man could have been dangerous. And he might come back. "He was wearing some sort of loincloth, I think. His arms and chest were bare, and so were his legs, clear to the hip."

Wes licked his lips. "I thought you said it was dark."

"Well, there was moonlight. And once I put my back to my gas lamp, I could see a little better."

"Oh."

She tilted her head.

"So," Wes said, "you say he looked to be in... er...fairly good shape."

"He looked like he belonged on a calendar." She pursed her lips in thought. "Maybe he really was a ghost after all," she said. "I never saw a real man look that good." Then she walked a few steps to the east, her back to Wes. "He rode off in this direction, and that was...uh...Wes?"

He looked up, seemingly surprised to see that she'd moved on and continued speaking. He was still standing in the same spot, blinking in what looked like shock and looking as if the heat was getting to him a bit, judging by the flush of color in his face.

"Yeah. I'm with you," he said. And he hurried up to join her.

* * *

The way she described Wolf Shadow had shaken Wes right to the core. And the way she looked when she described him was even worse.

For God's sake, she acted turned on by the guy.

But *the guy* was *him!*

Only, she didn't know that. And he didn't seem to know much of anything. And besides, she was scared, too. Scared enough so that she'd made him promise to arrive here before dark. Scared enough so that hint of fear in her eyes had been all it took to extract that promise, and maybe his liver, if she'd asked for it, as well.

He'd finished chores in record time after she'd gone. Then packed up his things and tossed them into the back of his Bronco. He'd gone back inside just long enough to write down his bid on the old Cumberland place, and then he'd sealed it in an envelope and dropped it off at the town clerk's office. After that he'd made a quick stop to check in on Turtle.

He'd arrived at Turtle's place shortly after noon, and the old goat was actually out of bed and dressed for a change. Seeing him looking more like his old self chased a good portion of the troubling thoughts from Wes's mind, and he even smiled. "You're looking better!"

"Because I know you intend to set up camp at the site, Raven Eyes," Turtle said. "And because I know you'll remain there until you've found a way to protect the sacred ground."

Wes shook his head slowly and took a seat at the small Formica-topped table in the trailer's kitchen. Turtle took a cold beer from the ancient fridge, handed it to Wes and sat opposite him. He sipped tea, and that alone let Wes know he wasn't completely recovered yet. "I'm going to try, Turtle, but I can't promise it's going to work. Taylor says—"

"Taylor?"

"Doc McCoy. She's the one in charge of the dig."

"Ah…Sky Dancer."

Wes searched Turtle's face, brows raised in question. Turtle's only answer was, "It is a good name."

Blinking, Wes shook himself. "Okay, if you say so. Anyway, she didn't say a thing about finding evidence that Emerald Flat was ever anything other than a regular village."

"It was," Turtle said, interrupting him. "It was sacred to the shamans of my clan. It is sacred to me."

"But why are you so sure all this is true?"

Turtle closed his eyes slowly, then opened them again. "I believe it is true. The why does not matter."

Wes sipped his beer and counted to ten. Then, as calmly as he could, he said, "The Wolf Shadow thing isn't going to work, Turtle. She isn't all *that* afraid of him."

"Yes, she is," Turtle said as if he knew it beyond any doubt.

Wes took a breath, bit his tongue. "Okay, she's a little afraid, but there's more."

"She's attracted to him," Turtle said.

Wes gaped.

"This is good, my friend. If she fears him, his power over her is strong, but if she wants him, it is even stronger. You must appear to her again as Wolf Shadow. Soon."

Wes shook his head. "She wants me out there so she'll have protection from him…er…me," he said. "She even made me promise to be there before dark. If that ghost shows up and I'm not in my tent, she's going to want to know why.''

"Then lure her away. Away from the camp. And while she's away, appear to her then. She can't blame you for not being close by if she's the one who leaves.''

Wes grated his teeth, shook his head. "She'll never go for it. Look, my setting up housekeeping out there on the flat is supposed to end the need for this Wolf Shadow nonsense. If I'm right there to watch what—''

"It's not enough.'' Turtle smiled serenely, sipped his tea. Then he closed his eyes and pressed a hand to his forehead. "I'm feeling weak again, my friend. Perhaps I got up too soon.''

Wes's frown vanished, swept away by concern for his friend. "We shouldn't even be talking about this,'' he said, getting to his feet, taking Turtle by the arm. "It gets you all stirred up. Come on, lie down. Take it easy. Don't worry about any of this, Turtle, I'm gonna take care of it.''

He put an arm around Turtle's fragile shoulders and eased him into the living area, three steps from the kitchen area in this cubbyhole of a place. He helped the old man onto the green-tartan couch that sagged in the middle, and pulled a woven horse blanket off the back to cover him.

Turtle asked, "Tonight, Raven Eyes? You'll try again tonight?''

"Yeah, tonight, sure,'' Wes said. "If it's humanly possible. Now rest, okay? Just relax. It's gonna be okay.''

After assuring himself Turtle was all right, for the time being at least, Wes had continued on his way here. To look into the huge ebony eyes of the woman he was supposed to be scaring off. And to learn that she liked horses and Western novels, and had a sense of humor, and was afraid of something. Something besides his ghostly visit. Herself, he thought. Her past. Her blood. She was afraid of it.

There was no way in hell he could lure the doc away from the camp that night. He watched and waited for an opportunity, stuck close to her side all evening, just in case she'd wander off, giving him an opening. He could get into costume in five minutes flat. There would be no time to "borrow" his brother's oversize horse this time, but if she knew horseflesh as well as she seemed to, that probably wouldn't be a good idea, anyway. Besides, he didn't need the horse. All he needed was an opportunity.

He watched her when the sun began its spectacular descent, sinking lower on the western horizon, painting the desert with a blaze orange brush. He saw the way she fidgeted and kept glancing off in the direction where his alter ego had made his first appearance. Getting nervous by the look of things. Pacing back and forth in front of her tent. Wes sat on the ground in front of his own tent, with an open notebook in one hand and a pencil in the other. He had planning to do, careful planning. The bank loan wasn't quite enough to cover the cost of all the renovations that old Cumberland place would need, if he were lucky enough to have put in the winning bid. He'd have to make the money stretch, cover the necessities first, and save the frills for later on.

Every once in a while he felt Taylor's eyes on him, glanced up fast to catch her looking at him. As if to assure herself he was still there. Close by. But when he met her gaze, she quickly covered whatever she was feeling with an "I couldn't care less" sort of expression.

Wes set his notebook aside and walked up to her anyway, nodded down at her small camp stove and the pan of water boiling on its single butane burner, and said, "It's gonna boil dry pretty soon."

She glanced down, frowned. "I forgot about it."

"Well, you have a lot on your mind."

She drummed up a scowl for him, and he wondered if he were right in assuming he'd been the thing distracting her.

Or maybe not. Maybe it was Wolf Shadow she'd been thinking of just now.

She ducked into her tent and emerged again with a sealed plastic bag full of dehydrated food, which she apparently intended to drop into the water for her dinner. He must have made a face, because she paused over the camp stove, and sent him a questioning glance. "What?"

Wes shrugged. "I just didn't expect you'd be so...citified."

"*Citified?*"

"Modern. Civilized. I mean, you're the one trying to find yourself in the past, aren't you?"

"You said that. I didn't." She glanced down at the bag of food, then back at him, and she looked puzzled. She was cute when she was puzzled, he discovered. "And what does that have to do with this, anyway?" she asked, lifting the bag.

He shrugged. "Maybe nothing. Or maybe..." Giving his head a shake, he looked at the area around him, dimmer now, bathed in the last pale blush of the setting sun. Scruffy-looking trees, and a small patch of forest to the northwest, with that pond and the cave where he'd hidden his props nestled inside. To the east was civilization. Walking that way would bring you to the dirt road and Turtle's trailer, and beyond that actual towns began springing up. To the south was desert. Not the kind of place most people thought of when they thought of desert. No sand or dunes. Just hard-packed ground and rock formations rising up like living things. Nothing much grew out there. Arid, barren land. Folks around here called this patch of nowhere the Badlands. And whether it was technically accurate or not, Wes thought it fit.

This flat was like an oasis. A gentle haven set within the harsh country. Lush greenery and life, right in the middle of no-man's-land.

"What is it, Wes?" she asked, coming to stand closer to him, searching his face, the plastic bag of food forgotten.

"I was just wondering…what it was like here a hundred years ago. Or two hundred."

"Or six," she said in a voice softer than he'd ever heard her use. "I was wondering about it myself, just last night. Six centuries ago is when the first Comanche people set up camp here on this flat."

He shook his head. "Bet they didn't eat from any boilable bags, Doc."

She frowned at him. "Of course not. They cooked over a central fire, over there." And she pointed.

"So why don't we?"

She blinked, surprised maybe by his suggestion. "Wes, it's dry here. It would be dangerous to…" But her words trailed off as she gazed toward the spot she'd indicated, and he thought she was picturing it, maybe.

"We dig down a little," Wes said, "surround the fire with stones the way our ancestors did."

Her eyes glowed in the dying breath of sunlight, just before it slipped lower and vanished amid the barren hills to the west. "We could have a few pails of water standing by, just in case."

Wes smiled. He couldn't imagine why he was smiling, or why he was so enthused over something as simple as a campfire. He and Turtle sat beside a campfire more often than not. So what was the big deal here?

"I'll gather some deadfall," he told her. "There's plenty in that little stand of woods."

"I'll get Scourge to help dig a trench. Let's keep it small, Wes." She looked up at him just before he turned away, and when their eyes met, something moved between them. A childlike excitement, a sense of adventure, something new. She smiled gently at him, and Wes's throat went dry. Then he turned and headed out in search of firewood.

And as he gathered branches and twigs from beneath gnarled, mystical-looking trees, Wes asked himself what the hell he was doing. He wasn't supposed to be playing Cub Scout with Doc McCoy; he was supposed to be convincing her the legend was real and then scaring her the hell away from here. But damn, when she flashed those big onyx eyes his way, it was tough to remember that. Okay, so he'd do the campfire thing. At this point it would look pretty suspicious if he didn't. But after that, it was back to the matter at hand. His best friend's life might very well depend on it.

Chapter 4

Why she agreed to the idea of building a fire in the midst of the site, she couldn't have said. There was really no logical reason for it. Then again, there was no real reason not to do it. The location of the central fire had already been excavated, and with the pails of water Wes had hauled up from the pond, any risk of the fire spreading was eliminated.

Still she wasn't prone to mixing work with pleasure, and a campfire was that. Pleasure.

Such pleasure.

Wes took her by the hand, a casual gesture that really shouldn't have sent her pulse rate skittering. Then he knelt and patiently showed her just how to arrange the dried leaves and twigs he'd gathered up. He added large twigs in a tepee shape above the kindling. Then he took two stones from his pocket, pressing one of them into her hand.

"What is it?" she asked, mesmerized.

"Flint," he told her as she handed it back to him. "Watch." Bending low, he struck the stones together, holding them close to the edge of a dry leaf. They produced a spark with each strike, until finally the leaf began to smolder, and then to glow. Wes bent closer and blew gently on the newborn fire until tongues of flame came to life. Then he straightened, facing her. "That's the way our ancestors did it."

She averted her eyes, just a bit uncomfortable.

Then her hands were caught in his larger ones, and the stones gently enfolded in her palms. But his touch was lingering and warm. Like a lover's caress, and it made her shiver. "Keep them," he said. "You never know when you might need them."

He took his hands away slowly, as if he regretted doing so, looked up into her eyes with a slightly puzzled expression in his—as if his actions had surprised him as much as they had her. Then he gave himself a shake and sat down to enjoy the fire. And Taylor did, too.

How had she lived this long and never known how good it felt just to sit under the stars beside an open fire?

The firelight painted every face with dancing light and flickering shadow. Full darkness bathed the camp all around them, and Kelly seemed to be enjoying the fire as much as Taylor was. In fact, sitting crosslegged on the ground, the desert's chill rippling up and down her back, while the fire's warmth blanketed her front, she found it easy to imagine that the dark shapes of the dome tents around her were actually pointy-topped tepees. And that the people sitting around the fire wore animal hides instead of denim and flannel.

Scourge wasn't as enthusiastic. Not at first, anyway. He sat there glumly, as if he were only doing so under protest. The looks he sent Wes's way when Wes wasn't looking were less than friendly, bordering on suspicious, in fact.

Wes sat beside Taylor. And she wondered if he had a clue what sorts of things were going through her mind right now. And whether he'd planned it this way. Maybe he was in cahoots with old Turtle. Subtly steering her toward things she'd avoided until now. Of course, knowledge about Comanche ways had been a necessity before even beginning this job. But the things she'd let herself study were words in books. Clinical accounts of the past. This…this was different.

If she closed her eyes, and just let herself float away in sensation—the pungency of the wood smoke, the snap and crackle and hiss of the fire, the heat of it on her face—she could almost feel them all around her. A village filled with people. Her ancestors. And instead of chilling her, the sensation warmed her.

But the warmth made her wary. She found herself mistrusting it.

"Our ancestors told stories on nights like this," Wes said, his voice deep and slow, making her think he was feeling the same things she did. But that was impossible, of course.

She nodded. "I don't know their stories nearly as well as you do, I'm sure," she said softly. Kelly was talking softly to Scourge, while he stared in silent contemplation of the flames. "I can recite facts and figures, tell you what they ate and how they cooked it. But the legends…" She sighed. "The People were later in developing a written form of their language than many other tribes. So much of what they believed in has been lost."

"Not as much as you think," Wes said, searching her face. "But what survived, survived because of nights like this one, and people gathered around a fire, sharing their tales, the old telling them to the young, generation after generation.''

When he looked at her, the reflection of the flames danced in his black eyes. And she didn't say anything, so he went on. ''Imagine what would have happened if the young refused to listen to those stories.''

He was referring, of course, to her. She'd told him how she'd avoided studying the Comanche ways all her life. ''Then the stories might have been lost.''

''Not 'might have been.' Would have been,'' Wes said. ''It's the oral tradition that's kept them alive. The stories, the history of a people.''

She nodded, knew what he was getting at. She was doing a disservice to her ancestors and maybe to her descendants by refusing to listen, to know.

''For a long time I didn't think it made a difference. Maybe to *them,* you know. But not to me, personally.'' He paused there, waiting.

''And what changed your mind?'' she asked. Kelly and Scourge had moved closer, abandoning their own conversation in favor of listening to hers and Wes's.

''I met an old man who liked to tell the stories. And I was either too polite or too dumb not to listen.''

Taylor nodded slowly, watching his eyes. Seemed once a person looked into those dark eyes, it got unreasonably difficult to look away again. ''And did it? Make a difference to you, personally?''

He dipped a hand into his jeans pocket, and pulled out a small woven pouch of black and bright red. The drawstring was knotted around one of his belt loops, she noticed. ''Made a lot of difference,'' he said. ''I know who I am now. Know where I come from.''

She was mesmerized by the way his big hand cupped the small pouch. Long fingers stroking the weave. And maybe it was the firelight, or the night air…but it seemed sensual, somehow. And she forgot to breathe for a minute, staring at the way his fingers moved.

"Could you tell us some of those stories?" Kelly chirped, jarring Taylor right out of the spell the night—and Wes—had spun.

Wes didn't answer her. He was staring at Taylor. "They're nothing to be afraid of," he said, very softly, so softly she wasn't certain whether the other two could hear him, or if his words reached her ears alone.

"I'm not afraid of any tales of the past," she whispered, but as she said it, a shiver ran up her spine.

"Then ask, and I'll tell you. Say stop and I'll stop."

She bit her lip, glanced over the flames at Scourge, who seemed to be straining to hear the words they spoke softly to one another. At Kelly, practically bouncing on the ground in anticipation. At her tent, out of reach on the other side. But not really out of reach. She could get up, walk away, let him tell his stories to the kids and try hard not to hear, the way she did when Turtle came and insisted on talking of the past, and The People and the old ways.

She met Wes's eyes again, and there was warmth there, assurance. He wouldn't say anything that would hurt her, his eyes seemed to promise. She swallowed the lump in her throat.

"Tell me," she said softly.

And he smiled. Taylor felt as if she'd overcome some kind of obstacle. It was one of those moments when you sensed your life—your world—was about to change. And a warm hand crept over hers where it rested on the cool ground, closed around it and squeezed. And when she looked up at Wes, he was looking away, as if he was deep in thought and totally unaware of the intimate gesture.

His hand moved away a second later, and he spoke in a voice that carried around the fire. "My friend, an old shaman, tells this one over and over again," he said. "I think it's his favorite."

Without thinking about it first, Taylor moved closer to him. She couldn't take her eyes from his face as he spoke. And he reached up, without warning, to gently remove her glasses, fold the arms and drop them into her shirt pocket.

"There was a woman, long ago, who had a vision. An eagle landed on the limb of a tall tree and spoke to her. And the things the eagle said frightened the woman to the core of her, but they brought her hope, as well. 'Hard times lay ahead for The People,' the eagle told her. 'And before your generation leaves this world, you will see such hardship and strife that very few of you will survive. Many of the ways of The People will be lost, forever.'"

Taylor nodded. "Smart eagle," she said softly. "He was all too right."

Wes looked serious as he went on. "This troubled the woman. But she remained where she was and bade the eagle go on. 'You,' he told her, 'will bear a daughter, who will bear a daughter, who will bear a daughter. And this child, the great-granddaughter of your heart, is destined to restore the past to The People to whom it belongs. For no tree can exist without all of its roots. And no people can flourish without all of its past.'"

Taylor almost winced at the way those words cut to the quick. She'd been trying to flourish without her roots, but all she felt was lost and alone. But her isolation was self-imposed. She didn't trust because she chose not to trust. It was easier—safer—than believing and being betrayed again.

"The woman asked the eagle how her great-granddaughter would accomplish such a thing, but the eagle only uttered the name of the young warrior the girl was to take as husband one day, a warrior not even born yet, and then he said no more. He spread his mighty wings and took flight.

"Part of what the eagle told the woman did indeed come to pass. She had a daughter. And her daughter had a daughter. And finally her granddaughter had a daughter.

"But the granddaughter died while her child was still young, and her relatives had no wealth to give to the child. Times were dire for The People then. Thinking they were doing what was best, they sent the young one away from her tribe and her people, and she was raised in the white man's world, learning only white men's ways."

Taylor shifted uncomfortably. "You're making this up for my benefit, aren't you?"

Wes frowned at her. "This is exactly the way it was told to me, I swear." Then he tilted his head. "Why do you think—?"

"Because it could easily be my story."

He held up both hands. "Hold on. Wait. I know, you think I'm making up a story around your life to guilt you into something you don't want to do. I know. I accused my old friend of the same thing when he told it to me."

She tilted her head, eyed him suspiciously.

"It could be my story, too, Taylor, with some very minor changes. I used to think that's why the old crock was so fond of telling it to me. I've decided otherwise, though. It's just one of a hundred tales he's told me over the past year."

She lowered her head, a little embarrassed at having accused him. And then lifted it again, because what he said was sinking in. If it could be his story, as well, then...

"So...we have one thing in common, you and I," she said.

"More than one thing." His eyes gripped hers for a moment, but then he lowered them. "Should I stop?"

It was just a story, she told herself. It couldn't hurt her. "No. Go on. What happened?"

She thought he might have sighed in relief, but she wasn't sure. When he looked up again, his eyes were distant, in the past, maybe. "The great-grandmother knew of the death of her granddaughter, and that the child was given to whites, for she saw these things in her dreams as she lay on her deathbed. Yet she didn't know where the child was taken, or how to reach her. She called the village shaman to her bedside, and she told him of all the eagle had said. And with her dying breath, she whispered the name of the young warrior her great-granddaughter was to marry, according to the words of the eagle. She begged the shaman to see to it that all would happen as the eagle had said it should, and he gave his word, that she might cross to the summerland in peace.

"But the shaman was afraid of the enormous task set upon his shoulders. To find this girl, and somehow bring her back to her homelands. To teach her the ways of her people, and convince her to take upon herself the task the eagle had said would be hers...much less to convince her to marry a young man she didn't know, one he might never be able to find...all of this seemed impossible."

Kelly was smiling and wide-eyed and rapt. Even Scourge was leaning forward a bit, listening.

"The shaman went on a vision quest on the night of the old woman's death. And he saw the Great Spirit, in the form of an eagle, just as the old woman had. The eagle spoke to him and said these words, 'You will not see death until you have fulfilled your vow.' To this day that shaman still lives. And still he seeks to complete his mission."

Wes fell silent, and sat staring into the flames. Taylor stared at his face for a long time, the shadows the fire created making him seem harder and more mysterious than before. When she finally looked away from him, it was to see the others around the fire, both staring at him exactly the way she'd been doing. Kelly looked as if she wanted to wrap up in his arms. Scourge seemed mesmerized.

"It's a beautiful story," Taylor whispered.

"It's intense," Scourge said. "Mr. Brand, you said a shaman told you this tale."

Wes blinked and looked up, as if he'd been lost in thought. Then he nodded. "Yeah. There aren't that many Comanche shamans left now, but I believe this one's genuine."

Scourge bit his lip. Wes frowned across the flames at him. "I can see there's something on your mind, kid. Spit it out."

Nodding fast, Scourge said, "I've read accounts claiming that the...er...the magic practiced by Native American shamans is...well, uh...beyond explanation." He shrugged. "It makes a person wonder, is all. Have you seen anything that...would make you...you know, wonder?"

Wes glanced sideways at Taylor, and she realized she hadn't taken her eyes off him, and wondered if she looked as moonstruck as poor lovesick Kelly did. There was a question in his eyes.

"I'd like to know, too," she told him.

Wes drew a breath. "You asked for it. But the first one of you who so much as chuckles, gets staked out in the desert for the night. Understood?"

Kelly shifted nervously. Scourge licked his lips and swallowed hard, but nodded.

Wes glanced at Taylor, as if he were speaking only to her, but his voice carried to everyone as it had before. "I was a skeptic. Never believed in anything I couldn't see. So when this shaman friend of mine started talking about magic, I just smiled and nodded. Figured I'd humor him. Turtle is an old man after all, and I—"

"Turtle?" Taylor blinked in surprise. "Turtle is this shaman you're talking about?"

Wes frowned, tilting his head and searching her face. "You know Turtle?"

"I've met him, yes. He just showed up here a few times for no apparent reason. I never did figure out what he wanted. He seemed harmless enough, and he was friendly, so I didn't mind."

Wes seemed thoroughly surprised by her revelation.

"I'm sorry," she said, and she reached out, impulsively, touching his hand, covering it with her own. It was such a natural act, she did it without thinking, as if she'd been touching him this way for years. And when she did it, he looked down at her hand on his and blinked. Taylor felt her face heat, and drew her hand away.

Something was happening here. Something…potent. And totally unexpected. What *was* this?

"I didn't mean to distract you," she said, but her voice was coarse and unsteady. "Please, go on. You said you were skeptical when he talked about magic."

"Magic," he repeated, still staring at her hand. Then he blinked and seemed to shake himself. "Right, magic. When Turtle talked about magic, I didn't argue, but I didn't buy it, either. I hadn't figured out yet that he could see right through me. So, one night when I was visiting him, I noticed he'd let the campfire burn down to nothing but a heap of cherry red coals. I reached for a log to toss on, but he stopped me. And he told me to sit and be quiet."

Wes paused, looked around. When he did, Taylor did, too. Kelly and Scourge were rapt. Wes picked up a stray length of wood, stretched out his arm and poked at a nest of glowing coals beneath the fire. "They were like these, those embers," he said softly. "Red-hot." He stared at the coals for a moment, then shook his head. "So I sat and waited. And Turtle, he stood looking at that bed of heat for a minute or two. I thought he was meditating or something. Then he closed his eyes. And then he just…he just stepped forward…into the hot coals. And I realized then that he was barefoot."

Kelly squeaked in alarm. Even Scourge's jaw dropped.

"I thought my heart stopped when I saw that," Wes said. "It turned my stomach over, and I had to bite my lip to keep from yelling out loud and startling him into falling flat on his face or something. I jumped to my feet, reached for him, but he just held up a hand, and gave me this serene look. And for some reason I stood still. And old Turtle…he just walked across those coals like he was walking barefoot through the cool green grass."

Scourge swore. Kelly elbowed him. Taylor had fallen into some kind of a trance. "Go on," she whispered, and this time her hand closed tight around his, as if by holding on to him she could hold on to the magic he was casting around her. It was the third time their hands had joined almost of their own volition tonight, but this time he turned his, threaded his fingers with hers, held on gently, before she could pull her hand away.

When he met her eyes, she saw that whatever this thing was she felt, he was aware of it. Feeling it, too, and knowing she did. Her heart rate increased, and her stomach felt knotted with fear. She barely knew this man.

"Not much more to tell," he said, speaking low. Still holding on, his thumb now idly moving up and down on the back of her hand. "As soon as Turtle stepped onto solid ground again, I made him sit and I got down on my knees to examine his feet and tried to remember the number for 911."

Scourge chuckled at that remark. But Wes's eyes never left Taylor's. "But there wasn't a mark on him. Not a burn, not a blister. Nothing." Wes drew a deep breath. "Turtle pats me on the head like I'm a little kid or something and says, 'Raven Eyes, you have much to learn about shamanism.'"

"And that was it?" Kelly asked.

"That was it," Wes said. "He just sat down in his usual spot, opened a fresh beer and acted like nothing had happened."

The fire popped loudly, and Kelly jumped a foot off the ground. Scourge leaned closer to her and said, "Boo," but she only scowled at him. Then Scourge shook his shaggy head and said, "That's intense."

"Yeah, it was intense, all right," Wes said. "Shook me up pretty thoroughly, I can tell you that much."

"It gave me chills just listening to you tell it," Taylor whispered, and when he looked at her, she knew exactly what he was thinking. That the chills running through her right now were not from his story, and that he was perfectly aware of it.

She gently took her hand from Wes's, and avoided his eyes. It was ridiculous, this sense that she knew him. That she...

Ridiculous.

The small group around the fire fell into a contemplative silence for a while, and first Kelly, and then Scourge withdrew into their tents, yawning and stretching as they went. The sounds of nylon zippers broke the incredible tone of the evening for Taylor, but she couldn't bring herself to call an end to it. Not yet. Not even when every alarm bell in her brain was ringing, and her practical mind was screaming at her to put some distance between herself and this mesmerizing man.

Instead she turned to him, studied his face, his black eyes. "Raven Eyes," she said softly. "Is that—?"

"It's the name I was born with," Wes said. "My mother gave it to me before she took ill and died."

"I'm sorry," she whispered. "But how did you end up with the Brands?"

He smiled. "I'm only half-Comanche, Doc. The other half is pure Brand." She frowned and tilted her head. "It's a long story."

"It's early yet."

His eyes danced over her face. "It's midnight." And then he touched her cheek with a forefinger. "And you don't like stories, remember?"

Taylor looked at her watch, and shook her head in disbelief. The time had flown past.

"But I'll save that one for another time," he said. "And as much as I'm enjoying sitting out here with you..."

"I know. You must be half-asleep."

"I've never been more awake in my life."

She felt her eyes widen, her pulse skip. "I...um..."

With one hand he touched her hair, very tentatively, just with his fingertips, catching a lock between them and rubbing it. He closed his eyes. "Where the hell did this come from, Doc?"

Panic took hold. Taylor got to her feet, reached for a pail of water and poured it on the fire, symbolically dousing the flames licking to life in her belly. "I'm not sure what you're talking about," she said, reaching for another.

"Yeah, you are." He heaved the third bucket onto the smoldering coals. The water smothered the fire, turning instantly into hissing steam. Wes stirred the remaining embers with the long stick he'd been poking the fire with all night. "But it's okay. You know you can bank the fire, but the heat's gonna stay around for a long while."

She didn't look at him. Couldn't. "Tonight was... unexpected."

"I know. For me, too," he said. Seemed as if he was going to let her off the hook then. Whatever this thing was between them, they didn't have to discuss it, analyze it, admit to it out loud. She didn't have to be vulnerable to him.

She *wouldn't let* herself be vulnerable to him. To anyone.

But even as she reminded herself of that, there was a part of her thinking how she'd never in her life enjoyed an evening the way she'd enjoyed this one.

"Our ancestors," she said softly, "really knew how to live."

Wes smiled at her, easing the tension with the warmth in his eyes. "That's arguable," he said. "Our ancestors would have followed this late night up with a freezing-cold bath in the water hole around dawn."

"Well, nobody's perfect." She examined the fire

again, satisfied herself that it was safely extinguished and turned toward her tent. But she paused at the doorway. "You won't...leave or anything...during the night, will you, Wes?"

He turned from his tent flap to catch her gaze. "I'll be right here, Doc. I'll be right here."

She nodded once. "Thanks." Then she ducked through the opening of her dome tent, and pulled the zipper down to shut out the cold.

Chapter 5

Wes Brand was scared half to death. He'd known a hell of a lot of women. Hell, he'd *had* a lot of women. But he'd never once felt this kind of chill set into his bones, way down deep where a man couldn't do a thing to chase it away. He'd never once looked into a woman's eyes and seen...

What had he seen in those onyx eyes that had him so thoroughly shaken? He closed his eyes and brought those gemstones into focus in his mind. And it was just like looking into them again. And he was seeing—himself, only the missing part of himself, that empty place that even finding his heritage hadn't filled. And he was seeing—damn, he was seeing hearts and flowers. Wanting a woman was one thing, but this was damned *dangerous*.

In his mind he looked deep into her eyes again. And he was seeing...

Babies!

Wes jumped to his feet, forgetting he was in a dome

tent too short to accommodate his height, and poked his head into the top. Holy mother of God, what was the matter with him?

Lord help him, he was losing his mind.

He took some deep breaths and tried to keep from hyperventilating as he very slowly lay back down and slid into his sleeping bag. He just wouldn't think about her. That was all. He'd just think about the ranch. The old...uh...Cumberland spread. He'd plan—that was what he'd do. He'd lie here and plan his future until he fell asleep.

He didn't fall asleep. He couldn't focus on the ranch when he kept seeing her eyes, and the firelight on her face. And lying there alone, in the dark, his thoughts turned from hearts and flowers and—God help him—babies, to things of a more earthy nature. His mind wandered where it damned well shouldn't, so that every time he came close to drifting off to sleep, he started to dream of what she'd look like with all that hair hanging loose over her shoulders instead of bundled up in back the way she wore it. He'd start to wonder what she'd feel like naked and twined around him, and what kinds of sounds she'd make, and what her mouth might taste like, and...

And then he'd be wide-awake again, and aching. And wondering just when any man had been hit as hard and as fast as she'd hit him, like a mallet between the eyes.

All right, so he wanted her. Bad. It wasn't the end of the world. And it was no reason to give up on the job he'd come here to do. Right? No. In fact it was just an added motive to get the job done. He had to scare her away from here in order to save Turtle's life and—if he were very lucky—preserve his own sanity. And while he was at it, he might as well attempt to keep his hands and his thoughts to himself. All of which might be too much for one ordinary man. It surely would be too much for any man he knew.

But, he reminded himself, he wasn't one ordinary man. He was two men. Hot-tempered Wes Brand, *and*—stepping into a nearby phone booth—the mystical, legendary Wolf Shadow!

Surely between the two of them, one could manage to get the woman the hell out of here before it was too late.

Too late for what? he wondered.

He pulled his sleeping bag up to his neck and tried to get some shut-eye. But as dawn crept over the encampment, he was still wide-awake.

She dreamed again that night. As she slept, Taylor felt the woman she'd always been slowly peeling away, layer by layer, until the woman who remained wasn't Taylor McCoy at all. She was Sky Dancer, a Comanche woman, sitting at the central fire of her village and listening to a brave named Raven Eyes tell stories that fascinated her. And she couldn't take her eyes from him, and she realized that he was looking at her just as often, just as intensely. He was the most intriguing man she'd ever known. And she wanted him.

This woman, this Sky Dancer, wasn't afraid of her feelings at all. So when the others retired to their beds for the night, and Raven Eyes rose to go to his own, she took his hand, and she told him with her eyes what she was feeling as she drew him slowly to her painted tepee.

He followed her, his dark eyes blazing, and inside, in the dimness, he swept her into his arms, and he kissed her hungrily, greedily, taking her mouth in a mimicry of lovemaking that made her insides melt and bubble. She threaded her hands through his hair, tugging loose the band that held it tied back. And when the satin masses spilled free, and he lifted his head slightly, she looked up at him...

And saw Wolf Shadow. His face frightening beneath its fearsome war paint. His eyes hard and distant. His touch cold, and his breath smelling of death.

She sat up in her tent, eyes flying wide, and she screamed in stark terror.

Almost before the sound died, her tent's zipper was yanked upward, and the flap shoved open. And then Wes Brand was inside with her, gripping her shoulders in the darkness, touching her face, asking her if she were all right. She didn't need the light to know who he was. The sound of his voice was burned into her mind, after hearing him tell those stories the night before. She knew him when he spoke. And she shamelessly clung to him, burying her face against his broad chest, holding him hard and trying not to cry.

She hated for *anyone* to see her cry.

He stiffened a little at first, but only briefly. In a moment his hands were stroking her hair, and her back and her shoulders, and he was speaking softly. "It's okay, Doc. Look, it was just a bad dream, all right? There's no one out there. And I'm right here. Okay? Hmm?"

Sniffling like a child, she nodded against his chest. Her nose and wet cheeks and lips brushing the bare skin as she did. Tasting the salt of it. Feeling its warmth. She went still, and so did he. Heat uncoiled in her middle and spread upward, downward, everywhere. She was sitting up, her legs folded to one side, her sleeping bag tangled beneath her. Apparently she'd fought free of it during the dream. He was kneeling, one hand at the small of her back, where only a tank top lay between her flesh and his. The other hand buried in her hair at the back. Her own arms had twined around his waist, and her face remained pressed to his hard, bare chest.

It was embarrassing to behave like this. She was a scientist. A professional.

She was burning up inside for a man she barely knew.

Her own breathing was getting soft and shallow. His heart pounded against her face.

"Are you okay?" he whispered.

"I…I think so."

"I'm glad one of us is."

He was waiting. Waiting for her. To move. To touch him, to kiss him or to pull away. Some signal. Some sign of what she wanted. And if she knew what she wanted, she might have given it to him.

Still he waited. And finally he said, "Doc, I'm clinging to my last shred of chivalry with my toenails. Another second and I'm gone."

Her fingers moved. Not away, though. Just splayed across his back. She moved her lips to speak, but only managed to caress his chest with them, emitting soft air and no words.

"There it goes," he whispered. He pulled back just slightly, looking down, catching her chin in one hand and tipping her head up. Parting his lips and moving nearer, and she thought that in an instant he'd be kissing her mouth, and then he'd push her back onto the sleeping bag, and he'd…

He stopped a hairbreadth from her lips. Clenched his jaw. Swore. "You're trembling. Your eyes are as wide as the Rio Grande. I'm scaring the hell outta you." And he backed away, took his hands away, his warmth, his touch. He sat there and pushed a hand through his hair, blowing air through his teeth.

Taylor was shaking even harder now. So she pulled

the sleeping bag up over her shoulders. "I...I don't know what's happening to me."

"You're not the only one, Doc." He gave his head a shake, met her eyes. "You okay?"

She closed her eyes and nodded. "It was just a bad dream."

He looked around, fumbling until he found her lamp and some matches. He filled the tent with light, carefully set the lamp on a small stool and then turned to zip the flap closed. She sent him a startled look when he did that, and he said, "Bugs. Light draws them."

"Oh." She swiped at her cheeks, embarrassed by the tearstains he might see there. And she noticed he was wearing a pair of boxers, and not another stitch. He was incredible. Firm and lean and muscular. And she revised her earlier opinion that no man alive could look as good half-naked as Wolf Shadow did. Because the living proof was right in front of her.

Wow.

When she got around to focusing on his eyes again, she noticed they were glued to her chest. And she remembered she wasn't wearing much more than he was. A snug-fitting tank top and a pair of panties. No bra, and she figured he knew that by now. It was none too warm in here, and he'd been staring at her chest plenty long enough to see the obvious. Besides, a second ago he'd probably felt the obvious. She pulled the bag around her more thoroughly.

He met her eyes again. And his hair was loose. And she realized with a start just how much this little scene was starting to resemble her dream.

"I'm sorry I woke you," she said.

"I'm not." He looked her up and down. "I've been

wondering what your hair looks like when it isn't bundled up in a knot.''

Her hand closed reflexively around a tendril that hung down below her shoulder. "I—"

"Maybe I should stay," he said. "Maybe you'd sleep better. Hell, maybe we both would."

She felt her eyes widen and her heart trip over itself. "I...no. Look, I don't do this kind of thing, Wes."

She closed her eyes, shocked by her own blunt statement. But at least she'd made it plain. "I don't even know you."

He nodded. "That's not what it feels like."

"I know." She bit her lip, shook her head slowly. "I didn't come out here looking for...I don't even want..."

"And you're scared witless. What I can't quite figure out, Taylor, is what scares you most. Wolf Shadow? Me? Or yourself?"

"You don't need to figure that out, Wes. It doesn't matter. Because this kind of thing isn't going to happen again."

"Are you sure? 'Cause I'm sure as hell not."

She didn't answer. Instead she got up, too hot, needing air, leaving the sleeping bag to puddle on the floor. She pushed the tent flap open and gazed outside. "The sun's going to be up in a few minutes," she said softly.

A low groan brought her head around, and she saw Wes's eyes roaming up and down her body. She bit her lip, reached for an olive drab button-down shirt and pulled it on. "Sorry," she said. But the wanting was still in his eyes, and she was more shaken by it than by Wolf Shadow in all his glory. "I think I'll do what my ancestors did and take a dip in the pond this morning."

"It'll be freezing," he told her.

"The colder the better," she said.

"I heard that."

She swallowed hard. "I just need to be by myself for a while. You...um...you aren't what I expected to find out here. This is all coming out of left field for me."

"Me, too," he told her. "Just so you know. I'm as...I'm as blown away by whatever the hell this is as you are." He drew a deep breath, closed his eyes in resignation.

A deep fear gnawed at her stomach. Taylor met his eyes. "Don't be. This is nothing. Look, Wes, I don't want to mislead you. I don't...I don't *do* relationships."

A frown creased his brow, but he said nothing, just watched her, waiting.

"I came here to do a job. When it's over, I'm leaving."

"I see." But he didn't. He couldn't. She was confused as hell, because she was feeling something here, something she hadn't felt before. But it was physical; that was all. So her hormones were raging, raising hell after a lifetime of lying around all but dormant. This didn't mean anything. It couldn't. She wouldn't let it.

When you loved...when you trusted...when you believed in other people, you got hurt. It was the way it was. She'd spent years drumming that lesson into her heart, and she wasn't going to forget it now. Not now. Not ever.

Wes was still studying her face. But after a long moment he sighed heavily and turned toward the flap. "I'll get the hell out of here and leave you alone, Doc. I didn't mean to...shoot, maybe I'll take the next turn at that icy pond water."

"Just so long as you wait until I get back here first," she said. "And do me a favor, Wes? Keep the A-Team from wandering out there for a while?"

"They'll wander out there over my dead body, lady." He smiled at her, but it wasn't a real smile. All for show. He seemed as mixed up right now as she felt. But the sight of that fake smile made her stomach clench all the same. Then he ducked out into the graying dawn.

Do it. This is your chance.

Dammit, Wes thought. I can't. I *can't*. There's something about her…I want her. I want to…

No. I have to get her the hell out of here. Make her leave. I don't like the way I feel when I look at her. It's too intense, too…

But she was leaving anyway. She'd made that perfectly clear, and Wes was damned if he knew why the idea bothered him so much. It was what he wanted. And it would be better for him, far better for him, if she left here sooner rather than later. Because if she stuck around much longer…

He wasn't going to want to let her go.

It would be cruel of him to frighten her again. She was already so shaken up she was having nightmares.

He thought of Turtle lying on that cheap couch, wasting slowly away. Turtle, begging Wes to save his life. Surely if the choice were between frightening Taylor McCoy and losing Turtle to death, it was obvious what he had to do. The risk to Turtle was far greater. The consequences to Taylor, far less severe. What was a little fear when a man's life was at stake?

Besides, if he scared her, she'd leave. Soon. Before this horrible feeling writhing around in the pit of his stomach got any worse.

He waited until she was out of sight, and then he sneaked around the outer edge of the woods, reentering beyond her, and making his way to the cave where he'd hidden his supplies.

Taylor looked around carefully. A little niggle of fear rushed up her spine when she thought of bathing in the water hole, out in the open like this. But it was dawn. Wes would keep Kelly and Scourge from wandering down here. And that nut who wanted her to believe he was a ghost wasn't likely to show up in the daylight. He'd wait until dark to bother her.

She thought about her dream, about the way she'd felt in it. Wild and free, unfettered by shyness or fear. The way the Comanche women who'd lived their lives here had been.

Her ancestors. Surely some of their blood ran in her veins.

She blinked at that thought. It was the first time she'd consciously acknowledged that she was of the same blood. It must be this place. It was getting to her. And maybe that was part of the reason she'd reacted to Wes Brand the way she had. Just some of her long-nurtured inhibitions dissolving away.

She shouldn't be ashamed of wanting a man. It was natural. She was a healthy woman. Why shouldn't her body react to the touch of a handsome man? Why shouldn't it? It would be the same with any man she found attractive. There was nothing special with Wes. It was chemistry, pure and simple. No more than that.

She felt better having convinced herself of it. Relationships scared the hell out of her. Chemistry, she could handle. She was the one in control of her own body, after all. She could deal with it, keep it in check.

But a tiny voice in the back of her mind was telling her there was something more than the physical going on here. Something deeper. She didn't want to hear that voice, so she silenced it, refusing to even consider what it had to say. But the doubt remained. She just wished she knew for sure.

She stripped off her clothes, stepped up to the edge of the water and dipped one toe in. The chilly water embraced her skin, and she drew a harsh breath. Cold. Freezing. If she hesitated, she'd never get in, and suddenly she wanted to. She didn't know if she were trying to prove something to herself…to Wes and Turtle, who probably didn't think she was worthy of calling herself Comanche. It didn't matter. She wanted to do it.

Drawing a deep breath, backing up a few steps, Taylor ran forward and jumped into the water, sinking under the frigid surface as her warm skin screamed with shock. When she came up again, every nerve ending in her body was tingling and goose bumps crawled over her arms and legs. She felt alive. More alive than she ever had.

By the time he heard Taylor splashing in the water, Wes's face was hidden beneath layers of brilliant paint, an eagle feather was braided into his hair and he was wearing, once again, a loincloth and a string of bear claws around his neck.

He felt pretty much naked. And it wasn't as dark this time as it had been before. She'd see him a lot more clearly. Bared flanks and all. He could imagine how amused she'd be if she recognized him. His face heated, no doubt in reaction to the idea of her laughing at it. But for Turtle, he could do this. And for himself. She couldn't stay here. He could make her leave. It was just a matter of getting into character.

I *am* Wolf Shadow, he told himself. I'm a legendary warrior, noble, fearless, doing what's right.

Yeah, right.

Stiffening his spine and assuming a more noble, war-riorlike posture, Wes stepped out of the sheltering trees and up to the water's edge. And then he realized what he should have realized sooner. She was naked, too. More naked than he was, as a matter of fact.

Why that didn't make him feel any more at ease, he could only guess. No, scratch that. It would be better not to speculate on the reasons for that clenching and tight-ening going on all over him.

He caught glimpses of her dark skin as she moved and played in the water and told himself to avert his eyes. But he couldn't look away. He could only stand there on the shore, in the mists of early morning, watching her as if mesmerized. She was a different woman out here. Al-most childlike in her frolicking. Smiling. She was smil-ing. And he stood there in silence, wishing he knew ev-erything about her, watching her and trying to figure out the change. Until finally she turned and saw him.

She went still, one hand flying to her mouth as if to catch the startled cry that squeaked out of her. Her smile died, and the fear that crept into her eyes was too much for him.

"I won't harm you," he told her, deliberately speaking in a lower than normal tone of voice. "I couldn't."

She blinked, and her brows drew together. "As if I'd believe that. Why should I trust a word you say?"

"Because I say you can."

Again her eyes narrowed. Then they traveled down his body, and lingered. She drew her gaze upward to meet his again, and now she seemed more confused or puzzled than angry. "Pretend to be a gentleman," she said. "Turn around, let me get out of here and..."

Wes turned his back to her before she could finish the

sentence. And he heard the water rippling as she moved toward shore. But having his back toward her did little good. He could envision her body, gloriously naked, beaded with water and goose bumps, nipples erect and hard. He bit his lip, and turned around again. She'd wrapped a large towel around her, under her arms.

She scowled at him. "You could at least give me time to get dressed."

"What I have to say to you will not take long," he said softly. Too softly. That kind of catch in his voice wasn't going to scare her. He was supposed to be intimidating her. So he added, "Besides, I like the way you look. Dress after I'm gone."

"Bastard," she said. And she took a step toward him.

Startled, Wes took a step backward, and held up one hand like some extra in an old Western, about to say "How." Only his line was, "Stay where you are."

She frowned, tilting her head to one side. "Why?"

Uh-oh. She looked suspicious. Time to pull out the big guns. Or arrows, as the case may be. "I've warned you to stop this digging, to leave this place." He made his voice deep and scary. He hoped. "You have ignored my words. What happens to you should you ignore them again will be no one's fault but your own."

"So you came here to threaten me again?"

Wes grated his teeth. Why was it she seemed so afraid of Wolf Shadow when he *wasn't* around, but when he *was*, she stood up to him like a bulldog guarding a T-bone?

"It's no threat, Taylor McCoy. It is only the truth. A warning. I have told you the sacred place is here, on this site. That has to be enough for you. Tell the elders not to sell the land. And then leave here. Today."

There. Any minute now he ought to see the fear creeping back into those black eyes. And maybe it was mean, but it would get rid of her before his mental state deteriorated more than it already had. And it would save Turtle's life.

The fear didn't come. In fact her expression got about 360 degrees angrier. Not liking the way this was going, Wes turned to walk away. His intent was to vanish into the mists as any self-respecting noble warrior would do, and then hightail it back to his tent.

It took him completely by surprise when a small hand gripped his shoulder from behind and spun him around. Taylor stood toe-to-toe and nose-to-chest, glaring up at him. "Don't you *dare* walk away from me, dammit. I want to know who you are, and what the hell you really want, or I'll—"

He'd only meant to set her away from him. To get some distance between them and protect his identity from that piercing ebony gaze. But his fingers somehow tangled in the towel, and it fell to the ground. Taylor stood in front of him naked, chest heaving, cheeks flaming. Her fists clenched at her sides as he stood there, paralyzed, unable to move or take his eyes off her incredible body. Every cell in his brain went to sleep, and every cell in the rest of his body came to screaming, aching life. Looking at her was like glimpsing heaven. And he couldn't think. He wanted....

"Damn you," she whispered, and she bent to retrieve the towel. Unfortunately, at the same moment, his knees gave out, and he dropped down onto them. She tugged at the towel, but since he was kneeling on it, it was useless. His eyes feasted on her breasts. And then she went still, and he saw the anger in her face easing, changing, and he saw something else replacing it.

He lifted his hands slowly, so slowly he was barely

aware they were moving. As if they were floating upward
on their own, until they closed around her small waist.
She inhaled, a short, wavering gasp. But she didn't move
away. Her wide eyes held his, no anger in them at all.
Not anymore. There was something else. A curiosity. A
question, though he wasn't sure *what* question.

"Never in my life," he whispered, his voice harsh,
"have I seen anything I wanted to touch the way I want
to touch you."

He slid his hands upward until his thumbs could run
along the bottom curve of her breasts, and then higher,
brushing over her nipples. A sound came from her. Not
one of objection, but one of need. And when he met her
eyes again, he saw the excitement burning in them, the
ever so slight flare of her nostrils as the breaths rushed
in and out of her.

He pulled her downward, and she dropped to her
knees. And with one last look at the fire in her eyes, he
lost himself. He wrapped his arms completely around her,
pulling her tight to him, one hand closing on her buttocks, one threading through her hair. Her breasts touched
his naked chest, and he pressed tight to her, bending her
backward and lowering his mouth to hers.

Ah, God, she tasted good. Salty and sweet and warm.
He ached for her. Ached in a way he never had. Her
body, totally naked, utterly vulnerable to him in every
way. Her mouth, parting to let him take what he wanted,
her tongue responding to each caress of his. He pushed
her down farther, until her nude body stretched on the
ground, and he lowered his own atop it, still feeding from
her succulent mouth. He wedged his knee between hers,
parting her legs, and lowering himself between them. He
was hard, throbbing, and he pressed himself into her and
cursed the loincloth and thanked his stars it was the only

thing between them. She arched her hips against him, and he thought he would die of wanting. He reached down with his hand, parting her folds and thrusting a possessive finger inside her. When she stiffened, he pushed deeper, and she was hot inside, hot and quivering and wet for him. He yanked the loincloth aside, lowered his hips to hers. The tip of him touched her and pushed the merest fraction of an inch into her hungry body.

And someone—Kelly, he thought—yelled, "Ms. Mc-Coy! Ms. McCoy, are you there?"

She stiffened, palms flattening to his chest and shoving at him. And Wes jerked away from her, wondering just what sort of insanity had claimed him. But he shouldn't wonder. He knew. Who was it who'd said God gave man a penis and a brain, and only enough blood to flow to one of them at a time? Whoever it was had been right. He sure as hell hadn't been thinking with his brain just now.

Taylor looked bewildered. Like a sleepwalker just waking up and wondering how she'd got where she was.

Twigs snapped under approaching footfalls. Wes looked up fast to see Kelly making her way toward them at a steady pace. But she hadn't spotted them yet. Then he looked down at Taylor, lying there naked and hungry and confused, panting with reaction and wide-eyed with fear all at once. He knelt, snatched up her towel and draped it over her body. Then he turned and ran off into the mists, disappearing just the way he'd planned to do.

Chapter 6

She sat up, wrapping herself in the towel, scrambling backward over the prickly grass to snag her shirt and panties from where she'd left them. She tugged them on frantically and clumsily, because her hands were chilled numb and trembling.

What had she done? What had she *almost* done? What had come over her just now? For the past hour she'd been analyzing her attraction to Wes Brand, telling herself over and over it was only physical and meant nothing, and doubting the truth of that mantra. When Wolf Shadow touched her, when he looked at her, she'd felt the same sizzling desire she'd felt for Wes. And she'd thought…she could let him kiss her. Just once, to prove to herself that her reaction would be the same. Prove to herself it would feel no different. That any attractive man could probably elicit a response in her, now that her sleeping libido had finally decided to wake up. She was thirty-five. Didn't they say women reached their sexual peak around this age? Wasn't that the one and only reason she felt the least bit attracted to the two men who'd dropped into her life out of nowhere?

Well, she had her proof. She was right; it was physical. Because Wolf Shadow's kiss and the delicious press of his body against hers had aroused her as much as Wes's touch had done. But my God, she'd let herself get lost in it. She'd kissed him back. She'd lost her mind for a few brief seconds. If Kelly hadn't come along when she had...

"There you are!" Kelly said, hurrying forward. "I was worried about you. After that thing with that Wolf Shadow character and all, I thought you shouldn't be out here all al— Ms. McCoy? Gosh, are you all right?"

"What? Oh. Fine."

Taylor was kneeling, buttoning up her shirt, but she paused to look at the way her own hands trembled. And she wondered what her face must look like. Her eyes.

"You look scared to death," Kelly said, confirming Taylor's suspicions, as she knelt in front of her. "Did you see that ghost again? Oh, gosh, you did, didn't you?"

"I..." Taylor blinked, searched the girl's face and finally shook her head slowly. "No. Of course not. It's just the water, it's freezing. I dove in without realizing how cold it would be, and it jolted me." She hugged herself, rubbing her arms for effect. If she frightened the students with much more of this Wolf Shadow nonsense, they'd want to pull the plug and leave. Might even run out on her. And she couldn't risk that.

Kelly frowned, her big blue eyes probing, worried. She was a sweet girl, even if she was making eyes at the same guy Taylor was interested in. No. The guy she *wasn't* interested in. It was her body that wanted him. There was nothing else there.

And how could Taylor possibly feel even that one brief stab of jealousy, when she'd just been making out with another man?

She couldn't believe this. All through school she'd been a loner. An island. A solitary woman with more interest in dusty tomes and historical accounts than human beings. She'd avoided getting personally involved with anyone. Male or female. Sexually or otherwise. She didn't even care enough to have any real enemies.

Now she was turning into a grade-A slut. Burning up for two men, neither one of whom she knew well enough to call an acquaintance. What was the matter with her? Maybe she should see a doctor. Maybe raging hormones could be controlled with a little pill.

She gathered up her towel, and the T-shirt she hadn't put back on. Wearing her long button-down and her towel, she started back for camp. She hoped she wouldn't see Wes. Wouldn't have to explain her appearance to him. He was so sweet. And maybe interested in her. And patient when she'd explained that nothing could happen between them. What kind of woman must she be to behave this way? How would he feel about her if he knew?

Didn't make any difference, she told herself. It didn't matter how he felt about her, because she didn't have any feelings for him.

She couldn't face him. Not yet.

"Did you notice that hollow in the ground over there?" she asked, grasping at straws. Stalling for time. She had to pull herself together.

"Where?"

Pushing her hands through her wet hair, Taylor led the younger woman to a perfectly natural dip in the ground, and pretended to examine it, rattling on about possible reasons for it being there while her mind raced everywhere else.

Kelly fell for it for a while, but soon she was looking at Taylor a little oddly. "Ms. McCoy, is there some reason you don't want to go back to camp?"

"What? No. What a silly thing to ask." Taylor avoided the girl's eyes.

"Oh. 'Cause I thought maybe...well, that Wes Brand..."

"What about him?" She'd asked it too quickly, her tone too sharp. Stupid.

Kelly shrugged. "I've seen the way he looks at you. That's all. But if it's him you're avoiding, you don't have to worry. He's not there."

Taylor blinked and stared at the girl blankly. "Not..."

"He left right after you wandered down here. At least, I think so. He seemed to be heading out when I glimpsed him, and I didn't see him again after that."

But he'd promised to keep everyone away while she... Oh, hell, what difference did it make? It certainly wasn't the biggest promise made to her that had ever been broken.

Taylor gave her head a shake, turned away from the girl and started back toward camp. Kelly kept pace with her. As they emerged among the tents, she saw no sign of Wes. Maybe Kelly was right and he had taken off. Thank goodness. She turned to Kelly. "Thanks for worrying about me," she said.

Kelly nodded. "You'd better dry off, or you'll catch your death." Then she glanced at the sun, a fiery ball peering up over the horizon. "Then again, it'll be sweltering here in no time anyway. Maybe you should just stay wet." She smiled and headed back toward her own tent. Scourge was sitting near the fire with a cup of coffee in his hand, and he nodded hello as Taylor passed.

Closing her eyes in relief, Taylor headed for her tent, peeling back the flap, ducking inside and sinking to the floor to lower her head to her hands.

"Doc?"

Taylor jerked her head up fast to see Wes Brand sitting on the small stool in her tent, looking genuinely concerned. His face was red, as if he'd just scrubbed it. And his hair was pulled back into its customary queue, held in place with that thong of his. He wore a ribbed tank top, with a denim shirt tossed over it, hanging unbuttoned, sleeves clumsily rolled to just below his elbows. And black jeans that fit so snugly they ought to be illegal.

She felt so guilty she couldn't look him in the eye. And why, for God's sake? It wasn't as if there was anything between them. Not really.

Then why did it feel as if she'd betrayed him?

"Are you okay?" he asked, getting up, coming closer. "Did something happen?"

"No!" She bit her lip, realizing how defensive she sounded. "I'm just...jumpy. That's all. I shouldn't go walking off by myself when I'm so keyed up. I jump out of my skin every time a rabbit scampers by."

He frowned. "But you're okay," he asked. "You didn't see that Wolf Shadow character again, or anything."

"No, of course not." She averted her eyes as she said it.

"Okay," he said. And something in his tone made her head come up slowly.

He was quiet for a moment, searching her face. Then he averted his. "If you did see him, Taylor, and you're not telling me—for whatever reason—" He gave his head a shake.

Did he know? Had he...oh, God, had he wandered down to the water hole and seen...?

She turned her back to him abruptly, pressing her fingers to her lips.

"Look, I'm not prying," he said softly. "It's just that if I'm going to find out what's behind all this, Doc, you're going to have to be honest with me. If you don't trust me enough to tell me everything, then I might as well give up the investigation and—"

"I do trust you," she said, interrupting him, so guilt ridden she could barely stand it. And for no good reason. She schooled her features to what she hoped was a semblance of calm, and faced him again. "Really. It's myself I'm having trouble with." When he frowned and searched her face, she opened her mouth to speak, only to stop when movement outside caught her attention. She turned to see Scourge and Kelly outside, fixing their morning meals, pouring more coffee. "And you're right, something did happen this morning."

"But you don't want to tell me about it," he said slowly.

She lifted her chin, swallowed hard. "You came out here to look into this when you had plenty of better things to do. The least I can do is tell you what you need to know to do it right."

"So...?"

She closed her eyes. "If there's one thing I can't stand, it's dishonesty."

"Then you're going to tell me." He looked down, and something crossed his face. Looked as if he felt badly about something.

"I don't want to talk about this here," she said. "Can we go somewhere...private?"

"Sure," he said. "All right, Doc. Okay. C'mon, I know a place."

What devil was driving him to ask her about what happened this morning? He must be totally insane.

And why the hell was it he felt compelled to take her where he was taking her?

He didn't know. He didn't know much of anything anymore. She was driving him so crazy he wasn't sure what he wanted from one minute to the next.

Wes drove the little khaki-colored Jeep because Taylor asked him to. He opened the door, got in and adjusted the seat. She sent him a frown. "What?" he asked.

She shook her head and faced front.

He started it up and pulled out, heading over the rough terrain that skirted the woods, and around them until he emerged onto the dirt trail that passed for a road. And when he pulled onto it, he reached up to adjust the mirror.

She swung her head toward him, making an irritated sound, but then bit her lip and looked away.

Wes tilted his head to one side, and his troubled mind eased just a bit. Or he was distracted from it at least. Because he'd made another discovery about Taylor McCoy.

"You don't usually let anyone drive this baby but you, do you, Doc?"

She shrugged, staring through the windshield, but not seeing anything, he thought. Not the Texas sage or the gradual leveling off of landscape, that buzzard circling some roadkill up ahead or the increasing greenery they were heading into.

"I think I'll change your radio station now."

She blinked and looked at him. Gave her head a shake. "Sorry. I was somewhere else."

"Where?"

She closed her eyes, lowered her chin an inch or two. Was that guilt she was feeling?

Wes squirmed inwardly. He was the one who ought to feel guilty, first for trying to scare her, then for losing his sanity out there in the woods with her. And then for asking her to tell him what had happened when he knew exactly what had happened. He supposed it was some sick, morbid curiosity on his part. He wanted to know how she felt about damned near making it with him.

No. Scratch that. With Wolf Shadow. Not him.

And he wasn't even sure what he was hoping to hear. Would he be gloating or green-eyed if she confessed to having relished every sizzling second in his arms? In *his* arms.

Sighing, he shifted down a gear and took a turn onto an even less traveled dirt road, heading up a slight incline. Taylor glanced up at him, her eyes exotic and wide and curious. The guilt or whatever she'd been feeling, momentarily gone. "Where are we going?"

Good. A change of subject. He was sick of thinking about his alter ego. "It's just ahead," he told her. And then he braced himself for her reaction when the Jeep bounded over the crest of the hill and the level ground rolled out like a lush green carpet for as far as the eye could see. When he'd brought his baby sister up here to see it, long before he'd ever decided to buy the place, she'd focused in on the dilapidated barn, listing slightly to one side, boards gray with age, roof flapping in the slightest breeze. And the house, with the shutters hanging crookedly like broken glasses on filmy, myopic eyes. The railing, clinging to the porch in places, sagging in others, sections missing. The peeling flecks of paint where there was any paint at all.

Jessi's reaction had been a grimace. As if she'd eaten some bad meat.

He pulled the Jeep to a stop in what had once been a driveway and now was bits of hard-pack in between patches of weeds. And then he turned to see what Taylor thought.

Her back was toward him, though. She was opening the door and getting out. And as bothered as she'd been before about their near copulation in the woods, she seemed to have forgotten all about it now. He got out, too, and walked around to join her, eagerly searching her face.

She wasn't looking at the barn or the house. She was looking beyond them, at the gently rolling fields, and beyond that to where the creek meandered lazily, a blue coil bisecting the green, glittering like diamonds in the Texas sunshine.

She opened her mouth, but all that came out was a whisper of breath. And then she blinked. "I don't think…I don't think I've ever seen anything this beautiful in my life, Wes."

He smiled so hard his face hurt. "You're kidding."

"No." She turned to face him. "How much land is attached to this place?"

"Five hundred acres." He waved an arm to encompass the area. "As far as you can see. It's nowhere near as big as the Texas Brand, but—"

She trotted forward without warning, heading up the rickety steps to the porch, and then pushed the door, testing it, pushing it some more. It squealed in protest, but she was stepping inside by the time Wes caught up with her. Rapping the walls with a fist. Running a hand along the time-worn, dirt-stained woodwork.

"Look at this workmanship," she said. "And it could be restored, I think. There's no sign of rot."

"I thought the same thing." He couldn't believe her face. It glowed. Her eyes lit and sparkled, and she couldn't seem to stop smiling.

"The foundation..." she began.

"Solid as a rock."

"And the roof?"

"Needs replacing. Wiring, too. Plumbing's in great shape, though, and the house is structurally sound. Most of the fixing up will be cosmetic."

She'd stepped into the large front room, and was staring up at cathedral ceilings with chipping plaster, the same awestruck look on her face he imagined most people got when looking at the ceiling in the Sistine Chapel. But she paused to bring her head level when he spoke. "Will be? Have you bought this place, then?" Her voice echoed in the emptiness.

"Not yet. But I've put in a bid on it."

"Well, if I had the money, Wes, I think I would, too."

"Like it that much?"

She moved her gaze from one end of the room to the other, then walked slowly through to the wide bay window in the back, chipped casing and all, and stared through at the view. "If I found a place like this," she said softly, leaning forward, elbows on the sill, "I don't think I'd ever want to leave."

And he thought, *Maybe I should give it to her, then.* But wait a minute. He *wanted* her to leave.

Didn't he?

"I'd stay here always. Fix it up, a little at a time. Barn first, though. The house could wait." She pushed herself away from the windowsill and turned to head back outside. Wes trailed along like a lovesick pup as she stepped lightly down the porch steps and turned to inspect the barn. "Is it in pretty good shape, as well?"

"Water and power were never put in," Wes said. "We'd have to—" He stopped short, and his jaw dropped. He blinked. Lord have mercy, what had he just said? Had he just said *we?*

"What?" she asked, turning, looking as if she hadn't noticed.

He licked his lips. "I'll have to wire it from scratch and run a water line to it. You can see the roof is bad. But the framework is sound. Just needs work."

"That would be what I'd do first," she said. "Fix up the barn."

He moved up beside her. "That's exactly what I plan to do," he told her, a little amazed she'd agree. "My sister said I was nuts. That the house is more important." They walked side by side as they talked, slowly, arms swinging.

"Depends on who you ask. If it were me, the barn would be the first priority. Because I'd fill it just as soon as I could."

Wes stopped, crossed his arms on the top of a wobbly fence post. "And what would you fill it with, Doc?"

She smiled, and he thought she had the prettiest smile he'd ever seen in his life. "You'll bring in cattle, no doubt. Beefers like your family raises. But not me. I'd raise horses."

His arm slipped, and he almost fell forward. Caught himself just in time to keep from slamming his chin on that post. "H-horses?"

"Appaloosas," she told him.

And he just stood there gaping.

Taylor leaned back against another fence post, this one looking a little more solid. Her hair was loose today for some reason, and the breeze up here pushed it around a bit, so it seemed alive. "I have a mare, you know. Jasper. Oh, and she is the finest mare you've ever seen in your life."

She looked at him, but since he'd lost the ability to speak, he kept quiet. Just nodded at her to go on.

"I have to board her, of course. I don't even have a permanent home. I don't get to see her nearly as often as I'd like to. But someday..."

"S-someday?" he prompted, glad he'd regained the talent for uttering one-word sentences, at least.

"Ever since I was a little girl, I've wanted a big place. Like this one. Maybe not quite this big. Just big enough for Jasper and me." She looked around, shaking her head. "Now that I've seen this, though, I think I'd expand on that dream a little. Heck, with a spread this big, I could raise them."

He tried to speak, cleared his throat, tried again. "You'd want to raise Appaloosas?"

She smiled at him, nodding hard. "Silly, isn't it? I'm an archaeology teacher without tenure anywhere, and I'm still dreaming those little-girl dreams." She shrugged and sighed deeply, gazing off into the distance. And the dream in her eyes was so real he could see it there. What startled him most was that he was seeing his own dream there, as well. "But you know, I've spent a lot of time waiting to find something better, and I haven't. Maybe I knew more about who I was as a little girl than I've managed to figure out since."

"You ever have her bred?" She brought her gaze back to him, and he added, "The mare?"

"Oh. No, not yet. I will someday, when I have a place

of my own and room for a colt. But you know, the stallion would have to be something special."

"I...um...I have one."

Her brows came together. "A stallion?"

He only nodded.

"An Appaloosa?"

Another nod. My, but his conversational skills were honed to a razor edge today! "Actually that's what I want this place for. That's why I bought him. He's going to be the beginning of my herd."

Her lips parting slightly, she shook her head. "I can't believe this." But the look of wonder died, and one of confusion replaced it. "It's almost scary, isn't it?"

"What, how many things we have in common?" He lowered his head. "Freaking terrifying."

She came closer, laying one hand on his chest, so lightly it felt like a nervous little bird, ready to take flight at the slightest hint of danger. Swallowing hard, Wes lifted his own hand to lay atop it. And then he met her eyes and thought she looked more scared now than she had when he'd been *trying* to frighten her.

"I...I don't think it means anything," she said, as if trying to convince herself. "It's just chemistry. And coincidence. It doesn't mean anything."

"What if it does?"

She drew a breath, lifted her chin higher. "I came out here to tell you about this morning."

Guilt hit him hard in the belly. He dropped his gaze, shook his head. "No, Taylor, look, you don't have to—"

"He kissed me." She blurted it. And then she pulled her hand away and turned her back to him. "He more than kissed me. And I kissed him back."

"Taylor, it doesn't—"

"Yeah, it does," she said. "Or...I thought it did at

the time." Facing him again, looking like a criminal facing the jury, she lifted her chin. "I don't know what's come over me lately, Wes. I don't act that way. I've *never* acted that way. And the only time I've even come close to feeling that kind of…thing…has been with you. So I thought it was just my body telling me it had been too long and it was time and it didn't matter who…" She closed her eyes, gave her head a shake.

"And what do you think now?" he asked her.

"I don't know." She blinked up at him. "When I'm with you I think…maybe…it's something more. But it's something I don't want. Something I've never wanted."

"Like you thought you never wanted to know about your people, Taylor? Your past?"

She lowered her head quickly. "Maybe."

Her hair fell over her face like a curtain, and impulsively Wes brushed it away. "Would it help to know I never thought I wanted it, either?"

"I'm afraid of this," she said softly.

"I'm terrified of this," he told her, and it was the truth.

"I thought when I told you…about Wolf Shadow, about this morning, you'd…"

He felt like an assassin. Like a liar. Like a fool. "It's okay." He lifted his hand to touch her cheek. If he'd blown his chances with this woman because of all that Wolf Shadow nonsense, he would never forgive himself. Ever. "Let's forget it happened, Taylor. Let's start over, right here, today."

Her smile was tremulous when she faced him again. "At least it's out in the open. Whatever this might be…" She sighed, shrugged. "If it starts with honesty, maybe it will be all right."

Honesty.

How many times a day did she use that word in a

sentence, anyway? It was important to her. Vital, he sensed that. Then he went warm inside, because she leaned up, and she kissed him softly on the mouth.

A kiss he deserved less than any man on the planet. Except maybe Wolf Shadow.

"Wes?"

He opened his eyes, met her wary, uncertain gaze.

"Will you take me to the Texas Brand? I'd like to meet your horse."

"You might have to put up with meeting the rest of my family while you're at it," he said.

"I think I can stand that."

He slipped his arm around her shoulders, and turning, walked with her back to the Jeep. It was an odd feeling, this thing. This new thing where he could put his arm around a woman's shoulders as casually as this. Or hold her hand. Or lean down and kiss her cheek. This…Lord, this was turning into a *relationship*. And Taylor had told him, up front, that she didn't *do* relationships. And until now, he'd pretty much felt the same on that score.

But he was worried. Scared out of his mind, really. Because he liked this thing, and he wanted this thing. But if his secret identity came out…it would be over. He'd lose her before he'd ever really had her.

It was amazing how much the thought of that hurt.

Chapter 7

They had to head back to the site first. Taylor said she needed to put in several hours at work on the dig before she could leave. Her time was limited. That reminder jabbed at Wes's gut. Things were changing. Everything was changing for him.

By the time they headed to the Texas Brand, it was getting toward noon. Taylor was too conscientious to take a break before lunch hour, even though she wasn't punching a time clock and Wes was pretty sure the kids could have handled the morning on their own.

It would be just like that family of his to invite her to stay to lunch. And he was real nervous about that. He didn't want his siblings needling him about past mistakes or his infamous temper, or telling her stories that would curl her hair. His past was a sore subject, and he wasn't sure enough of Taylor yet. Hell, the whole town had pretty much turned against him after the robbery. Even when the conviction was overturned, Wes suspected most folks hadn't changed their opinion of him. And he didn't want Taylor to judge him the way the others had. Couldn't bear the idea that she might change her mind about him, once she knew the truth.

They took his Bronco this time, and Wes climbed into the passenger side before she could beat him to it. She paused beside the door and looked down at him, her long straight hair hanging through the open window. He wanted to stroke it, but resisted. He didn't want to scare her by coming on too strong. She'd been hesitant when he'd nearly kissed her in the tent before.

But she hadn't been hesitant at all with Wolf Shadow. Damn, he was being stupid. But it was true. She was different with him.

"So what is this," she asked, "you tired of driving?"

"I drove yours, so you get to drive mine." He smiled up at her, hiding the doubts that kept creeping in. "Besides, I want to make sure you know the way...so you can come back."

She smiled back at him and headed around to the driver's side. When she got in, she adjusted his seat, fiddled with his mirrors and twisted the radio dial though it wasn't even turned on yet. He was, though. "There," she said. "Now we're even." And she cranked the engine to life.

Wes gave directions for the shortest route to the ranch, and she drove, smiling in pleasure when the Bronco bounced beneath the arch and into the driveway. She nodded in pleasure. "What a place," she said. "Just as impressive as the first time I saw it."

"You like it better than the other one?" Why was he suddenly so sensitive about everything she said?

"Not by a long shot, but this is nice, too."

He almost sighed in relief. She brought the car to a

stop behind Garrett's gargantuan pickup truck, and looked at Wes a little nervously.

Wes jumped out and hurried around to her side, opening her door. "Come on," he said. "If you meet my horse before my family, they'll feel slighted."

"Wouldn't want that." She took the hand he offered and got to her feet, and then she paused, looking down at their joined hands, blinking as if she was seeing something she'd never seen before. Then she met his eyes and he knew. It wasn't something she'd never *seen,* but something she'd never *felt.* He was feeling it, too. He'd have laughed in the face of anyone who told him love at first sight could happen to him, but he was beginning to think this thing with Taylor was damned close to that.

The screen door creaked, then it banged. "Wes? Hey, I didn't know you were coming home for lunch. And you brought company!" Chelsea smiled and wiped her hands on the apron she was wearing. "You're in luck," she said, smiling her killer smile at Taylor. "It was my turn to cook."

"Is that a slam on the Brand men's culinary talents?" Wes asked. Then he glanced down at Taylor. "Don't let her fool you with that housemother getup she's wearing. Chelsea's a lot more than chief cook and bottle washer around here. Even if she *hasn't* acquired a respectable Texas drawl just yet." He sent Chelsea a wink.

She came down the steps and extended a hand. "I'm Chelsea Brand," she said. "You must be Taylor. I've heard a lot about you."

Taylor shook her hand. "I can't imagine how."

"Oh, I get around. Actually I'm studying for a psychology degree over at the university. The professors there have been bandying your name about campus since you started on the Emerald Flat dig. You have a terrific reputation."

"That's good to know," Taylor said, and Wes saw her chin lift just a little. She was proud of that reputation, and she should be.

The door banged again, and little Bubba toddled onto the steps, reached for his mother, teetered. Wes lunged quickly and scooped the pudge up before he could take a tumble. "Hey, Bubba! How's my best buddy doin?" He tickled Bubba's ribs, and got a squeal out of him.

"Eat," Bubba said.

"You *always* wanna eat," Wes returned.

Chelsea shook her head. "Taylor, meet my little boy, Ethan. Though the men in this house refuse to call him by his proper name."

"Hello, Ethan." Taylor came closer and stuck out her hand. Bubba shook it, apparently quite pleased at being treated like a grown-up.

"Who?" he said.

"Taylor," she told him. "Tay-lor. Can you say 'Taylor'?"

He grinned at her. "Tay-*lo!*" he said. Then he turned very seriously to his uncle, his little brows furrowed as he lowered his forehead to Wes's and stared him square in the eyes.

"He likes her," Chelsea said.

"Me, too," Wes replied. Then wished he hadn't, because Chelsea, when he glanced her way again, was grinning as if she'd just won the lottery. Lord help him now.

"Well, come on inside and let's feed this starving toddler before he wastes away," she sang, and she slipped an arm through Taylor's and walked her up the steps and into the house as if she were a long-lost sister.

By the time Wes carried Bubba inside, Taylor was being ushered into a chair at the kitchen table, and Chelsea was sending silent messages to Garrett with her eyes. Wes's brothers were already sitting, and it looked as if they were all picking up on Chelsea's unspoken announcement that Wes had finally found a woman he liked.

They rose as Taylor sat. Two giant maples and a whip-cord sapling, all inspecting the poor woman as if she were a cow they were considering buying. All smiling and nodding at one another as if they'd decided she'd be good for the herd.

Wes tucked Bubba into his high chair and performed the introductions. "You've already met Garrett," he said to Taylor, pointing.

"Chelsea's husband, right?" Taylor smiled. "Good to see you again."

"Pleasure's all mine, Taylor," he said, and they all sat down.

"The big blonde in need of a good barber is my brother Ben," Wes said, "and the puny one there is Elliot, runt of the litter."

"Thanks a lot, big brother," Elliot said. But he sent Taylor a grin.

Wes took the only seat they'd left him, the one next to Taylor, and Garrett started passing dishes around. Taylor said, "This isn't everyone, is it? I remember I met a sister...Jessi, wasn't it?"

"Yeah. Jessi lives in town with her husband, Lash, and their new baby girl," Chelsea filled in. "She's a veterinarian."

"Right, I think I drove past her clinic one day. Her husband is your deputy, right, Garrett?"

"He is when I can get him to give up daddy duty long enough to be. Right now he's more into changing diapers than keeping the peace. Fortunately we don't have a lot of crime around here."

Chelsea nodded hard. "Quinn, Texas, is the best place in the world to raise a family."

Wes sent her a scowl. Gee, next she'd be ordering invitations. "I have another brother," he said. "Adam works for a bank in New York City."

"I'll never keep everyone straight." Taylor smiled and helped herself to a scoop of mashed-potato pie.

"Sure, you will," Chelsea said. "But we're talking too much about us. We're all dying to hear more about you. Where are you from, Taylor?"

"I grew up in Indiana," she said. "But now I don't really call any one place home. My work takes me all over."

Chelsea frowned. "As highly as they speak of you at the university, I figured you must have tenure somewhere."

Taylor shook her head. "I haven't wanted tenure. Been waiting to find the perfect place first."

Chelsea smiled and glanced at Wes knowingly.

"And how is the dig going?" Garrett asked. "Any more trouble from your ghostly visitor?"

Taylor's eyes met Wes's. "Not really," she said. And he knew she didn't want to talk about Wolf Shadow with his family right now. He couldn't say he blamed her.

"I'm watching things," Wes said, to save her from having to say any more. "I don't think he's gonna bother Taylor again." Truth was, he meant it. His Wolf Shadow days were over.

After lunch Wes managed to extract Taylor from the grip of his family—though they seemed reluctant to let her go. He walked with her out past the stable to where the horses grazed in the back pasture, and she leaned on the gate beside him when he whistled to Paint.

The stallion galloped toward them, slowing to a high-stepping trot as he approached, shaking his mane. The show-off.

Taylor reached up to stroke his neck. "Look at him," she said. "Wes, he's fabulous."

"I know." The horse blew and stomped when Taylor stopped petting him, fussing until she started up again. That made her laugh, a sound like ice and crystal. Wes swallowed hard. "I have an idea, if you want to hear it."

"I think I know what it is already," she said. "But tell me anyway."

Wes turned to lean his back against the gate, scuffing the dust with the heel of his boot. "Well, you said you were boarding your mare someplace. I was thinking, once I get that barn in shape, you might want to have her trucked out here. I'd keep her for you for nothing."

"And breed her to Paint, here," she said, nodding. "But not for nothing, Wes. I couldn't do that."

"Sure you could. I—"

"No." She turned, too, leaning back against the gate just as he was. Paint leaned his head over and nuzzled her hair. Smart horse. "I'd have to pay you." She laughed at the horse's attention and reached up to rub his face. "I'd give you the foal."

Wes straightened and pushed his Stetson back farther on his head. "I couldn't take your colt, Doc."

"Sure, you could. Heck, Wes, I can't care for one horse, let alone two. What would I do with it?"

He drew a breath and sighed. Taylor straightened up and thrust her hand out. "So do we have a deal, or what?"

He looked down at the toes of his boots, looked up at

her again. "Okay. Deal," he said. And he clasped her
hand in his. But instead of shaking, he drew her slowly
forward, and pressed his mouth to hers. Light and gentle.
Long and lingering. But careful.

When she lifted her head, she looked as bewildered
and enchanted as he felt. Lord, but he was sinking fast
with this woman.

"You know what I like about you?" she asked softly.

Wes shook his head. "I can't even imagine."

She smiled a little. "You're gentle," she told him.
"You kiss me like you're afraid I might break. And
you're real."

"Real?"

"Straightforward," she said. "No games or acts.
Just...honest. That means everything to me, you know.
Honesty."

Wes swallowed hard and tried to still the panic in his
belly. She was sincere, meant what she was saying. But
in her eyes he thought he saw more. Anticipation. Ea-
gerness. She wanted to explore the feelings flowing like
a deep river between them as badly as he did. Wanted to
know just how deep that water was, and what lay at the
bottom...and where that river was going to take them.

Wes just hoped there wasn't white water waiting
around the bend.

There wasn't, of course. It was more like Niagara
Falls.

Wes was a special man. It didn't take much to see that.
He was gentle. He was sweet and kind and so, so very
gentle. She'd seen him with his little nephew. The careful, expert way he'd held the chubby toddler as if it were
something he'd been doing for a long time. And when

little Ethan looked up at his uncle, there was adoration in his eyes.

She liked everything about him. Everything. His family. Their teasing did nothing to conceal the love that lay underneath. It was something she'd never had, that closeness.

That afternoon she rejoined her group, and they wrapped up work on the quadrants where they'd been digging, and set up guidelines for the next. Small squares, roped off with light string. Wes had said he had to leave for a while. Didn't say where he'd gone. Didn't say what he was doing. It didn't matter.

Good God, was she saying that she *trusted* him? It was amazing to her that she could know a man for so short a time and trust him even slightly. She'd vowed *never* to put herself on the line like this for any man—or for anyone at all. Was she beginning to trust Wes? And was she putting herself at risk as she'd sworn she would never do by letting herself?

As the day wore on into late afternoon, with Taylor crouching in the square she'd assigned herself, sifting earth through a screened tray, breaking clumps of soil with her fingers and tossing pebbles aside, her fingers closed on something hard. Frowning, she grasped it carefully, setting the tray aside and reaching for her small brush, and methodically she began brushing the dirt away. Slowly a medallion emerged. An uneven oval of metal...gold, she thought, pounded flat. Symbols and designs had been carved into the gold all around. And in the center an almond-shaped, smooth piece of turquoise, with a perfect black circle painted in its center. Like an eye, set in gold. With a small black pupil. There were holes bored into either end of the oval, and she suspected a thong had been threaded through each end, to hold the eye around its owner's neck.

It was beautiful. And her first thought was that she couldn't wait to show it to Wes.

That made her pause and blink in surprise as her fingers caressed the smooth turquoise. Usually her first thought would be radiocarbon testing of the metal to determine its age, or perhaps what the stone had signified. Now it was of Wes. Lord, the way he'd crept into her thoughts was incredible. And frightening. And maybe…maybe right.

And at the same time, completely without her permission, an image flew into her mind. Of Wolf Shadow, sitting tall on his magnificent horse, this pendant gleaming on his naked, muscled chest. His eyes boring into hers and glazed with desire. His hands on her body. His mouth…

"Dammit, what's wrong with me?" She ordered the image away, but not before she'd felt the effects of it. Her body heated and her belly clenched. How could she be feeling so much—for the first time in her life—for one man, and still be so powerfully hungry for the touch of another? How could she care emotionally, as well as physically for Wes, and want to make wild love to someone else? It made no sense. Wes and that other man were total opposites. Wes was so tender, so sensitive. Wolf Shadow was wild and untamed, and dangerous.

"Where's Mr. Brand?" Scourge's voice interrupted her confusing, faithless thoughts. Guiltily she closed her hand around the pendant, dropping it into the deep pocket of her khaki trousers before turning to face him. Kelly stood by his side, shifting from one foot to the other a little nervously.

"He had some things to do," she said. "He'll be back

later on. Why, is something wrong?'' The two certainly looked as if there was. Kelly chewed her lower lip, and Scourge couldn't quite meet her eyes.

"Well, come on, speak up. What is it?"

Kelly drew a breath, looked at Scourge and sighed. "We went into town today, to pick up some bottled water. We were running low."

"And?"

"Well, we mentioned to the man in the store that Wes Brand was up here helping us out. And the guy just started talking."

Scourge cleared his throat. "It isn't like we were asking about him or anything, the guy just...he just talked. You know how older people like to talk."

Taylor frowned, waiting for them to go on.

"Ms. McCoy, you aren't like getting involved with this guy, are you?"

"Kelly, I really don't think that's an appropriate question." Taylor averted her eyes. "Just what did this fellow in town say to get you two so stirred up?"

Scourge lowered his head. "He said Wes was the black sheep of his family. That he'd done time in prison for robbing a bar and beating the owner half to death."

Taylor sucked in a fast, loud breath. Closed her eyes. It wasn't true. Not Wes. Not the gentle man she'd been getting so close to. "You shouldn't listen to gossip." But she turned away.

"He also said Wes killed a man a little over a year ago. With a knife."

"It's ridiculous!" She faced them again, getting angry now. "Don't you think he'd be in jail if any of this were true?"

"Maybe not...his brother being the sheriff."

"Oh, for the love of—"

"He does carry a knife. A big one, tucked in his boot. You must've noticed it," Scourge said slowly, not meeting her eyes.

She'd noticed it. But that didn't mean... "I don't want to hear any more slander about Wes Brand. I can't believe you two listening to small-town gossip and swallowing it whole like this. You're old enough to know better."

"But, Ms. McCoy, the man wasn't slandering Wes. He was...it was like he was praising him or something. Said if he ever had trouble he'd want Wes on his side and—"

"And that alone should tell you his story is nothing but garbage. Kelly, Wes Brand came here to protect us, for heaven's sake! He put his own responsibilities aside to spend time here, just to be sure we'd all be safe. He..." She pushed one hand through her hair and shook her head. "Look, that's enough. I'm not going to discuss this anymore. Gather up what you've got and get busy cataloging it. We'll stop in an hour for something to eat, okay?"

Scourge shook his head and made a disgusted sound in his throat as he turned and stomped away. Kelly started to go, too, then turned back. "It's just that we're concerned about you, Ms. McCoy. We didn't mean to upset you. I mean...we've never seen you look at a man the way you look at Wes. And if he's bad news...well, we just thought you ought to know."

Taylor looked at the innocence in Kelly's blue eyes, and her anger cooled to a simmer. "I'm glad you're looking out for me," she said. "But that's *my* job, remember? I'm a grown-up. I've been doing it for a while now."

"Okay. But...be careful."

She nodded. When Kelly left, Taylor brushed off her

hands and headed for the solitude of her own tent. And then she sat down on her sleeping bag, grated her teeth and prayed that Wes didn't have some secret side he'd been hiding from her. She'd begun to let herself think that maybe he was the man she was meant to find. But what if she hadn't seen the man he really was?

And if she had to ask him directly, and it turned out to be true, how could she trust him to be honest with her about anything else? How would she know when he wasn't lying, but simply hiding the truth?

And if she asked him about this and it turned out to be a pile of lies...would he forgive her for being so suspicious?

She gnawed on her lower lip. How could she handle this? How?

"It's over, Turtle. She's not leaving the site, and this Wolf Shadow nonsense isn't going to convince her to. I can't do it to her. Not anymore."

Turtle sat outside tonight. Wes had encouraged him to get up off the ratty plaid couch and come out under the stars to sit beside a fire as they'd made a habit of doing for the past year. The fire Wes built snapped and danced, and Turtle sat on his favorite lawn chair with a woven blanket wrapped around his shoulders. He sipped tea again tonight. And Wes was still very worried about him.

"Why, my friend?" he asked, then he closed his eyes, and the firelight painted his papery lids. "No, don't tell me. I'm still a shaman. I can see."

Wes frowned and sat still in the other seat, an old metal folding chair that had seen better days. He took another sip of his beer and waited.

"You care for her," Turtle said.

Wes choked on the beer.

Turtle's eyes came open, and he smiled slightly. "It is good," he said.

"Not if it means you're going to wander off into the desert and sit there until you die of dehydration and exposure, old friend. I'm here to tell you, I won't stand for that."

Turtle nodded slowly. "I've had a vision, Raven Eyes," he said. "It might be that my failure to protect the land will be forgiven...if you will remain there. Watch over it. See that the possessions of our ancestors are treated with respect, and honor."

Wes set his empty beer can aside and stared at Turtle. "Taylor wouldn't treat them any other way," he said. "You have my word on that."

"Not enough. You must be there. Remain until she is finished with her digging into the past."

The firelight danced on his face, making it appear red and orange rather than weathered bronze.

"And if I do, you're not going to go on this death march of yours? I have your word on it?"

Turtle blinked slowly. Very turtlelike. "If the time comes when I must go to await the spirits, my friend, I will come to you to say goodbye."

"Guess I can't ask for more than that," Wes said, but he was thinking that he'd hogtie the old shaman if that were what it would take to keep him safe.

"It's dark," Turtle told him. "You should go to her now."

Wes nodded and got to his feet, picked up his empty beer can and tossed it into the barrel that was overflowing with them. "Gotta empty that for you next time I come over," he said. "Remind me, will you?"

Turtle nodded again, and turned to stare solemnly into the flames.

* * *

When Wes had gone, Turtle slung his blanket off his shoulders. It was working. The long-ago words of the eagle to Sky Dancer's great-grandmother were being fulfilled. She would marry the man chosen for her. She would marry Raven Eyes. And then Turtle would teach them the old ways, together. He'd keep the promise he'd made to her grandmother as the woman lay dying.

There was still more to be done. So much more. He had to be sure Sky Dancer could be trusted not to violate the sacred ground, should she find it. He had to be sure the elders wouldn't sell the land to Hawthorne, in case she didn't find it. But he wouldn't take any action just yet. He had a feeling Raven Eyes and Sky Dancer must be the ones to work all of this out. To make the legend come full circle. Then prosperity would surely come to The People. And the spirits of Wolf Shadow and Little Sparrow would find one another, and peace.

He took a hasty sip from his cup, grimaced and spit in the fire. Tea. Awful stuff! He reached for a beer from the six-pack on the ground, took a long swallow and set it aside. Then Turtle got to his feet and began to move. Slowly at first, in rhythmic steps danced for centuries. A dance of celebration. His voice rose to the skies in the tongue of his ancestors, and his pace increased as he danced in joy around the fire.

Chapter 8

It was dark and he hadn't returned. And part of her was afraid Wolf Shadow would show up before Wes did. And part of her hoped he would. The guilt that rinsed through her over that thought was sickening.

Then her tent flap opened and Wes stuck his head inside, and Taylor sighed in what she sincerely hoped was relief.

"You're back."

"Sorry it took so long. I had to check in on a sick friend." He came closer, sat beside her.

She smelled beer on his breath. Sick friend? Then she closed her eyes and told herself not to let Kelly and Scourge's gossip make her start doubting every word Wes said. So he'd had a beer while he'd been gone. So what?

"Is anything wrong, Doc?"

She looked up at him, faked a smile. "No," she lied. Then she sighed. "I don't know."

Looking worried, Wes searched her face. "Tell me."

Taylor drew a deep breath. "I guess...this thing is moving a little too fast for me, Wes. I have all these feelings and..."

"And?"

She closed her eyes. "And I barely know you." She opened her eyes and looked at him. "I really don't know anything about you. Your past, or..."

Wes sighed, lowering his head. "My past." He said it softly, and she knew then that there was something. A chill went up her spine. Wes licked his lips and met her eyes again. "It isn't pretty, Doc. Truth is...I didn't want to tell you."

"Why?" she whispered.

Wes reached out, stroked her hair. "Because I'm scared to death of losing you before we find out...just what we have here. I'm afraid you'll change your mind about me the way everyone else in this town did."

He was really afraid she would. His dark eyes were so vulnerable right now. She gave her head a shake. "Honesty is more important to me than any mistakes you might have made in your past, Wes." And right then, she meant it. "I'm not going to change my mind."

"Yeah, well, don't say that with so much conviction just yet."

"All right." She shifted a little closer to him. This need to be near him, to be touching him, was overwhelming, and new and frightening. "Then tell me. But...hold me while you do."

Wes slipped his arm around her, and she leaned back and sideways, her head cradled on his shoulder. It felt good to be held in his strong arms. So good.

"I've done time in prison, Taylor."

She closed her eyes. Damn. It was true. She should have known nothing this good came without a price.

"I've never been known as a reasonable man," he told her slowly. "And for a while, I ran with a pretty rough crowd. I must've been about seventeen when some of the boys and I were drinking and raising hell one night. We got tossed out of the bar by the owner, and he was none too gentle with us. Well, I spent that night trying to stay on my horse long enough to get home. See, the one thing I did have in my brain back then was enough sense to take the horse instead of the car when I knew I'd be drinking. But to tell the truth, it was probably less out of any sense of right and wrong than it was because I knew Garrett would kick my young butt black and blue if I did otherwise."

She thought she heard a smile in his voice. Maybe what he had to say wouldn't be so bad. "And what happened?"

He held her a little tighter. "The boys went back to that bar after closing. Beat the owner within an inch of his life and cleaned out the cash box. It was dark. The owner swore up and down all of us had come back that night, but I swear to you, Taylor, I wasn't with them. Course, I had no witnesses, no alibi. Got myself convicted and did two years' hard time before one of the boys finally admitted the truth. I got a new trial, and the conviction was overturned."

She sat up a little, turned and looked into his eyes. He was telling the truth. She could see it. "That's it?"

He nodded.

"And you thought..." She shook her head slowly.

"Most people around here don't believe me," he told her. "And they've known me all my life. You've only just started to get to know me. Why should you believe me when—?''

''I believe you,'' she said.

Wes stared so hard into her eyes she thought he was seeing into her soul. ''Why? Taylor, you said I was gentle, honest. But I'm not. I've got a terrible temper. The whole town knows it. And I doubt there's a gentle bone in my body.''

''You're gentle with me,'' she said.

He licked his lips, shook his head. ''I'm different when I'm with you. I've been different since I laid eyes on you, Doc.''

''I know. I've been changing, too. It's not like me to trust someone, Wes, but…I'm finding myself…trusting you.''

He averted his face when she said that, and a niggling doubt crept up her spine. There was more he was keeping from her. She knew it right then. And maybe it had to do with that other bit of gossip Scourge had so willingly passed along. That he'd killed a man. But it couldn't be true. He was opening up to her, being honest with her. She had to let herself trust him. And pray it wouldn't be a mistake. It was time, she told herself. It was time to believe in someone again.

''You keep saying that,'' he said after a moment. ''About trust…about honesty being so important to you.'' He met her eyes. ''You've been lied to in the past, haven't you, Taylor?''

''Hasn't everyone?'' She blinked and looked away. But then she bit her lip and faced him again. He'd shared some of his secrets with her. Maybe not all of them…yet…but some. If she were going to make this work, she was going to have to do the same.

She returned to her former position, settling back into

his arms. "My parents—the McCoys—they never told me I was adopted." She drew a deep breath and let it out slowly. "I think I was around eight or nine when the questions started occurring to me. I was so different from them. My skin and my hair. But when I asked them about it, they just changed the subject, completely avoided the issue."

"Aw, hell, Taylor. What were they thinking?" His big hand stroked slowly down her hair. And again.

"But I could never get past the feeling that there was this big secret being kept from me. And it seemed like everyone was in on it but me. Kids in school, teachers, parents of my friends when I visited. I could sense it, you know?"

She felt him nod, and snuggled closer. "In seventh-grade health class we were studying genetics. And according to what I was reading from the textbook and hearing from the teachers, there was no way in hell a copper-skinned, black-eyed, raven-haired baby could be produced by a blue-eyed blonde and a blue-eyed red-head." She felt a tiny twisting in her stomach. It still hurt now and then, even after all this time. "I think I suspected it before then, but to have it confirmed like that...in school...all my friends looking at me like they'd known all along. The teacher suddenly backpedaling and trying to cover. But they knew. I could see it so clearly. I ran out of the classroom in tears. Mom had to come to school and take me home. And they still didn't want to tell me the truth. I had to practically force it out of them."

Wes shifted, pulling away from her for a moment and moving so that she reclined in the V of his legs, resting her back against his chest. His hands locked at her waist. He bent to kiss the top of her head. "It was because they loved you," he said. "They were afraid of losing something by telling you."

"I know that now. But then…well, I was pretty devastated." She laid her hands over his, squeezed them. "I guess that's why honesty is so important to me. It has been ever since then. Maybe it gets too important sometimes. If someone lies to me…I just can't ever trust them again."

He stiffened a little. She turned his hands over and threaded her fingers with his. "It was about that time I started to withdraw. I don't need a psychologist to explain that to me. I just didn't like being close to people anymore. I think I was subconsciously wondering what they were hiding from me, what secrets they were keeping. After all, if the people I trusted most in the world had lied to me, how could I believe there was anyone who wouldn't?"

"So you were a loner. Just like me."

"Yeah. But after a while I thought I could get past it, learn to trust again. I saw a therapist, for quite a long time, and eventually I opened myself up again. Let myself trust him. Told him everything I felt and thought and wanted and dreamed of."

"And it helped?" Wes asked.

Taylor drew a breath and sighed. "I had an affair with him." She said it quickly, to get it over with. She'd never told a soul about this. "I thought I was in love with him. And he encouraged it, talked to me about our future together, used all my dreams against me." She shook her head, closed her eyes. "Then I found out he was married."

Wes swore softly, held her a little tighter.

"I withdrew more than ever after that. Just sank inside myself, poured all the energy I used to spend on relationships into my studies, my degree and later my career. But it's never been enough. I thought it was. For so long I thought it was all I needed. Just me. No connections, not with people, not with my…my heritage. But now…" She turned in his arms, looked into his eyes. "Now I want more. And I think…I think I want it with you."

He ran his hands up her back, under her hair, fingers sliding over her nape and sending chills down her spine. And then he kissed her. As tenderly as before.

Taylor put her hands on his head to cling closer, and the kiss deepened. He slipped his tongue between her lips and tasted her mouth. And Taylor thought finally…finally he was making her feel the way she'd felt with Wolf Shadow. Aroused, and liquid, and shivery. She kissed him back. She touched his tongue with her ðwn, and twisted his hair around her fingers.

And then she lifted her head away, staring into his shining eyes.

"I don't deserve you," he told her. "They say I have the worst temper in seven counties, Doc. You sure you want me?"

"Are you trying to scare me away, Wes?"

"No." His gaze roamed from her forehead to her chin and up to her eyes again. "I won't hurt you, Taylor. I couldn't."

And in that instant his voice sounded exactly the way Wolf Shadow's had. He'd said those same words to her, in almost exactly the same way. And he'd sounded…

"Are you ready to make love to me?" he asked her, and now his voice was softer, raspier. A whisper.

She blinked, unsure, confused. "I…I'm not sure."

He closed his eyes, drew a breath, then opened them again. Leaning forward, he kissed her forehead. "If you're not sure, then you're not ready." He smiled gently at her. "And that's okay by me. I'll wait forever if I have to. But I think it might be best if I headed out of this tent now."

"Oh."

He kissed her nose. Then her lips, lingering there, suckling upper, then lower in turn. Then he released her with a sigh, and got to his feet. "We have a lot more to talk about, Doc. There are still things about me…" He closed his eyes, shook his head. "But we have time."

And he left, calling good-night over his shoulder as the tent flap fell behind him.

She *did* want him. She *was* ready.

No. No, she wasn't. Wes was right; they had time. And there was still something he hadn't told her about. It was shadowing his eyes tonight. She'd spotted the secret first when she'd told him how important honesty was to her, and again when he'd said there was more they had to talk about. She knew that look. That look of a secret hiding in a person's eyes. She'd grown up with that shadow peering out at her from the eyes of her parents. She'd seen it, sensed it there.

"Right, and I've been suspicious of every person I've met since." She pounded her fist into the sleeping bag beneath her, turned over, closed her eyes. Told herself she was overreacting. Wes had no secrets. He wasn't hiding anything. It was her. And she was going to ruin what could be the best thing that had ever happened to her if she kept doubting him this way.

She knew she would. She'd ruined budding friendships, even a couple of relationships with men after only a couple of dates, by being so untrusting of everyone she knew.

She had to get past this. Maybe talk to someone. She'd

always vowed never to try therapy again, after her dev-astating experience with it in the past. But maybe it was time she tried it again. Because she didn't want to take chances with this fragile, precious thing. She couldn't risk it.

Maybe…maybe she could talk to Chelsea.

Yes. That was it. She'd felt instinctively drawn to that small, auburn-haired woman. And Chelsea was studying for a degree in psychology. So maybe…maybe it would be worth trying. Before she screwed everything up with Wes.

Wes. The man she thought she might be falling in love with.

Chelsea refilled Taylor's cup with coffee, and returned to her seat in Jessi's kitchen. Taylor marveled again at the closeness of this Brand family. Chelsea had simply told Jessica that she needed a private place to talk, and Jessi hadn't batted an eye or asked a question. Just opened her door and let them both come in. Said Lash had taken the baby to the pediatrician for her immuni-zations, and that she would be out in the clinic if they needed her. And that was that.

It must be nice to be able to count on people the way this family could count on each other, Taylor thought, with a twinge of envy. She'd never been able to convince herself anyone would be that trustworthy, there for her, no questions asked, for any little thing that might come up. It was incredible. She'd lost the ability to trust fully in her parents. Oh, they'd mended things, saw each other often, got along well. And she loved them. But it just wasn't the same as it had been before.

And this closeness, this intimacy, was something she craved.

"This isn't really my area of expertise," Chelsea said, stirring her coffee and leaning back in her chair. "But I want to tell you how much it means to me that you could come to me with all this."

Taylor lifted her brows.

"I mean it, Taylor. No matter what happens, or doesn't happen with you and Wes, I want you to think of me as a friend. And anything you say to me isn't going any further. I promise."

Taylor nodded. "So what is your area?" she asked, sipping the coffee, enjoying her time away from the site and wondering how soon she'd screw up this new friendship Chelsea seemed to be offering her. "I don't think you said before."

"No, I didn't. I specialize in domestic violence. When I first came out here, I…well, I was a lot like you, actually. But it was only men I couldn't trust. Garrett included."

Taylor blinked in surprise, stopping with her cup halfway to her mouth. "You…you'd been…?"

"Battered?" She closed her eyes briefly. "I saw my mother die when my father took his rage too far. And then my sister was murdered by a man who'd claimed to love her. Little Ethan was her baby…his father was her killer."

"My God." Taylor's hand snaked across the table to close around Chelsea's before she'd even realized she was moving it.

"I'm okay now," she said. "Really. And so is Ethan. I like to think my mom and sister are, too, somewhere. Anyway, after I married Garrett, I saw a need in this area. So many small towns with so few resources. So I got involved with a domestic-violence hot line, and got some basic training in how to counsel the women who called.

It wasn't long before I realized I didn't know as much about how to help them as I would have liked. Garrett encouraged me to go after this degree, if it was what I really wanted. And it was."

Taylor shook her head slowly. "You must be an incredible woman, Chelsea Brand."

Chelsea smiled. "I like to think so."

They both laughed, and Taylor thought she felt more relaxed than she had in ages.

"Actually, Taylor, I don't think your inability to trust is an unusual reaction to the kind of betrayal you felt your parents had dealt you. And that therapist should be in prison for what he did. It's amazing you don't have more problems than just this."

"So what should I do?"

Chelsea tilted her head. "Not to sound biased, but Wes is as honest as the day is long, Taylor. If there's something you want to know about him, just ask him."

"But he might think I don't trust him."

"Well, you don't. You can't just yet, because of what you've been through. Be honest with him about that. That kind of trust is something that has to be nurtured and it will grow over time. I guarantee it."

"I still think he's keeping something from me."

Chelsea frowned. "I can't imagine what. You said he told you about his prison time. That's been a thorn in his side for a long time, I can tell you that. But he's been different since you've been around. Calmer. More serene or something. Actually he's been steadily getting over his rotten temper for even longer. I think that old Indian who befriended him has a lot to do with that." She sipped her coffee. "Of course, Wes thinks the rest of us don't know about that. But he'll tell us, when he's ready. Why don't you tell me what you think it is? I can see in your eyes there's something."

Sighing, Taylor lowered her head. "You'll think I'm horrible just for asking."

Chelsea laughed, bringing Taylor's gaze sharply back to her. "Honey, when I met Garrett, I punched him in the face and accused him of murdering my sister. You got nothing on me. Now spill."

"You didn't."

Chelsea nodded.

Taylor took a deep breath. "Some of the students heard a rumor in town that Wes had killed a man a year ago, with a knife. And I've seen that bowie he carries in his boot." There. It was out. She studied Chelsea's face, but there was no shocked reaction. No outrage. No righteous indignation.

"Oh, hell, *that* can't be the big secret you think he's keeping. Listen, I was there."

"So was I," a deep voice said. Taylor stiffened and turned to see a man she'd never met before, whipcord lean and handsome, carrying a pudgy baby girl with dark swirls of hair and huge blue eyes. He had to be Lash, Jessi's husband. He held up one hand. "Didn't mean to barge in. Honest. And I just came in this minute, all I heard was what you two just said. Scout's honor."

Chelsea smiled and shook her head. "I gotta get an office or something. Lash, meet—"

"Taylor McCoy," Lash said. "I'd know her anywhere. Jessi's done nothing but talk about the beautiful woman who's got her hotheaded brother acting like a pussycat." He smiled, his brown eyes warm. "Now that I've seen her, I think I understand how such a miracle could come about."

Taylor sat still, not sure what to say or how to act.

"I'm assuming this was a private conversation. Look, I won't repeat a word, but as long as I'm here, can I tell you about that day, Taylor?"

Taylor opened her mouth, closed it again, nodded once.

"Good." He came inside and settled the baby in her cradle and handed her a rattle. "Maria-Michele, you be good while Dad gets Uncle Wes outta hot water, okay?"

The baby gurgled and cooed in response to her father's voice, and Lash ran a hand over her curls before turning to join them at the table.

"Lash can give you a better version of events than I can anyway," Chelsea said. "See, I was busy being held at gunpoint by the man who killed my sister. And Garrett was trying to get to me in time to save my life."

Before Taylor could choke out her surprise, Lash went on. "Right. But the maniac had snipers lined up to take Garrett out. Wes and the rest of us were trying to remove them from the equation. Now, Jessi had just tackled one guy when—"

"Jessi?" Taylor gaped, wide-eyed.

"Oh, yeah. She's a hellion when someone she loves is at stake. Hell, that's why I take little Maria in for her shots. I'm afraid Jessi would punch out the doc for pricking her." He grinned and winked. "Anyway, she took one guy out, and I turned to see another one lifting his rifle and taking aim at Garrett. I couldn't get to the guy in time, and Garrett didn't even know he was there. Wes spotted him, though, pulled his knife and threw it just as the guy's gun went off."

Taylor looked from Lash to Chelsea and back again.

Chelsea said, "If Wes hadn't done what he did, my husband would be dead right now. Even the FBI agreed no charges should be filed against Wes. He just did what he had to do to save his brother's life.''

Taylor lowered her head and shook it slowly. "I feel so horrible for thinking...even for a minute..."

"Hey, Wes is no angel," Lash said. "But he's a decent guy."

"But, Taylor, if you're sure he's keeping something from you, it's obvious this isn't it. He'd tell you all of this just as readily as we would. It's not a secret. The whole town knows about it." Chelsea shook her head. "So if he *is* keeping something hidden, it must be something even *we* don't know about."

The front door opened, and Jessi came in, made a straight line for her husband and ended up wrapped tight in his arms. They kissed like lovers. And when he released her he said, "I was just telling Taylor that she ought to come by for dinner sometime."

Jessi grinned. "Oh, she will. I've got a feeling we're gonna be seeing a lot of her. *If* my brother has half a brain, anyway."

Taylor lowered her chin to hide the way her cheeks heated. "Thanks for that, Jessi."

"Stick around for a while?" Jessi asked. "You can help me feed Maria her lunch. I might even make you a sandwich." She winked. "I want to get to know you better, make sure you're up to the Brand-family standards and all that."

"Watch it, Taylor," Chelsea said. "Once she decided I passed muster, she wouldn't let me leave until I married into the family."

Taylor smiled. "I think I like you people," she said. "I'll stay if I get to hold the baby."

Taylor was thoroughly disgusted with herself for thinking there was even a slight chance the things Kelly and

Scourge had told her about Wes were true. She must be sicker than she thought to mistrust a man like him. He was honest. And kind. And with a family like the one he had, how could he be anything else? No, the more she thought about it, the more certain she was that Wes wasn't keeping any secrets. And that meant the problem was all hers, and by God, she was going to deal with it this time. Get over this habit of being so suspicious.

Because he meant something to her. He meant…a whole lot to her.

And maybe, just maybe, this lingering attraction she still felt for Wolf Shadow was just one more way she was subconsciously trying to sabotage her own happiness. It was probably all some very deep psychological thing that she couldn't untangle alone. But she would. Chelsea would help her.

She came back to camp feeling guilty, but determined not to wrong Wes with her suspicious mind again. And then she remembered the medallion she'd uncovered yesterday. She hadn't cataloged it yet, because she'd wanted to show it to him. And now would be the perfect time. It was the least she could do to make up for the rotten things she'd been thinking.

She got the turquoise eye from her tent, emerged and scanned the area, but saw no sign of him. The kids were doing paperwork in the shade, and she knew they'd attack the actual digging again in a short while when the sun wasn't beating down quite so fiercely. But Wes wasn't with them. Shrugging, she headed to his tent. The flap was unzipped, so she pushed it aside and stepped in.

No Wes. She felt a rush of disappointment, but told herself she shouldn't expect the man to be here at her beck and call at any given moment of the day or night. She turned to leave, tripped on the tent flap and caught herself before she fell, but the medallion flew from her hands, landing in a muddy bit of dirt directly in front of Wes's tent.

"Damn!" Taylor knelt, snatching it up, checking it quickly for damage and scowling at the mud all over its surface. She ducked quickly back into Wes's tent, searching for something to wipe the pendant clean, and spotted a washbasin in the corner, with a cloth tossed inside it. Snatching the cloth up, she carefully wiped the bits of dirt and mud from the pendant, sighing in relief when it seemed to be unharmed by her clumsiness.

But then she frowned, because the cloth left a streak of yellow on the stone. What the hell...?

Taylor rubbed the stain off with her thumb, then shook the washcloth out and stared at the odd blotches of color smeared all over it. It looked like...

She blinked in shock. It looked like the paint Wolf Shadow wore on his face. It looked like...

"No." She slapped the cloth back into its basin and backed away from it as if it could infect her. "It's my cynical brain working overtime again. He couldn't be..."

But what else would explain this? It isn't like he's been painting in here. It isn't Halloween. He's not an actor. So why's he got bright-colored stains all over his washcloth?

But what sense did it make to think Wes had been the man behind the makeup? Why would he want to scare her away?

God, had it been Wes she'd very nearly made love to in that quiet glade? *Have I been feeling guilty for being attracted to two men, who are really one and the same?*

Taylor pressed a hand to her suddenly throbbing forehead. This was ridiculous! How was she supposed to know when she was using her common sense and seeing the obvious, and when she was letting past betrayals make her unduly suspicious? And how the hell was she going to find out for sure which was the case this time?

But how could she doubt it, when the proof was right before her eyes? She recalled Wes's words to her the night before, the way they'd sounded so much like Wolf Shadow's. And his kiss...and the way his touch fired her body to life just the way...

Was it true? Oh, God, he had lied to her. She'd let herself trust him, and he'd lied. The pain that twisted her insides was nearly unbearable, and tears burned hot paths down her face.

But what if...what if there was the slightest chance she might be wrong? How could she be sure?

It came to her slowly, but it came.

She had to see Wolf Shadow again.

And when she did, she'd look into his eyes and she would know. She couldn't look into Wes's eyes and not know him, not after all this.

God help him if he'd been deceiving her all this time.

And God help her.

Chapter 9

Wes had bundled up all his Wolf Shadow paraphernalia and got it the hell away from the site. It had been tucked in that cave near the pond, but that was far too close for comfort. Under his bed, back at the ranch was the best he could do for now. And there it would stay, until he could find time to toss it into a bonfire, at least. He didn't want to risk what he had going with Taylor. And he wasn't going to. She'd never find out the truth. And now there was nothing standing in the way. He was going to wine that woman and dine that woman until she melted in his arms; that was what he was going to do.

A finger of guilt tickled at the back of his neck. He knew he ought to just tell her. Just come clean and have it over with. Hell, she'd probably react to just about anything better than she'd react to being lied to.

But what if he told her, and lost her?

Maybe he should wait. Tell her later, after they were on more solid ground. Maybe if she…if she…

He was a rat. He never should have started all this. But he'd make it up to her. He'd sweep her off her feet. He'd make her see that it didn't matter, that what was growing between them was more important than any stupid mistake he'd made. And he'd start tonight.

He was practically rubbing his hands together in anticipation as he traipsed up over the slight incline and headed overland to Emerald Flat that evening wearing his newest pair of Wrangler jeans and his best boots.

She was sitting near a campfire. Seemed she'd taken a liking to campfires since he'd built one the other night. She—or somebody—had built another in the same spot, though it wasn't even dark yet. And Taylor sat on a seasoned log and stared unseeingly into the flames. She looked worried.

He aimed himself in her direction, only to be stopped by a scrawny hand on his shoulder, and turned to see the hairball looking at him with what he probably thought was a mean look on his face. From Wes's point of view, it looked more like indigestion, but he didn't think that was the kid's intent.

Wes stopped, glanced down at the hand on his shoulder and narrowed his eyes. The hand fell away. Wes turned his gaze on the kid. "You got something you need to say to me, son?"

"I'm not your son, mister."

"You got that right," Wes said. "No son of mine would be traipsing around with an earring in his nose, unless he wanted it replaced with a bull ring." Wes started to walk past him. The hand landed on his shoulder again.

"You know, Stanley, you keep sticking that hand where it don't belong, you're liable to lose it."

The kid flinched at Wes's use of his given name, rather

than his nickname. "I want to talk to you," he blurted, but the hand fell to his side again.

Wes's temper bubbled up a little. But he managed to keep it to a simmer. The doc seemed to like Scourge, and Wes wasn't about to mess things up with her over the punk. "So what's on your mind?"

"Ms. McCoy."

Wes grinned a little. "Well, forget it. I got there first."

"I'm serious here, Brand. You better watch your step with her."

The simmer changed to a boil. "And just why is that?"

"'Cause I don't want to see her getting hurt, that's why. And I'm not gonna stand by and watch you keep jerking her around the way you've been doing."

Jerking her around? "Kid, I'm restraining the urge to kick your skinny ass for you here. But maybe it'd be nice if you'd tell me what the *hell* you're talking about now, while you're still able, just in case."

The kid swallowed hard, but lifted his chin. "She's been sitting there like that for over an hour. And I think she was crying earlier, in her tent. And she doesn't deserve…"

Wes swung his gaze to Taylor, shoved the kid aside and strode up to her, suddenly feeling the cold fingers of panic poking him in the gut. "Doc?"

She blinked and looked up at him. And damned if it didn't look as if maybe she *had* shed a tear or two today. She worked up a welcoming smile for him, but it was about as steady as a hummingbird in a hurricane. He dropped down on one knee in front of her, searched her face. "Taylor, what's wrong?"

She sniffed, shook her head. But when she met his

eyes, there was something there that scared the life out of him. "I hope you won't hate me for this," she said.

"Not a chance, lady." He clasped both her hands in his. They were cold, trembling. "Come on, tell me what's wrong. It's not going to be as bad as you think."

She closed her eyes. "You won't say that after you hear what it is."

Wes went stiff. God, was she going to tell him to take a walk? That she didn't want to see him anymore? That she'd changed her mind?

She lifted a hand, stroked his face. "I can't go on with this relationship," she said softly, tears brimming in her beautiful eyes. "Not until I..." Biting her lower lip, she shook her head.

"Not until you what, Taylor? Damn, don't leave me hanging this way." His heart had already dropped to the vicinity of his stomach. He was sorely afraid she was about to drop a boulder on top of it.

"Not until I see *him* again."

"Him?"

She took a deep breath, lifted her chin. "Wolf Shadow."

Wes blinked and managed not to let his jaw hit the ground when it fell.

"Wes, what I feel for you is...is so powerful, so intense. But...but you deserve more."

"I didn't ask for more," he said. "Taylor, you don't have to—"

"Yes, I do. Wes, I have to see him one more time. I have to prove to myself that whatever odd attraction he stirred in me is dead now that we're...together. For my own peace of mind, Wes. Can you understand that?"

He looked at the toes of his boots, shook his head.

"No," he said softly. "No, ma'am, I sure don't understand."

"I'm sorry, Wes. I think...I think this will be good for us. Once I put him behind me...I'll be free of him forever. And there won't be anything in the way of you and me."

"It doesn't make any sense to me," he said, staring into her eyes, a plea in his own.

"Lord forgive me if I'm wrong," she muttered.

"Taylor?"

"Please, Wes. Just give me some time. I need time to think and to sort out my feelings. And seeing him will be all the verification I need. I can't commit to you the way I think I want to until I prove to myself that I can live up to that commitment. Be as faithful as you deserve me to be. I have to see him, calmly tell him that it's you I want. If I can do that, then I'll know I'm okay."

He let his chin fall to his chest, sighing in resignation. "If you have to, you have to."

She nodded. "Maybe...since there's no way of telling when I'll see him again...or even if I will—"

"Oh, you will." He clamped his mouth shut after he said it.

"But who knows when? I think it might be easier if you moved back to the ranch until—"

"Forget it. I'm not leaving so that bastard can waltz in here and—" Wes stopped talking, replayed what he'd just said in his mind and frowned. Damn. "I'm losing my freaking mind here."

He turned and went into his tent, angry and hurt and jealous as all hell. Of himself.

Wes strode into the house that night without a word to anyone, heading straight up the stairs to his room. He felt the eyes on him. Garrett's curious gaze, and Chelsea's concerned one. But neither spoke, and maybe they sensed the turmoil going on inside him.

He couldn't believe it had come to this. That Taylor felt she had to see Wolf Shadow. It gnawed at him, and he couldn't shake the idea that maybe she preferred his alter ego to him. That maybe it was that legendary ghost she really wanted, and had been him all along. And it was stupid to feel that way; he knew that. But dammit, if she were so determined to see Wolf Shadow again, then he had no choice but to don the costume one last time.

He slung his bedroom door open and stalked inside, knelt beside the bed and groped underneath for the bundle that held his secrets safe from prying eyes.

And there was nothing there.

"You wouldn't be looking for this, now, would you, big brother?"

He came to his feet and whirled to see Jessi standing in the doorway with his satchel dangling from one hand. His temper heated up. "What are you doing with that?" He surged forward and snatched it from her hand. "Dammit, Jess, you know better than—"

"Than what? Huh? To worry about my brother and try to find out what's wrong?"

"To snoop." He tucked the bag under his arm, hoping to heaven she hadn't gone through it.

She stared at him hard, crossing her arms over her chest. "How could you do it to her, Wes?"

Hell, she had gone through the bag, then. "Look, you don't have a clue what's going on, so just—"

"The heck I don't! You're the one who scared that woman half out of her wits in that godawful getup. What

I don't have a clue about is why. And I'm not leaving this room until you tell me."

"I'm not telling you anything. This isn't your business, Jessi." He tried to keep his temper in check. He adored his little sister, but her meddlesome ways could make a saint see red. "Leave it alone, Jess."

She thrust her chin out, and he knew damned well she wasn't going to oblige him. "You can talk to me, or you can talk to Garrett," she said. "But I can tell you now, he won't be too pleased to have to arrest his own brother for trespassing and whatever else you've been up to out there at Emerald Flat. So what's going on? Why are you trying so hard to ruin the best thing that's ever happened to you, Wes?"

Sighing hard, Wes sank onto the edge of his bed, closed his eyes. "I'm not tryin' to ruin it. I'm tryin' to save it." He peered up at Jessi, but she was still standing there with that stubborn look in her eye, so he told her. He told her everything, and it actually felt good to get it off his chest. When he finished, she came to sit down beside him, and she looked up at him, shaking her head.

"You're going at this all wrong," she told him. "What you gotta do is throw this dang costume away and tell Taylor the truth."

"Hell, I can't do that."

"She'd understand, Wes. Just tell her the way you told me. Tell her about old Turtle and his illness and all. Tell her—"

"You don't get it. She *likes* the guy."

Jessi cocked her head. "Turtle?"

"No. Wolf Shadow. She...she's attracted to him."

His sister made a fist and knocked lightly on the top of his head. "Hello? Anybody home in there? The guy is you, Wes."

"Yeah, but she doesn't know that."

Frowning hard, Jessi said, "I wouldn't be so sure about that theory. The woman isn't stupid."

"She doesn't know. I'm sure of it, and dammit, Jess, I have to keep it that way. She wants to see him one more time, and by God, I'm gonna see to it she does. Let her get the damned ghost out of her system so we can get on with things."

"And you think that's what's gonna happen?"

He lowered his head. "I hope that's what's gonna happen."

Jessi shook her head. "I never realized just how clueless the Brand men were. Lord, but you all need keepers."

"I have to go." He got to his feet, satchel still tucked under his arm.

"Don't do this, Wes. It's bound to blow up in your face, I'm telling you."

He shook his head. "I got no choice." And he headed out without waiting for her arguments, because they made too much sense and he was already scared witless about what he was going to do. She was wrong, no matter how logical she sounded. Dead wrong.

He hoped.

Taylor waited until Wes was out of sight, and then she followed him. On foot. She cut through the woods to watch as he walked down to his car and took the long way around, the only way on and off the flat by car. And then she stationed herself there, where she'd be sure to see him when he came back.

It was over an hour. But he did return. He pulled the truck off the trail into a copse of brush almost as if he wanted it hidden, and then he got out, slung a pack of some kind over his shoulder and began hiking toward the woods where she crouched.

Catching her breath, Taylor ducked behind some dead-fall, and waited for him to pass. He hadn't seen her. Good. His steps never faltered. And he walked like a man who knew exactly where he was going. She gave him a few seconds, and then she crept out of her hiding place and followed.

Once she stepped on a twig, and it snapped. She lunged for a tree, flattening herself to its bark for cover, and when she peered out, she saw Wes standing in the distance, looking back, listening. She all but held her breath as she waited, and waited. But eventually he gave his head a shake and turned away again.

Relief made her almost too limp to move, but she was determined to know the truth. For sure. Tonight.

And in a few more minutes she did. Wes clambered up a shallow slope not far from the pond, and then disappeared. Taylor crept closer, pushing tangled undergrowth aside to find the entrance to a cave. And there was a light coming from within. Narrowing her eyes, she peered around the corner to see Wes sitting cross-legged on the stone floor, a kerosene lamp glowing in front of him, a mirror propped up against a rock. As she looked on, he pulled his hair free of its usual thong. Then he dipped his fingers into a jar of color, and smeared stripes of bright yellow over his face. Before her very eyes, Wes turned into Wolf Shadow. And it was good that she'd seen it because she never would have believed it otherwise.

She withdrew in silence, lowered her head, felt the burn of tears in her eyes, but only for a moment. Seconds later anger surged up to overwhelm the disappointment. Damn him. He obviously had some ulterior motive here, some hidden reason for wanting to sabotage the dig. And she couldn't help but wonder if his alleged feelings for her were as phony as the costume he was wearing tonight. Just another part of his scheme. A way of putting himself right in the middle of the dig, maybe getting in position to resort to some other means of stopping the project in case his scare tactics didn't work.

Why? She couldn't for the life of her imagine why.

But maybe the why of it didn't even matter. He'd lied to her. He'd betrayed her, when she'd trusted him in a way she hadn't trusted anyone in a very long time. And it hurt to feel this disillusioned yet again. But she'd deal with the hurt later. Right now the man needed to be taught a lesson he wouldn't soon forget. How could she ever have thought she could be falling in love with him?

She slipped down to the edge of the pond, brushed the tears from her eyes, and she waited. And within a short while, his footsteps came softly on the dried leaves and bristly grass behind her. Drawing a breath, telling herself she could play at this game of charades as well as he could—better than he could—she got to her feet and turned to face him.

She had never looked more beautiful, Wes thought, or more vulnerable, than she did right now. He felt like slime. Lower than that. But dammit, what choice had she given him? He was doing this for her...for them.

She looked at him as if she were seeing him for the first time, and he thought she set her jaw. "I was hoping you'd come tonight," she said, her voice barely more than a whisper.

"For the last time," he told her. "I can't come to you again after this." He didn't move closer. God forbid she should recognize him now, when he was about to put this stupid scam to rest forever.

"Why?" Taylor came closer, but stopped two feet from him, those piercing dark eyes of hers skimming his face.

"I am not real, Taylor. I'm a phantom. A myth. I don't even exist."

"We both know that's a lie." She came still closer, and this time she touched him, her palm skimming lightly up his outer arm. "You're as real as I am."

He drew slightly away, because her touch rekindled memories of the last time he'd been with her here. What had nearly happened between them. And he wanted her so much he ached with it. But not as some ghostly apparition. Not like that.

"You're wrong. I only came tonight to say goodbye," he said, and his voice had gone hoarse. "You deserve more. A real man, who can give you all that I can't. I'm going, Taylor, and you won't see me again."

She swallowed hard, met his eyes. "If that's the way it has to be."

He nodded. "It is."

"Will you do one thing for me before you go?"

So close. So close to ending this charade. Wes felt a shiver dance up his spine. "If I can."

"You can," she said, and she averted her eyes. "I need to know that what I...feel for you...is as nonexistent as you claim to be."

"It is, Taylor. It's only a fantasy."

"Prove it to me, Wolf Shadow." She lifted her head, met his eyes and came closer, until her toes touched his. And he realized for the first time that she was barefoot, as he was, and damned near moaned at the erotic thrill that rushed through him at that simple contact. Skin to skin. Warmth and softness. "Kiss me," she said. "Just kiss me once more. A goodbye kiss."

He shook his head from side to side, told himself to move away from her, and remained standing right where he was. "It would prove nothing," he whispered, even as her hands crept up around his neck and her fingers threaded into his hair.

"Maybe not." She pressed her body to his. "Maybe I just want to make sure you know what you'll be missing." She fit her mouth to his, and she kissed him, gently, softly. Too softly. She drew away to stare into his eyes, and then she kissed him again. Drew away again. Kissed him again. Drew away. "C'mon," she whispered. "You know you want to."

When her lips danced over his yet again, Wes lost whatever willpower he'd had. And most of his sanity, as well. His arms locked around her waist, and he bowed over her, covering her mouth with his. Her taste drove him mad, and he pulled her tighter to him, his tongue diving inside her mouth, his hands anchoring her hips to his.

Her hands rose between them to push him away, but he ignored their gentle pressure, and kept kissing her. And finally she pulled her head to the side, muttered, "Stop. Enough, it's enough."

But Wes didn't think it would ever be enough. Still he let his hands fall to his sides. She was breathless, wide-eyed, and if she wanted him as much as she seemed to, he'd probably just blown his plan all to hell.

She took a step away from him. "Goodbye, Wolf Shadow," she said.

And he was left to frown after her, puzzled, confused, disgusted with himself for ruining everything and with her for letting him. Didn't she have any sense of loyalty at all?

She turned once more to look back at him. "Maybe some night when you're so lonely you can hardly bear it, you'll realize what you gave up tonight."

"I already do," he muttered, but she was already hurrying back through the woods out of sight. Damn. He'd lost her. He'd...

No, wait a minute. Wolf Shadow had lost her. Maybe that meant there was still a chance...for Wes.

Taylor slammed into her dome tent, yanked the zipper closed and fumbled in the darkness for a gas lamp until she finally got the thing lit.

Damn him!

And damn *her*. How could she still feel so crazy in his arms when she knew full well how he'd tricked her and lied to her? How could she have lost herself in his kiss the way she had? God, she still wanted the bastard. Even knowing the truth.

She was sick. She was seriously sick to feel anything for him now.

But she did. Leaving him behind in the forest had been the hardest thing she'd ever done. She should have been repulsed and disgusted to have to carry out her act. Instead she was more turned on this time than she had been before. And maybe that was because she knew the man she was kissing was really Wes Brand. So that now all the things she'd felt for him, and all the things she'd felt for Wolf Shadow, had combined into a burning desire for them both—for one man who had for some reason tricked her into believing he was really two.

Dammit, she hated feeling this way.

But she could control it. She could get past it. She'd

dealt with lies and betrayals before and survived it, hadn't she? She could do it again. But nothing, *nothing* infuriated her more than being made a fool of. And this time she was going to get a pound of flesh in return. Wes was going to live to regret the day he'd tried to pull one over on Taylor McCoy.

Damn. Why did it hurt so much?

She cried herself to sleep. And she dreamed a very strange dream. In which she saw a woman who looked like her, lying very still on the cold ground. Eyes open, but unseeing. And a man—a man who looked like Wolf Shadow—kneeling beside her, crying. The dream wrenched at her on a deep level she didn't understand, and she woke with a start, sitting up fast and wide-eyed.

"Just a dream," she muttered, pushing her hair out of her eyes. She sat still, consciously calming her breathing, waiting for her heart to slow down to a normal rate again. But there was a smell. Wood smoke, pungent and soothing somehow. A fire's glow painted the front of her tent from without. The yellow flicker managed to permeate the fabric, and she could feel the warmth making its way inside, as well. And the invitation was too much to resist. A glance at her watch told her there were only a couple of hours until morning. No one would be out there. Hard to believe the kids would have built up a campfire and left it burning, but apparently someone had.

She slid out of her sleeping bag, and slowly pushed the tent flap open to peer outside. No one was there, so she stepped out, drawn closer to the fire's warmth and the snapping and crackling that was like a night song. She stood close, her back chilled while the front of her soaked up the heat.

And then a woolen blanket was gently draped over her shoulders, and she caught her breath, looking up quickly.

Wes smiled down at her, but the smile didn't reach his eyes. Her heart started to melt. She hardened it. He'd lied to her, deceived her, probably hadn't felt a thing for her at all. She couldn't forget that. No matter how the fire-light painted the angles of his face or lit up his eyes.

He lifted a hand to her face, ran the pad of his thumb over her cheek. "You've been crying," he said.

She shrugged and averted her eyes. "The dig's been a big disappointment. I haven't found anything but what I'd expect to find in a normal Comanche village. It's...frustrating."

"But that's not what's bothering you."

Taylor stared into the flames, because it was easier than looking into his eyes and wishing he'd just tell her the truth. "No."

He pressed a palm to her cheek, turning her head toward him, probing her eyes with his. "Tell me."

Taylor drew a breath, fought to keep her chin high, to make her voice firm and emotionless. "I saw him tonight. Wolf Shadow. He said he wouldn't be coming back again, and I believe him." In spite of herself, her gaze lowered to the ground. "So there's no reason for you to stay on the site any longer."

He was quiet for a long moment. Not touching her. Just standing there, so close she wished he would. Then he said, "I would have said there was a damned good reason for me to stay." He bent a little, dipping his head so he could get a look at her lowered eyes. "But maybe I was wrong about that."

"Maybe you were." The breath rushed out of him. Taylor looked up to see him standing there, eyes closed tight as if he were in pain.

Without opening them, he whispered, "Is it because of him? Are you—?"

"Am I what? In love with him?"

Wes's eyes flashed open, and she saw the jealousy flash in their depths so plainly it was unmistakable. She frowned in confusion. How could he be jealous of her feelings for a man who was...who was him?

"Are you?" he asked, and he held her gaze, his own burning.

"How could I be? I've told you how important honesty is to me, Wes. How could I possibly fall in love with a man who won't tell me who he really is, or why he wants me to leave this place? A man who claims to be a ghost when I know perfectly well he's as real as...as real as you are."

It was Wes's turn to look away. Was he ashamed, then? She hoped so. He ought to be.

"If it isn't him," he said, his voice low and measured, "then what, Taylor? I thought...I thought we had something."

She shook her head slowly. "Maybe we did. Or maybe it was wishful thinking. I don't really know what I believe anymore. This whole thing with Wolf Shadow has me questioning everything I think is real."

"I don't—"

"I'm the only one who saw him, Wes. He says he isn't real, so what if it's true? What if he isn't real? What if nothing I think of as reality is real? How can I trust my own feelings? And if I don't trust mine, how can I trust yours?"

"You aren't making any sense."

"I'm making perfect sense and you know it."

He went still, silent, searching her face.

"I think you've been keeping as many secrets from me as Wolf Shadow has, Wes." She lowered her head. "So there it is. I won't be lied to. I won't. I can't."

Silence. Long, tense silence, and she waited. His hand came to her shoulder, but she shrugged it away, took a step to put distance between them, turned to look at him. "So are you ready to tell me the truth yet?"

And he was starting to get it. She could see it in his eyes, a slowly dawning horror. "What do you want to know?"

She shrugged. "Oh, I don't know. Maybe you can start by explaining why you felt it necessary to make a complete fool of me. To make me believe I was falling for two men, when they were actually one and the same."

It was as if all the life went out of him. His shoulders slumped, his head lowered. "You know." It was a flat, toneless statement.

"Yeah," she said. "I know." She turned toward her tent.

Wes caught her shoulders and turned her to face him again. "I don't know what you're thinking, Taylor, but it's wrong. I can explain all this. Once you understand, you—"

"It's too late for that."

"It's not."

She put her hands on his, removing them from her shoulders, and dropped them at his sides. "The time to explain all this, Wes, was the first time you kissed me and made me think it was real. Or when you took me up to that ranch and convinced me we shared the same dreams. Or when—"

"Dammit, Taylor, all of that *was* real."

"It was a fantasy," she said. "That's how our friend Wolf Shadow put it, wasn't it? I think I'd call it something else, though. A lie. It was all a lie."

Again she turned. And again his hand came to stop

her, on her arm this time. Facing her back, he said, "I don't want to lose you, Doc."

"You never had me, Wes. So losing me isn't an option."

He ran his hand gently up and down her outer arm. Taylor shivered and drew away. "You still want me," he said.

"Go to hell."

"I will. If you walk away now, I will."

She didn't turn, because if she had, he'd have seen the rivers of tears gliding silently down her face. She just went forward, into her tent, zipped it tight and left him standing there.

Chapter 10

When she emerged from her tent again, Wes's tent and belongings were gone, along with his truck. Taylor stood by the blackened logs and snowy ash of the dead fire, and for just a moment let herself wallow in disappointment. He'd left. She'd told him to go, and he'd just packed up and gone. Somehow she hadn't pegged Wes as a man who would throw in the towel so easily. She'd expected him to stay. To try to explain himself. Maybe lose that hot temper she kept hearing everyone talk about, but had yet to see firsthand.

But he'd done none of those things. And she shouldn't care. She'd read Wes all wrong. Had never really known him after all. He was a quitter, readily accepting her statement that it was over, that it was too late.

Or maybe he'd never really cared enough to keep trying.

"Damn you, Wes," she whispered. "I thought you'd at least explain..."

Her head came up sharply at the odd little tremors she felt beneath her feet. A sound, like distant thunder rolling nearer, made her frown and squint into the rising sun in the distance. And then she paused, because the sunrise was so stunning. A giant red-orange ball rising slowly from the desert, painting everything from the sky to the trees to the parched ground with color. As she watched, something took shape near the very center of the spectacular fireball. A form, growing larger, right where the sun kissed the desert floor.

Taylor shielded her eyes with her hands. It was a man on a galloping horse. With the sun behind him like some artist's concept of the perfect backdrop, she could only see the man in silhouette. Like a shadow, black hair flying loose in the wind as he leaned over his horse, urging it faster, racing nearer. Man and animal moving as one magnificent shadow.

Shadow. Wolf Shadow?

Her eyes burned from staring into the sun that way, and she had to avert them. But when she did, it seemed those hoofbeats got suddenly louder and the ground vibrated with them. And when she looked up again, Wes was bearing down on her. His hair wild, his chest bare, his skin reddish gold in the blush of sunlight. But he wore faded blue jeans, and there was no paint on his face. She glimpsed something around his neck, a pouch of some sort, on a thong. And then she realized she should have been moving instead of staring at him this way. Because he suddenly let out a cry worthy of any legendary warrior, and leaned sideways as his horse thundered past. Taylor felt an iron grip around her waist and then she was hoisted right off her feet, and deposited again on the horse's back. She was awkwardly balanced between Wes's legs in a bad imitation of riding sidesaddle, and her hands gripped his shoulders in a knee-jerk reaction to keep from falling to the ground.

Not that there had been any danger of that. His hard forearm still pressed to the front of her waist, forcing her body tight to his unclothed chest. He whooped again, kicked the stallion's flanks, and they surged forward at dizzying speeds. She was vaguely aware of Kelly and Scourge lunging out of their tents and shouting after her. And then all that was behind them.

It was with a little shiver of apprehension...and something else...that she realized where they were heading. The animal's hooves were throwing parched dust up behind them now, as they galloped out into the desert, into the Badlands, toward the rising sun.

She lifted her head, fixed a glare on her face, though it was difficult with the wind whipping her hair into her eyes, and making it dance around Wes's face, as well. "What in hell do you think you're doing?"

"Did you think I was just going to walk away?"

She'd thought exactly that, but she refrained from saying so. "Wes, this isn't going to make any difference."

"No?" He slowed the horse a bit, drawing back on the reins, angling him in a new direction. Slowing some more until the Appaloosa stopped running, and was trotting instead. The running was easier. Now she was bounced up and down like a Mexican jumping bean.

"Dammit, I'm going to fall."

"Sit astride, then," he said, and without waiting for her answer, he closed his big hand on her inner thigh, and pulled her leg over the horse's back. Only she wound up sitting backward, facing Wes, one of her legs anchored over each of his. She might be sitting astride the horse now, but she was basically straddling Wes, as well. And he'd planned it that way.

Damn him.

"I brought you out here to show you something."

"I'll bet."

The horse stumbled, jarring her up and down again. Wes's hands closed on her hips, and she would have believed it was an instinctive reaction on his part, except that they tightened there, pulling her to the hardness of him. Pressing her close. And he closed his eyes, and swore softly. And then he kissed her.

One hand slid slowly up her back until his fingers spread through her hair to hold her head. The other remained on her backside, kneading gently, keeping her close. His lips nudged hers apart, and his tongue slid into her mouth. And while her mind was telling her that she hated him, her body was responding the way it had before. Her blood heated and her heart hammered in her chest. Her arms crept around him, hands pressing to warm skin and hard muscle. Her lips opened to let him inside. Her hips moved when his did. The horse had stopped moving, but she was barely aware of that. She only knew Wes was making her forget everything except the fire between them. Making her want him when she didn't want to let herself.

He pressed himself to her, and she let him, and it made her angry that she still wanted him this much. And then he drew his head away from hers, looking down at her, his eyes as glazed and passion filled as hers must have been. He closed them slowly, releasing his breath in a soul-deep sigh. "That wasn't part of my plan," he said.

She couldn't look at him. Wasn't even sure what she was feeling. "You have to tell me why."

But before he could answer, she heard a voice, very distant and faint. A chanting song, in perfect Comanche, sung by a voice hoarse with age.

"I'll show you why," Wes said, and gently he turned her around so that her back was toward him. Then he nudged the horse's sides, and they moved up into the rocky, barren hills, ever higher over twisting, barely discernible paths. Pebbles clattered behind them.

She saw a thin ribbon of gray smoke ahead, and then, as they drew nearer, the painted tepee that had been erected, and the form hunched before it. An old man, sitting on the ground near his small fire, chanting in his native tongue.

Wes drew the horse to a stop and got down. Then he closed his hands around Taylor's small waist and lifted her to the ground. Turtle didn't seem to notice them there. The minute he'd gone to the old man's trailer and found it empty and locked up tight, he'd known where he would find him. Damn.

"What's this all about?" Taylor asked, but Wes shook his head, took her arm and drew her forward.

Without looking up, Turtle said, "I knew you would find me, Raven Eyes. But why have you brought Sky Dancer with you?"

Wes sat down beside his friend, and Taylor followed suit, sitting, as well. "Turtle, I'm not going to let you do this."

But the old one only shook his head. "I am a shaman whose medicine has turned bad," he said. "This is the only thing I can do. My time has come."

"Look, we tried this your way. It didn't work. Now we're going to try it my way. Talk to her, Turtle. Tell her why she has to stop digging on the flat. It's what you should have done in the first place."

For the first time Turtle lifted his head, his faded black

eyes leveling on Taylor. Wes could see her scanning his face.

"If Turtle had something to tell me, he would have told me before now. Instead of just telling tales and giving out nicknames."

"Sky Dancer is your name," Turtle said. "Not a nickname. Your true name."

Her brows came together. "I don't understand."

"You don't want to understand. You come here to do your white man's work, but all the time you fear your own soul. You fear the touch of your ancestors. You pray you'll never know them."

Taylor blinked, got to her feet, turned toward the horse. "I don't have a clue what new game this is you've cooked up, Wes, but I'm going back. On foot if necessary. I'm not falling for any more of your tricks."

"Taylor—" Wes began, but the old voice interrupted him.

"I was there when you were born, Sky Dancer. I knew your mother. And your grandmother before her."

Taylor went utterly rigid. "My *mother* was Leandra McCoy."

"Loving the one does not mean you cannot come to know of the other." Turtle turned to Wes, while Taylor stood there, back to them, hair flying like a satin flag in the desert breeze. "I will take your advice, my friend. I will tell her the story. If she will listen."

Wes nodded, got to his feet and went to her. "Taylor, please. Hear what he has to say. Please."

She remained stiff, but slowly she turned. "All right. I'll listen. But don't think any yarns you cook up are going to make me stop this project. I've been made a fool of once. It isn't going to happen again."

Turtle nodded slowly, patting the ground beside him.

Taylor sat down. Wes could see the wariness in her eyes, the suspicion. God. She didn't trust him now as far as she could throw him.

And Turtle began.

"Wolf Shadow was a shaman. Young, but taught at the feet of the old wise men of our clan for most of his life. His parents knew from the time he learned to speak, that this was the path he would walk, and so he learned. He knew the ways of good medicine and bad. He was a healer. And the spirits spoke to him in visions few other men had the power to see. But the spirit of the wolf called him brother, and he could see. He knew where our hunting parties would find success. He knew when disaster was about to befall them. And his prophecies always came true."

Taylor glanced at Wes, but he only shrugged. "This is new to me, as well." Then he turned his gaze back to Turtle. "Go on, old friend."

Turtle nodded. "Wolf Shadow fell in love with a young woman. And he set about to win her for his own. But the girl was an odd one. Determined to remain alone, to live her days without a man or children. And some said it was her very strangeness that made Wolf Shadow as devoted as he was. He brought gifts for her. Meat and ponies and blankets. Yet she denied him. He tried to impress her with his strength and skill in riding and fighting, but to no avail. It was only when Wolf Shadow took ill that her heart softened. She cared for him herself, refusing to allow any others into his tepee, and it's said that she fell in love with him then. When he was well again, the two were as one, never apart. And their happiness was said to fill the entire village with joy just at seeing it. Everyone became involved in the preparations for the ceremony that would join them."

Taylor had heard the story before. But Turtle was embellishing more this time, she thought. Turtle fell silent for a moment, staring into the dying flames of his small fire, breathing deeply. It was almost as if he could see the story he told, unfolding in the fire.

"But before they were joined, she was killed when the white man's horse soldiers raided the village. It was said they attacked to avenge some Indian raid on their towns, but our village was a peace-loving one. At least, it had been, until then. Wolf Shadow never smiled again, after that day. He became a warrior, raining vengeance upon the soldiers at every opportunity."

"You've told me this before, Turtle," Taylor said. "They were never married."

"Wolf Shadow spent days at her burial spot, hiding away many of the things sacred to the two of them. The heart he'd shaped of turquoise and given to her, the beaded moccasins she'd made for him. He declared that spot to be sacred, and vowed no one should set foot there or desecrate the ground. Before he set out on the raid that would be his last, Wolf Shadow told the villagers of a vision he'd seen while mourning over the body of his love. He said that because their love had never been consummated, neither of their spirits would find peace. He claimed he could only be freed when one of his descendants found true love with one of hers, completing the circle begun so long ago."

"Descendants?" Taylor glanced toward Wes, who'd gone still and silent.

"One of Wolf Shadow's nieces was given to Little Sparrow's nephew. But it was never true love. Only the village shamans knew, of course, but the spirits of the two lovers remained in turmoil. Ever seeking, but unable to find one another."

He looked Taylor in the eye, his own eyes clouded and sad. "Her resting place is in danger, Sky Dancer. You must stop this digging. Wolf Shadow has suffered enough. Moreover he charged the shamans of our line with the task of keeping that place safe, and I am the last of those. If I fail..."

Taylor got to her feet, paced toward the fire, stopped. "Turtle, you could have told me all of this a long time ago. I asked you, and other Comanche elders, if there were objections to excavating Emerald Flat. You all said there was nothing. The elders *asked* me to come here."

"Umm." Turtle nodded, lowering his gaze again. "They were determined to go through with the sale to Hawthorne unless they found proof that Little Sparrow's resting place was here. Hawthorne wanted a team of his own choosing. I was able to convince the elders to agree to the dig only if they could choose the scientist themselves. Hawthorne has his own reasons for wanting this land, none of which are known to us. It was I who told the elders to contact you, Sky Dancer."

"You...?"

"The legend of Wolf Shadow and Little Sparrow is sacred, and told again only to Comanches descended from their village and clan. And again there was the chance that once you knew of the sacred articles to be found, you would seek all the harder for the place where they've lain since the time of my grandfathers' grandfathers."

She turned slowly to face Turtle, brows lifting. "It's been that long?"

"Three centuries, and more," Turtle told her.

And she slanted a suspicious gaze toward Wes. "But the artifacts we've been uncovering on the flat are less than half that old. My research says the village is far older, but so far I've found nothing to indicate—''

"The village remained," Turtle said, nodding slowly. "The People lived there, each generation after the one before. Until they were herded like cattle onto the reservation. But that spot where Wolf Shadow buried Little Sparrow went untouched from the time she was lain down. And eventually the whites saw fit to return this bit of land to The People, because they saw it as barren and of little use to them."

Taylor nodded slowly. "Then this sacred spot wasn't *in* the village, but somewhere outside it."

"Taylor?" Wes searched her face when she turned to look his way. "For God's sake, you aren't seriously considering looking for it, are you? Not after what Turtle just told you. You can't—''

"If I don't find the spot, the land will be sold anyway," Taylor said. "Besides, how can I believe all of this isn't another lie? I want to know the real reason you two want me out of here. Until I do, the dig goes on as planned."

Turtle lowered his head. "Then I've failed."

For just a minute Taylor looked alarmed. But then she gave her head a shake. "Everyone knows you two are best friends," she said to Wes, with a nod toward the old man on the ground. "You cooked this up as another way of scaring me off. I'm not falling for it, okay? You think you can lie and trick me the way you have and then expect me to fall for the very next game you set up?" She shook her head, her eyes flashing. "No way. I'm the least gullible woman you're ever likely to meet, Wes."

When she turned to begin trudging off toward the flat, Wes shot forward, gripped her shoulders, made her face him. "This isn't a game, dammit. *Look* at him. He's waiting to die, Taylor. If you go on with this dig…'' He let his words trail off, because he saw no hint of surrender in her eyes. "You really don't believe a word he said, do you?"

"Not a word." She looked away. "And I can't believe you'd try to take the things I told you and twist them around to use against me this way. But I don't suppose I should be surprised."

"Taylor, that's not what this is about."

"The hell it isn't. It's one big guilt trip. Heap it on and you figure I'll buckle just to make up for neglecting my heritage all these years. Ignoring it. Well, I don't want it, Wes. For a while I thought I did, but…" She shook her head. "I'm damned well not going to give up on this dig out of guilt. So forget it."

She meant it. He'd destroyed any hope she'd trust a word he said, and Turtle was apparently judged guilty by association. He glanced toward where his horse stood patiently. "Take the horse," he said. "Get back to camp where you belong. I'll take care of Turtle."

"Fine. You two can sit here and start plotting your next scam." She walked away from him, mounted the horse with ease and whirled him around toward the site. With one last glance back at Turtle, she dug in her heels.

The dig continued at the village site through the day. Aside from a few bits of pottery, nothing major came of it. Taylor let Kelly and Scourge work, and closeted herself in her tent. Scourge had begun work on a map of the village based on what they'd found, and Taylor studied it, trying to decide where this so-called sacred spot might be located, if it even existed. Chances were it was as bogus as the rest of Turtle's tale.

But as determined as she was to ignore the old man's

story, it kept coming back to her. So much so that she was compelled to go through every account she'd brought with her, concerning the history of the Comanches in this area. Nowhere did she find mention of the location of Little Sparrow's resting place. The question was, what was the real reason Wes and Turtle were conspiring against her? What hidden truths were their lies covering up?

And what if she was wrong?

She closed her eyes and thought of the dream she'd had, of Wolf Shadow crying beside Little Sparrow's grave.

God, what if she was wrong?

There was no convincing Turtle to leave his morbid vigil. Wes tried everything from pleading with him to screaming at him, but nothing helped. At least he'd convinced his friend to eat something. He'd bagged a rabbit and cooked it over the fire, and Turtle had eaten a healthy portion. He was drinking the water Wes had brought out here, as well. But the fire was pathetic, and there wasn't a hell of a lot of wood to be found in the area, so keeping it any warmer would be impossible. He draped blankets over Turtle's shoulders and walked off through the rocks in search of more fuel. He'd been talking until he was hoarse, all day, trying to get Turtle to give in, but to no avail. It would be dark soon. The old man would freeze without a decent fire to keep him warm. And Wes wasn't willing to let that happen.

He was furious with Taylor. Wanted to shake her until she understood that this was for real. But every time his anger reached the boiling point, he reminded himself that her skepticism was his own fault. He'd courted her trust, and then broken it. Even knowing how much it galled her to be lied to. And she was right. She had told him things in confidence. Only to find out he'd been lying through his teeth all along. Could he really blame her?

He spotted some rotting branches that had fallen from a scrawny, sickly tree that had somehow grown here among the rocks, and he bent to begin picking them up, one by one. One branch seemed anchored in the ground beneath a huge boulder, and Wes yanked hard on it to pull it free. When it came, a shower of pebbles and dirt tumbled free with it, and Wes saw the concave shape that had been painstakingly chiseled into the rock, then covered over with smaller stones.

He went still. There was something in there. Something... Wes reached his hand into the opening and touched it. And the shape was smooth and cool against his fingers. He drew the item out, and saw it. The turquoise heart Turtle had described. With the figure of a sparrow etched into its blue-green face.

His heart beat faster as the stone seemed to warm in his hand. Wes quickly replaced it where it had been before, and shoved the pebbles in around it to hide it again. My God, this was the place. This was where Little Sparrow had been buried, and where her lover had sat for days mourning her. This was the spot no white man was ever to defile.

And here he was, invading it.

A sound made him whirl almost guiltily, and Wes glimpsed a man standing in the distance. For a second he thought he was looking into a mirror. But that would only have been right if he'd braided an eagle's feather into his hair, and wore buckskins instead of blue jeans. Aside from that, though, the image was his own. Standing about a hundred yards away, just staring at him, with eyes that looked haunted and unspeakably sad.

Wes blinked, rubbed his eyes and looked again. But this time there was nothing there.

"It's the desert," he muttered. "Been hotter than hell all day, and I probably didn't drink enough. Mirage. That's all."

Again he checked to be sure he'd concealed the treasure he'd found. And then he gathered up the wood he'd dropped, and returned to Turtle.

He could wait this thing out, hope Taylor never found the pendant. She'd pack up and leave, and when she did, Turtle would quit with this death watch he was on. She'd leave. She'd walk away believing he'd lied to her again. Believing he'd used her deepest feelings against her.

Or he could show her what he'd found. It would prove he'd been on the level and maybe give him another chance with her, which was what he wanted more than anything in the world. And if she knew it were true, she'd do the right thing.

Wouldn't she?

Could he risk that she might not?

He thought about the look in the apparition's eyes. Thought about the heartbreaking story Turtle had told him. And wondered just what in hell was the right thing to do.

Taylor waited until everyone was asleep to pull on her parka and hoist the heavy pack onto her back. Wes's horse was grazing contentedly where she'd picketed him, near the pond, but she'd have to see to it he got back to the ranch tomorrow. She'd kind of figured Wes would come back for him today, but he hadn't. And more and more, doubts were creeping into her mind.

She couldn't rest. Not until she just checked in. Just in case she was wrong, she had to make sure that old man was still all right. No dig was worth him losing his life over, even if she did think his story was just another ploy to get rid of her.

When Wes kissed her…God, he kissed her as if he meant it. It had felt as if…as if it were right somehow, being with him, being cradled in his arms. How could he kiss her like that just as a prelude to setting her up for his best scam yet? How could it feel so genuine if it were nothing more than a small part of a very big lie?

As much as she wanted to forget that kiss, she couldn't stop replaying it in her mind. Living it again. Feeling his hands in her hair and his mouth on hers.

She walked into the desert, under the moon, leaving the horse behind because he might make some noise and give her away. And part of her insisted it was just to check on the old man. But she knew deep down that she was really looking for a way to believe. She wanted to believe. Wes had made her want that. And she was probably just setting herself up for one more disappointment. But if there was a chance…if there was a chance…

Sky Dancer is your true name.

She had to see Turtle again, find out what he'd meant by that. She'd said she didn't want to know…and maybe she didn't.

But want to or not, she had to know.

She had to know.

Chapter 11

"You found wood." Turtle spoke softly, stating the obvious while Wes added a couple of branches to the dwindling campfire.

"Yeah."

"And?"

Wes pulled his gaze from the fire long enough to send a startled look Turtle's way. "And nothing. I found wood. We'll need it before the night's out."

Turtle didn't answer, didn't nod in his usual slow-motion manner. He narrowed his eyes instead, probing until Wes had to look away.

"If you'd agree to come back to the trailer, pal, I wouldn't need to be hunting high and low for wood in the first place."

"You don't need to. I've told you to go."

Wes resumed pacing. "If I go, you'll sit here and freeze to death, you stubborn son of a—"

"You saw something. Besides wood," Turtle said.

Wes stopped in midstride, turning slowly to face the old man. Turtle met his gaze and smiled. "It's in your eyes. Don't worry. Wolf Shadow would not object to your being there."

Drawing a breath and letting it out slowly, Wes moved over to where Turtle sat and hunkered down beside him. "You know, sometimes you have me all but convinced you're pulling my leg, and then you turn around and haul some mystical rabbit out of your hat and make me crazy."

"I am Turtle, last shaman of the Emerald Flat Clan. I'm surprised you still doubt me at all."

Wes lowered his head and ran a hand across his face. "Yeah. Well. This latest thing…having me put on that getup and try to scare her off…it wasn't like you."

Turtle lowered his head quickly. "People say desperate times call for desperate measures."

"Still…"

"Would it ease your mind to know I am not certain I was brought here to die?"

Wes frowned. "I don't get it. I thought that was the whole idea.…"

Turtle shook his head. "I saw him," he said very softly, watching Wes's face as he said it.

Wes drew a blank. "You saw who?"

"Wolf Shadow."

Tipping his head skyward, Wes rolled his eyes. But despite himself, a shiver ran up his spine. "Don't you think that horse is dead, Turtle?"

"I saw him. He told me to come here and to wait. I assumed it was death I was awaiting, but now I'm not so sure. Perhaps there was some other reason."

"What other reason?" Wes started to get to his feet to resume pacing. Pacing was good. Kept him from thinking about Taylor, and how damned much he wanted her. How much he missed her now that she'd decided to hate his guts. "To drive Wes Brand nuts, maybe? To give the both of us pneumonia?"

"To make Sky Dancer stay here."

He stopped short, his back to Turtle. "Make her stay? Hell, Turtle, this whole scheme of yours has only made her detest the sight of me."

"Not true." Turtle got to his feet and walked slowly toward Wes. "It was my scheme that brought her here."

"Yeah, so I gathered. Maybe it's time you told me why."

Turtle shrugged and turned away. "I promised her grandmother, as she lay dying, that I would see Sky Dancer returned here, and that she take as husband the man her family had chosen."

Wes turned. "You brought her here to marry her off to one of your relatives on the reservation?"

Turtle only looked at him with a slow, turtlelike blink.

Wes felt his jaw go stiff. "The hell you will."

"I must. I gave my word. She is the last descendant of Little Sparrow's family. She's the last chance there will ever be to bring peace to Wolf Shadow's spirit."

"Taylor?" Wes took a second to digest that. Taylor, the woman so afraid to embrace her heritage. Talk about irony. "So you've got some husband all picked out for her, have you?"

Turtle smiled while Wes reminded himself that beating the old coot senseless wouldn't do either of them any good.

"Yes. If I can bring the two together, then I haven't failed after all. It's as much a part of my destiny as protecting the sacred ground where Little Sparrow lies waiting for her spirit's release."

Wes was simmering. He'd be boiling over soon. All this time, all this scheming, and Turtle had an ulterior motive all along. Damn him. He'd sat still and watched Wes fall head over heels for the woman, while plotting to fix her up with someone else. The rotten, scheming, conniving goat.

"Maybe you'd better tell me who this guy is," Wes said. "So I can kick his ass up front and get it over with."

Turtle returned to his place and sat down.

"He is pleasing to the eye. Young women seem drawn to him. Besides, it is her destiny. She will agree." From somewhere under the blankets around his shoulders, Turtle pulled out some herbs and tossed them into the flames. A soft plume of fragrant smoke puffed out as they ignited, and Turtle used his hand to cup the smoke and pull it toward him, smoothing it over his face and head.

Wes lowered his head. "You're crazy, you know that? There's no way she'd…" He brought his head up again, eyes narrowed. "Has she met this guy yet?"

Turtle sat a bit straighter, eyeing the smoke as if he saw something there. Then he turned to Wes. "She is out there. You should go to her."

Wes tilted his head. "Yeah, I'll just waltz right up to her tent and tell her she's gotta marry some—"

"No," Turtle said. And he waved an arm toward the desert. "Out there."

"Out there," Wes repeated, frowning. Then his heart tripped over itself, and his blood chilled. "Out *there?*"

Stupid, stupid, stupid. Taylor thought it would be a simple matter to hike out through the Badlands and spot the cluster of boulders that grew into a rocky hill. Problem was, there was more than one rocky hill out here.

She hadn't realized. So she'd walked straight to the first one she'd spotted, which, as it turned out, had been the wrong thing to do. Now it was getting dark, and the chill was seeping straight through her clothes. She couldn't see her footprints in the patches of barren ground that stretched between clumps of solid rock, and every cactus looked the same.

She figured she had two choices. Try heading back the way she'd come and hope she didn't veer off track in the darkness, or camp here for the night and make the best of it until dawn. She was truly torn over which choice to make. The confident professional in her thought she could probably find her way. The little girl she seldom acknowledged was afraid of getting lost in the wasteland. But there was another part of her, a new part, telling her that spending the night out here would be okay. Her ancestors had lived here. They'd survived. It might even be exciting.

Okay, then. She'd stay. Spend the night right here in the wilderness, under the stars, no one for company but herself. And maybe…her past.

She closed her eyes, battling a shiver of unease and shaking her thoughts away. If she were staying, she'd need to do some things. She remembered Wes building the fire at the campsite, showing her the old way of stacking the wood, and using two flint rocks to spark the kindling to life. Could she do it? She didn't have a match or a lighter on her, so she supposed she had no choice but to try.

Hoisting her pack higher on her shoulder, Taylor walked higher up into the shelter of the rocks, looking around for a perfect spot. She found it in a half circle of boulders that stood like guardians, keeping out the wind. Good. She shrugged free of her backpack and dropped it to the ground. Something moved where it landed, and she shuddered as a snake uncoiled and slithered away, disappearing beneath a nearby boulder. Too nearby. She took her pack to the farthest point from where the slimy thing had vanished, scanned the ground warily and dropped the pack again. Now, for the fire.

She looked at the barren, rocky ground with a sinking sensation in her belly. Where was she going to find kindling or wood out here?

She supposed she could get by without a fire at all. She had a warm coat, and blankets in her pack. She'd intended them for the old man. As she thought of him a finger of guilt wriggled up the back of her neck. Damn. She hoped he was all right. But Wes was with him, right? Wes wouldn't go off and leave him alone if he really were waiting to die out there. Not that she believed any of that, but…

A coyote's heartbroken wail drifted from somewhere nearby, and she bit her lip. Maybe it wasn't a coyote. Maybe it was a wolf. Blankets or no blankets, she wanted a fire. To keep the critters at bay.

She started off, keeping careful track of where she was going and looking behind her often so she could find her way back. It wasn't pitch-dark. The moonlight made for great illumination, but it never hurt to be cautious. She wouldn't wander far. If she could find some wood nearby, great. If not…

Sky Dancer…

She came to a dead stop, bringing her head up sharply. What the hell was that? Her eyes scanned the moonlit rock formations as her heart accelerated. It had sounded as if someone had whispered that name the old man had given her.

No. It had to be the wind. And her own suddenly active imagination. Nothing more.

Sky Dancer...here...

The coyote—or wolf—yipped brokenly and then settled into a warbling howl. His relatives decided to join in. Taylor was beginning to feel as if she were playing an extra in some old black-and-white werewolf flick. Or was this Wes, up to his old tricks again?

She caught a flicker of movement, higher on the hill. And for just a moment the moon seemed to illuminate a form. Delicate and feminine, wearing a doeskin dress, bleached nearly white, with fringe dancing in the breeze just as her long hair was doing.

Taylor's heart flipped over. She'd seen this woman before. But... She lunged closer. But the form was gone.

Wes. Now he'd employed some female assistance for his ridiculous mind games. She clenched her fists at her sides and stomped forward. "Damn you, Wes Brand, when I get my hands on you I'll—"

Soft laughter filled her ears...or maybe it was her mind. And she realized she'd never told Wes about having seen the woman. He didn't know. So how could it have been part of his plan? She stilled again, straining to hear, but the sound faded until it became part of the wind whispering through the branches of a gnarled and twisted tree.

A tree. And a couple of others just beyond it. That meant wood.

Taylor rubbed her arms and looked around her as she walked on. And when she reached the small copse of stunted trees, she noticed an elongated rock formation that was nearly white. It stood upright and had a shape that from a distance, she supposed, might look like a person.

Yeah. A person with hair and a fringed dress. And a whispery soft voice. "You're losing it, Taylor."

She sighed. She really didn't want to believe Wes was still trying to frighten her with ghostly visitations, but she didn't want to think she was imagining things, either. The third possibility didn't even bear consideration.

It was Wes. It had to be. He was such a jerk.

She strode ahead and found a treasure trove of broken limbs and piles of tiny twigs and dried leaves for kindling. She carried these back to her spot, and made several more trips, until she had a nice-looking supply of firewood for the night.

The canine chorus was getting more raucous by the minute. Sounded as if they were working themselves up for a night of hell-raising, to her. She just hoped she wasn't on their list of things to do, under the appetizer category.

She bent over her pile of twigs and leaves, gathering bunches of them into her hands and piling them carefully in the center of the spot she'd chosen for her fire. Then she added larger twigs, leaning them against one another tepee style with the kindling beneath them. She left room enough for her hands on one side. Then, kneeling beside her creation, she took the flint from her pocket. And against her will, she remembered watching Wes as he used the stones with so much skill. Remembered his hands touching hers in a deliberate caress as he gave them to her. And the way the firelight had painted his face and danced in his eyes.

She closed her eyes and licked her lips. This was no way to get over the lying sneak. Just light the damned fire, she told herself. She struck the stones together once, twice, again. The third time produced a spark. Okay, good. She struck them again, and this time the spark caught one tiny edge of a dried leaf. A red glow ate into the leaf, and she bent closer, blowing gently, until a thread of smoke rose from the pile. Then a single tongue of flame licked to life, and it caught at the kindling. Taylor sat back on her heels, smiling as she watched the fire grow. It was slow, but steady, and soon the twigs were burning with loud snapping sounds and an aroma so sweet she could almost taste it.

She went to her woodpile for some large pieces, bending to grab what looked like the perfect limb—and then she froze in place, arm still extended, as the rattling sound pierced her nerves like a blade. Moving only her eyes, Taylor looked around her. The snake was coiled very close to where her hand still hovered, its tail vibrating. Her heart stilled, and she held her breath. It was within striking distance of her hand and maybe her forearm. She knew enough about rattlers to know that she would never make it back to camp if it bit her. But if she pulled her hand back quickly enough, it might miss. Might not even strike at all. If she could just jerk her arm out of reach, she might be okay. All right, then. On three. One…two…th—

"Don't move, Taylor."

Wes. Her breath rushed out of her, and her hands began to shake. "Jesus, what took you so long?"

"Stay still. Stay perfectly still."

She didn't look toward him, didn't answer him again. She heard a soft hiss, something against leather, she thought. Then before she could draw another breath, something flashed in her peripheral vision, and then thudded into the woodpile. The rattling stopped abruptly. Still frozen in place, she looked toward the snake again. It lay still, its head cleanly severed. A large silvery knife stood embedded in the branch she'd been reaching for, its handle still quivering from the impact.

"You can move now."

"Speak for yourself."

Wes's hands closed on her shoulders, and he turned her around, pulled her close as her body lost its fear-induced stiffness and went limp instead. He held her hard, and she let him, for the moment. It felt too damned good to object. "You okay?"

"Yeah." She hated to do it, but she pulled herself out of his incredible embrace and stood facing him.

"Nice fire," he said.

She glanced at the fire, then at the woodpile. Damned if she was going to stick her hands in that direction again. Wes seemed to read her thoughts, though, and he picked up a few larger branches to add to the flames. Then he settled himself down on the ground as if he planned to stay and visit awhile.

"So what are you doing out here," she asked him. "Shouldn't you be with your partner?"

Wes looked up, no doubt hearing the sarcasm in her tone. "What, you're not gonna thank me?" She glared. He shrugged. "Turtle said you were out here somewhere and sent me after you. Good thing, too." And he nodded toward the decapitated reptile.

Taylor shuddered. "Could you get rid of that thing?"

"Could," he said. "Depends on how hungry you are. Rattlesnake tastes—"

"Just like chicken?"

Wes grinned at her, and she caught herself smiling back for a second. She sighed heavily and looked away. Damn, why did he have to turn out to be a liar? It could have been something special with him.

Wes got up, pulled his blade from the log and used it

to lift the snake's remains and toss them out into the darkness. "Waste of a perfect dinner if you ask me." He wiped the blade on some of her dry leaves and then replaced it in his boot.

"I'd rather go hungry," she said. "But since I have plenty of food with me, I won't have to."

"Oh, yeah?" Without asking permission, he bent to unzip her pack, and began pulling out the contents. "I guess you do have supplies here. Food. Water. Blankets." He glanced her way, waiting for an explanation, she guessed. She only shrugged and looked away.

"Looks like you were either planning a little camping trip...or bringing this stuff out to Turtle and me."

She rolled her eyes. "Turtle," she said. "You could sit there and starve for all I care."

"I knew you were just a softy under all that ice, Doc. You were worried about us. Admit it."

"I was worried about the old man," she said.

"So you thought you might have been wrong when you called him a liar?"

"I never called him—"

"Did so. Maybe not in so many words, but that's what it amounted to." Wes spread one of the blankets on the ground in front of the fire, sat down on it and patted the spot beside him. She hesitated. "Hey, I'm not gonna bite you. Besides, I want you close by in case another snake comes along."

Taylor betrayed herself by quickly scanning the ground around her feet.

"Or a scorpion. Nasty little buggers, you know."

"You just never get tired of trying to scare me, do you?" But she did sit down beside him. And then she wished she hadn't. Being close to him was no good for her. Made her want to be closer.

"Taylor."

She turned to look up at him, and that damned firelight was making his eyes shine like before. He must know how good he looked in firelight, she figured.

"I'm sorry. No, don't look like that. I mean it." He pushed one hand through his hair, and she noticed that it was loose. He hadn't tied it back. "I don't know how the hell I let Turtle talk me into going along with that damned plan, but I did. He's...he's important to me. When you care about somebody, well, it's awful easy to screw up."

She sighed and looked away. Looking into his eyes was too much.

"Like I screwed up with you," he said softly. "If I could take it back, Doc, I would."

Without looking at him, she said, "Then what was tonight all about?"

"Tonight?" He shrugged. "I guess I thought if you saw how serious Turtle was about all this, you'd understand why I—"

"No, not Turtle and his deathwatch and his stories. I'm talking about tonight, here. That little act out on the bluff." She turned to look at him and saw nothing but confusion in his eyes.

"I don't know what you're talking about," he said.

She sighed in disgust. "Sure, you don't."

"Taylor, I just got here. I left Turtle two hours ago, hiked back to the site and then followed what was left of your trail from there." He searched her face. "Did something happen, Doc?"

She closed her eyes, shook her head.

"Stupid question," he said. "If nothing happened, you wouldn't be asking me about it, would you?"

She shrugged. "I saw something. Or I thought I did.

Hell, Wes, it was either you and your head games or my own imagination, and at this point I'm not even sure how I'd know."

His hand touched her hair, stroked it away from her face. "I did a number on you, didn't I? Doc, I swear, whatever you saw, I wasn't involved. You're getting nothing but the truth from me, from here on. I promise."

She lifted her head, his hand still lingering in her hair, and met his eyes. "I'd really like to believe that."

"What can I do to convince you?"

Her breath came out in a slow sigh. "Nothing, Wes. Not unless you can take away all the lies I've ever been told. All the times I trusted when I shouldn't have."

"No," he said. "There's a way. And I'm gonna find it, Doc. I messed this thing up and I'm damned well gonna fix it."

The coyotes wailed, sounding closer than before, and Taylor stiffened.

"You want to go back to camp?"

She shook her head. "I want to spend the night here, like my ancestors did." She saw his eyes widen in surprise. "I'm thinking...maybe...it's time."

He smiled slowly. "I'm staying with you, then."

"I didn't mean—"

"I know. I didn't, either." His thumb stroked a slow circle on her cheek, and then his hand fell away. "I'm just here for the snakes."

"And the scorpions," she said, and she felt lighter than she had before. The confusion, the emptiness she'd always felt inside her, seemed to melt away tonight, under the stars. And she had a feeling being with this man might have a lot to do with it.

"Turtle...he told me some things after you left. Things you maybe ought to know."

He was asking permission, she realized. She reached for her pack and the food she'd brought along, dragging it closer, taking out the packets of dehydrated meals. "You can tell me over dinner. I brought enough for two."

"Even though you were only worried about Turtle, and I could starve for all you cared?" There was a gleam of mischief in his eyes.

"Hey, you can always go after that perfectly good rattlesnake you threw away."

He made a face. "I never was much for chicken."

They ate, and Wes told her everything Turtle had said to him. About her famous ancestor, Little Sparrow, and about her being the last blood relative of her line. And finally about Turtle's belief that she should marry one of Wolf Shadow's descendants to free the spirits of the starcrossed lovers.

She took it all pretty well, he thought. Though she seemed to lose her appetite about halfway through his account. When he finished, she was quiet for a long time. And then she said, "Turtle...said he made this promise to see that I came back here and fulfilled what he calls...my destiny?"

"Yeah, that's what he said. And for what it's worth, I believe him. I know him pretty well, Taylor. And I can't think of any reason for him to make all this up."

"But you said he was the one who put you up to scaring me off. It doesn't make sense."

Wes nodded, and hoped he hadn't just blown any chance he had of regaining her trust in him. "I know. I asked him the same thing. Seems while he saw it as his mission in life to get you back here, he also made a vow to keep Little Sparrow's resting place undisturbed until her spirit is free again. I guess getting you here was fine, but having you digging on that particular spot wasn't. He was hoping to convince you the legend was real, and that the site was there, without you actually having to find it. He wants you to tell the elders the spot is here, so they won't sell.''

"I can't do that," she said. "It would be dishonest, if I didn't know for sure. And, Wes, those people need the money they'll get from this sale."

"I know," he said. And the guilt loomed up in him. Maybe he should just tell her where the site was. But what would that do to Turtle?

Staring into the flames, she nodded slowly. "I suppose his thinking makes some kind of sense."

"To Turtle, it does."

She turned her face to his, and Wes found himself marveling again at the depth of her dark lashes, the intelligence in her black eyes. "Who did he make this promise to? The one about me, I mean."

Wes drew a breath. "You sure you want to hear all this?"

She nodded.

"Okay. He said he promised your grandmother. Said he knew her, was with your mother when you were born."

She blinked several times, but that was her only reaction. "He knew my birth mother." Then she lowered her head. "The woman who gave me up."

"The woman who gave you life, Taylor. And she didn't give you up. She was sick, dying. And she knew it. She did everything she could to find a loving home for you. A good home. And hell, Taylor, back then times were pretty bleak for the Comanches on the reservation. So she sent you away from all that. She wanted you to have everything. But your grandmother made Turtle promise to see to it you came back someday. She wanted you to know where you came from, get in touch with your roots.''

Taylor searched his eyes, and hers were narrow, and unless it was a trick of the firelight, slightly damp. ''Turtle told you all that?''

''Yeah. He did.'' He wanted to pull her into his arms and kiss her pain away, because he could see how much she was hurting. He hated seeing her hurt. ''But that's about all he told me. Doc, if you want to know about your family, I imagine Turtle could tell you just about everything there is to know.''

She sniffed, averting her face. ''All this time I thought she just didn't want me. I thought she just gave me away. And I blamed her....''

''For what, Taylor?''

She shook her head, bit her lip.

''Come on, talk to me. Don't you think all this baggage has been weighing you down long enough? Unload it, Doc. Dump it right here.'' He patted his shoulder. ''Right here.''

She looked at his shoulders, then looked away. ''It was tough, you know? I went to a small school. Not another Native American in the place. And the kids—hell, Wes, you know how kids can be—they started making remarks about my red-haired dad and my blond, blue-eyed mother. Saying I must've been left by Gypsies and garbage like that.''

He could feel her pain, hear it in her voice. It wasn't a grown-up kind of hurt; he knew that. It was the pain of a little girl, confused and lied to. She looked up at him, eyes huge and glittering. ''I loved my parents.

Trusted them. So I believed them.'' She lowered her head and shook it slowly.

Wes sighed. Damn. It was still with her, the memory of that hurt. As fresh as if it were yesterday, he could tell. "It must have torn you apart," he said, and he stroked her hair again. Seemed he couldn't get enough of its silky texture sliding across his palm, around his fingers.

"It wasn't the knowledge that I was adopted," she said. "It was the betrayal. It was suddenly knowing the two people I'd trusted most in the world had lied to me, for all of my life. And I think I blamed my birth mother, in a way. I think that's when I decided I'd never want any part of my heritage."

"That's not surprising."

"It's screwed up a lot of friendships, this thing I have about trust. Every time I get close to anyone, it gets in the way. Either I think they're lying when they aren't, or I catch them in some harmless fib and overreact." She met his gaze head-on. "Or I actually start to trust them, and they..."

"They let you down," he said. "God, I'm sorry, Taylor. I'm so sorry."

"You can stop apologizing," she said. "I believe you."

Wes's heart leapt. "You believe me?"

And her gaze went wary. "I believe you're sorry. I don't know what else might happen, Wes, but I don't want you to spend every minute apologizing to me."

"I'd apologize till hell froze over if it would help."

She drew a breath, licked her lips. "I want to get past this," she said. "I want to trust you again, Wes. I really do. I just..."

"Just...?"

She closed her eyes. "Just don't know if I can."

"Ah, Taylor..."

Her eyes opened and met his, and maybe she saw him thinking about kissing her. Maybe she noticed the way his gaze kept dipping down to her lips, caressing them, tasting them in his mind. Because she stiffened her shoulders and moved a bit farther away from him. She stretched out on the blanket he'd put on the ground, pulling her backpack under her head for a pillow. "I don't want to think about my problems or your shenanigans any more tonight, okay?"

"Okay. We'll talk about something else. Anything you want."

Her eyes were closed. Wes got up and grabbed the second blanket, still folded on the ground. He shook it out, and spread it over her, and when he did, she hunched up her shoulders like a cat when you pet it just right. She looked relaxed, more relaxed than he'd seen her. And beautiful. Her hair spread like a black pool around her, and all he could do was stand there and stare, and think if he couldn't get her back, he'd never get over it. He'd see her like this every night, in his dreams, for as long as he lived.

"Tell me about your ranch," she said.

"The Texas Brand?"

She shook her head slightly, not opening her eyes. "No. *Your* ranch. The one you're buying."

"Ah, that one. Well, fact is, I bought it."

Her eyes popped open. "You did?"

"Yeah. The bids were opened today, and I won. Not that I imagine there was much competition. The loan from the bank will be enough to get started on the renovations, too."

"Barn first," she reminded him.

"Barn first," he said with a nod. "I've already ordered the supplies. I'll be able to start work any day now."

She smiled. Lips curving seductively upward, laugh lines deepening at the corners of her eyes. "It's going to be something."

"Sure is."

"What are you going to call it? Texas Brand Two?"

Wes rubbed his chin with one hand. "No. Actually it deserves a name as beautiful as the land that it's a part of, don't you think?"

"You have something in mind?"

Her voice was getting sleepy. Slower and thicker. Sexy as hell. "Yeah. I think I'm gonna call it Sky Dancer Ranch."

Her eyes opened suddenly. They met his, held them, but she didn't speak.

"Turtle says it is your real name. The name your birth mother gave you."

"I didn't realize...."

"There's a lot you don't realize just yet, Sky Dancer. A whole lot." He reached out, closed his hand around hers and just sat beside her, feeling its smallness, its warmth. Then Taylor opened her hand to lace her fingers with his, and she squeezed.

She fell asleep that way, while Wes sat there, looking at her, aching clear to his bones and hoping to God there was still a chance for him.

Chapter 12

A snuffling sound woke her. She had no idea how long she'd been lying there, sound asleep. Wes lay beside her, very close beside her. And beneath her. She'd cuddled closer in her sleep, so her head rested on his shoulder and his arm curled around hers. He was warm, and he smelled good. Wood smoke clung to his skin, but there was something more. His shoulder was bare beneath her face. And if she moved slightly, she could taste his skin on her lips. For a long moment she lay there debating the wisdom of doing just that.

She still wanted him. Whatever else happened, she thought she probably always would.

Then that snuffling sound came again, and she went a little stiff, and turned her head slowly. The fire had died to mere embers. And an animal was pawing at her backpack, no more than a yard from where she lay. Sniffing and pawing. Its head halfway inside the thing. It looked like an underfed dog, but she knew better.

Wes's arm tightened around her. The moonlight had fled now. It must be nearly dawn.

Moving slowly, Wes turned until his lips brushed her ear, and whispered, "No sudden moves, okay?"

She nodded once. And Wes pulled his arm from beneath her and sat up slowly. The animal yanked its head from the backpack and looked at him. Wes sat perfectly still and looked back.

It seemed like a standoff.

Taylor lay still, shivering under the blanket, though not from the cold. "Coyote?" she whispered.

And Wes gave his head a nearly imperceptible shake, side to side. No. Not a coyote, then. So that left...

"Wolf?" Her voice was a squeak, and the animal's ears pricked forward.

Wes kept his gaze focused on the wolf's eyes. Held them hard, even when the animal bared its teeth in a snarl and the fur on its back seemed to bristle upward. It lowered its head and shoulders slightly, as if in preparation to spring on them, and emitted a low and endless growl.

Wes didn't move. He just sat there, staring. Taylor wanted to tell him to get that damned knife out of his boot and make use of it. But she didn't dare to speak, and doubted she'd manage more than a meaningless grunt if she tried. Her throat seemed to swell shut with fear. She could barely breathe, let alone speak.

Very slowly Wes got to his feet. How he managed it in such slow motion was beyond her, but he did. Inch by inch he straightened until it seemed he towered above her from her vantage point, flat on her back. Then he moved forward, stepping over her, first with one leg, and then the other. So that he stood between Taylor and the wolf. And all the while he never broke eye contact.

The growling stopped. Peering around Wes's legs, she

could still see the wolf. Its snarl died, and its head tipped upward as it stared into Wes's eyes. It spent a long moment like that. Neither moving, nor making a sound. And then suddenly the wolf simply spun around and ran away into the darkness. Taylor glimpsed its upturned tail as it bounded away, and then nothing more.

She lay still, shaking her head slowly. "What did you just do?"

When Wes sat down again, he did it suddenly. As if his muscles had just decided to go limp. Taylor pulled herself into a sitting position, getting in front of him so she could see his face. His eyes were closed, and he sighed heavily.

"Wes?"

He looked at her, shook his head. "I don't know, exactly. It's something Turtle taught me. Damn, I'm glad it worked."

"Glad...what worked?"

In something like wonder he was looking off in the direction the wolf had taken. "I'd tried it with horses. An eagle once. But hell, I didn't really think it..." Again he shook his head, pushing both hands backward through his hair. "A wolf. Never thought I'd have call to try it with a wolf. Damn."

He was talking more to himself than to her. She reached out, touched his face, just to remind him she was there. It worked. He looked into her eyes, and she could see he was shaken. Maybe more shaken than she was.

"Wes. Tell me what just happened here."

He closed his eyes, opened them again. "I talked to him."

"You talked to him." She frowned and looked at where the animal had been crouching. Then back at Wes. "To the wolf."

He nodded. And he looked dead serious. Taylor battled a shiver, and then forced a smile that had to be shaky at best. "What did you say? 'Please don't eat us'?"

Wes shook his head and looked at the ground. "I sound like a lunatic."

"Not unless the wolf talked back," she said, trying for a light tone, even though she still couldn't stop shaking.

Without looking up he said, "He did."

She threaded her fingers into his hair, tipping his head up again. "Okay. So you're a lunatic. A lunatic who saved my life twice in one night." A little of the tension faded from his face. "You stepped in front of me," she said. "That animal could have—"

He pressed his forefinger to her lips. "I'd step in front of a train for you, Doc. Haven't you figured that out yet?"

He took his finger away from her mouth, staring into her eyes. And then he lowered his head, and put his lips there instead.

It was so right. So perfect. And she didn't care that he'd lied to her, or that he talked to wolves. It didn't matter. All that mattered was this. Touching him. Kissing him. Wanting him with everything in her.

She slipped her arms around his shoulders. His crept tighter around her waist. When his lips nudged hers apart, she shivered, and when his tongue slid over hers, her heart seemed to melt. She was in his arms, and it was where she wanted to be. Where she'd wanted to be for some time now. And she held him close to her as she lay down, so that he came with her, his body covering hers. When he moved his hips, she felt his hardness pressing into her, and when he took his mouth away, he whispered, "Tell me to stop, Taylor."

He stared down into her eyes, and his were on fire.

Black fire. Raven Eyes. It didn't have to mean forever. He knew she wasn't ready for that. He wouldn't expect anything. Just this…just tonight.

She ran her palms over his chest. And then she said, "Make love to me, Wes."

His jaw went tight. He closed his eyes. And then he kissed her again. Deeply, thoroughly, and the gentleness in his touch grew into something more as he tugged her T-shirt up and put his hands on her breasts. And then he was kissing them, too. Suckling her, groaning deep in his throat. She tipped her head back, closing her eyes and letting him feed at her nipples. Her breathing ragged, she ran her hands over his chest, and his back, and then lower, slipping a hand between his legs and caressing the hardness there. She freed him from his jeans, and touched him. Hot and ridged and hard. She closed her hand around the tip of him, and he shivered. And then he backed away, sitting up, and he reached slowly down to pull her shirt over her head.

She shivered in the cold. Wes took her hands and drew her to her feet. But he remained kneeling down. And then he reached for her pants, unfastening them, sliding them down over her hips, looking at her as he did. She shuddered, but without shyness, stepped out of them. And then he peeled her panties away in the same slow manner, his eyes devouring her. When she kicked the panties aside, he touched her there, and he whispered, "I want to taste you."

Her stomach clenched. He put his hands on her buttocks and drew her closer. And then he pressed his mouth to her, nuzzling her there, pushing her open with his mouth, and then tasting her with his tongue.

Fire shot through her body, and her knees trembled and then buckled. She fell to the ground, but he followed, parting her legs with his hands, and burying his face between them. Stroking deeper with his tongue until she clasped his head and moaned softly in the night.

He kissed a path up her body, putting his hand where his mouth had been seconds ago, stroking up inside her, making her shudder and cry. And then he pressed himself into her, and she felt filled, not just physically, but spiritually. When he sank himself all the way into her body, she arched her hips to take him. And he wrapped her up tight in his arms and kissed her again as he moved. She knew it had never been like this for her before, and never would be again. She moved with him, arching against him, holding him with every part of her. And when she climaxed, he did, too. And it felt as if their souls were fused together in this fire. As if they'd never be able to exist again on their own.

Wes lay beside her, holding her close, as the sun rose over the desert. A ball of fire. Every sunrise here was a spectacular light show. Wes wondered if the sunrises would be visible from his ranch. He thought so. What an incredible way to wake up each morning.

If she were there beside him.

Without Taylor's face, bathed in the fiery glow of dawn, the sunrises would lose their appeal.

He was in love with her.

The thought of losing her, of spending his life without her, became nightmarish to him then. And without warning, he thought of his brother Ben, and he nearly choked on the sudden tightness in his throat. Ben still mourned his wife, Penny. Every day he must think of her. Every morning he must wake up alone and remember waking with her in his arms. And the urge to hug his oversize brother hit Wes almost as powerfully as the urge to stay where he was, with Taylor snuggled close to him.

Then she sat up, and pulled the blanket over her, a little self-consciously. She looked nervous. Sated, but scared.

"It's okay," he told her, reaching up to stroke her hair. "I know it didn't mean anything."

And she lowered her head. "It meant something, Wes. It just didn't mean…everything."

He understood. He'd won her body, and even her affection. But not her trust, and not her heart. Not yet. "There's one thing you might not know about me, lady," he said with a smile.

"You mean besides the fact that you double as Dr. Doolittle and talk to animals?" She smiled back, seemingly relieved that he wasn't asking for promises, that he was taking last night for what it was and nothing more.

"That I thrive on challenges," he told her.

"But you're wrong," she said. "I'd already figured that out. I knew it the second you showed me that ranch of yours."

"You calling my new place a challenge?"

She shrugged. Wes sat up and sighed. "Better than my kid sister. She called it a dump."

The sun rose higher, and their smiles died as he got lost in her eyes. And before he slipped and said something stupid way too soon, scaring her off for good, Wes tore his gaze away. "We ought to get back. Your kids will be worried sick. Scourge might even decide to play hero and go wandering into the desert looking for you. I don't have time to hunt for hairballs."

"He wouldn't do that," she said. "He's too smart."

"He has a crush on you," Wes said. "Bad enough I have to compete with whatever Comanche stud Turtle has picked out for you. I have to contend with a Don Juan with peach fuzz to boot."

"Don't forget about my ghostly admirer," she said. "I really kind of like him." Her eyes were filled with mischief.

He chucked her under the chin. "He really kind of likes you, too," he said. "Damned if I ever thought I'd be jealous of myself."

She laughed softly. "Serves you right."

"You're right, it does."

He liked this. This easiness that had returned between them. And it was more than it had been before. Deeper. She seemed comfortable with him, relaxed. As for him, well, he was falling harder with every smart-ass quip she tossed his way. The guarded, solitary scientist had melted away. The woman underneath was so irresistible he could barely keep his hands off her.

"Better get dressed," he said. "Search party could show up any time." He got up, buck naked, and walked around picking up her clothes, which had somehow ended up scattered hither and yon. Then he brought them to her, and saw her eyes devouring him. He swallowed hard.

"Take away the clothes," she said, "And there's really no difference between Wes Brand and Wolf Shadow."

"Just a few hundred years is all. Or am I sagging more than I realized?" He pulled on his jeans.

She didn't return his grin this time. Instead her eyes narrowed. "Wes, will you tell me something?"

"Anything. I told you, nothing but honesty from now on."

She nodded, and he thought maybe she was about to

put his vow to the test. "What did that wolf say to you last night?"

He blinked. Then drew a deep breath, lifting his head, and bringing his gaze level with hers again. "He... uh...he called me 'brother.'"

Biting her lower lip, she nodded slowly.

"Am I going to regret being honest, Doc? You going to recommend I talk to a shrink now?"

"No, Wes. Not when I..."

"Not when you what?"

She shook her head. "It'll sound foolish."

"More foolish than talking to wolves? C'mon, Taylor, this honesty thing has to work both ways."

She met his eyes, nodded hard. "You're right. It does." She lifted her chin. "I think I saw...Little Sparrow last night." She turned then, and pulled on her shirt, maybe to avoid his eyes.

"That's what you were talking about when I first got here."

She nodded and picked up her khaki trousers.

"And you thought it was me? What, in drag?"

Pulling the pants up to her hips, she stood and tucked her shirt in, then fastened them up. "No. I guess I thought you'd drafted another conspirator. But I shouldn't have, because..."

"Because?"

Dropping her hands to her sides, she faced him. "Because it wasn't the first time. I saw her once before, just prior to coming down here for this dig." She frowned hard. "Wes, it was like looking into a mirror. Only, translucent. And then she just faded like mist."

He thought then that he should tell her about his own encounter with someone he thought might have been Wolf Shadow. The real one, not his own little interpretation of the role. But then he thought better of it. Honesty was fine, but she didn't trust him yet. And if he blurted this out, she might chalk it up to yet another trick on his part. He'd tell her, yes. But not just yet.

It was like looking into a mirror.

Her words rang in his ears. He'd had the same eerie sensation at the single glimpse he'd had of...whatever he'd seen last night.

"I think," she said, "that you should talk to Turtle about this wolf thing."

"I was thinking the same thing." He finished dressing himself, and began shaking out and folding the blankets, stuffing them into her pack, slinging it over his own shoulder when it was filled. He took a long drink from the canteen and then handed it to her. "I'll take you back to camp, and then I'll head out to check on him. I don't like him out there alone, especially with a pack of wolves so nearby."

"It was only one wolf," she reminded him. "Besides, Wes, if you can talk a wolf out of attacking, old Turtle can probably make him roll over and play dead. He's a shaman after all. Shamans are known for their animal broth—" She bit her lip and met his eyes, her own widening.

"Animal brothers." Wes finished her sentence for her. And he didn't blame her for the wide-eyed look. He was feeling pretty wide-eyed himself. He didn't know what all this meant, and frankly he wasn't sure he wanted to know. It was scaring the hell out of him. Almost as much as his feelings for Taylor were doing.

Chapter 13

Wes walked Taylor back to the camp, received a scathing glance from Scourge and grinned at the kid in return. He borrowed a few supplies from the site, stuffing them into Taylor's backpack. Then he turned to the woman he'd made up his mind was going to be his own. "I'll be back later on."

She nodded. "Go on, go see about Turtle. I'm as worried about him as you are."

Impulsively Wes swayed forward and brushed her lips with his. Then he turned toward where Taylor had his horse anchored for the night and climbed aboard. "I know you hate my guts for this, Paint. We'll head home for your morning oats soon, I promise."

Paint shook his mane and nickered as Wes untied him, slipped his bridle in place and then mounted. He glanced back at Taylor once as he headed back into the desert. She was speaking rapidly to the kids, gesturing, her face firm. Not defending that kiss, he hoped. More likely telling them to mind their own business. And he smiled.

As if she felt his eyes on her, she turned, and met his gaze. And for a long moment they remained that way. Just looking at one another. Wes could feel something moving between them. From her eyes to his and then back again, like a current gaining amps with every circuit. He touched the brim of his hat, and rode away, though it was the last thing in the world he wanted to do.

But she needed time. And he needed Turtle. Because something very strange was happening, and he needed to talk it through.

He found his mentor still sitting in the same spot near the fire. He must have moved once or twice, because the fire hadn't dwindled. He'd tossed logs on, then. But to look at him, you wouldn't have thought so. He was like a wooden sculpture, sitting cross-legged on the ground with the woven blanket draped over his shoulders. If his voice—slightly hoarse now—hadn't been raised slightly in song, Wes might have been startled to see him sitting so still.

Wes drew Paint to a halt and slid from the smooth white back. And as he did, Turtle stopped chanting and looked up. "You found her," he said.

Wes nodded and turned to the pack he'd slung over the horse's rump, pulled it off, then unbuckled and opened the flap. He pulled out a battered old coffeepot, the canteen full of water and a can with some coffee inside. The items rattled and clanked as he found the two tin cups in the pack, and with his arms loaded, he strode over to the fire. "Taylor's fine. She took it into her head to bring some supplies out here last night, and took a wrong turn. Wound up camping out at No Man's Bluff."

Hunkering down, Wes dropped the items on the ground, opened the canteen and filled the coffeepot.

"You stayed with her?"

Wes heard the speculation in Turtle's voice and glanced up sharply. "Yeah."

The old man averted his eyes, but Wes thought he'd spotted a twinkle in them first. Couldn't be sure, though. He hadn't expected it. He'd figured Turtle would be angry, if anything, at the idea of Wes spending the night with her. Screwing things up for the prospective bridegroom Turtle had picked out for Taylor.

Odd. Wes poured coffee into the pot's basket, guessing at the amount since he hadn't brought a spoon to measure it. Then he slapped the lid on and settled the pot on a thick forked limb amid the flames.

"Something is on your mind," Turtle said. "Sit down and tell me."

Wes sat, eyeing Turtle and wondering yet again about the old man's instincts. He always knew what Wes was thinking, or it seemed that way to him. "Yeah, there is something," he said. "A wolf got into Taylor's camp last night."

Turtle nodded slowly. "Only one?"

"Only one."

"You had a fire?"

"It was burning low, but still burning." Wes sighed. "I tried that thing you taught me. Holding his eyes and speaking to him with my mind."

"Ah," Turtle said.

"And I thought he answered me."

Turtle's head came up, eyes narrowed on Wes's face. "He called you brother?" the old man asked.

Wes frowned hard. "How could you know that?"

The old face split in a grin of long, straight teeth. "Because it is what the Tortoise called me when he came to me seventy years ago.''

Wes grinned. "Sure, he did. We don't have any tortoises in these parts. You're playing with me again, aren't you, pal?"

Turtle shook his head. "It wasn't a tortoise. It was the spirit of the tortoise. I was napping in the sunlight when a shadow fell over my face, and I opened my eyes to see him standing beside me, blinking slowly. And I saw his powerful beak and thought he might snap my hand off if it pleased him.''

Wes studied Turtle's face. "You aren't kidding, are you? So is that why they called you Turtle?"

"I was born early, and weak, and wasn't expected to survive. But I lived all the same. So my mother named me for the animal she knew as the survivor, for his hard shell of protection, and for the longevity of the creature."

"I see." But Wes wasn't really sure he did.

"Raven Eyes, do you know that every shaman has a spirit guide? Some have many. Some, only one. The animal spirit presents itself to the shaman in its own time, and often tests his courage. As the spirit tortoise tested mine. As the spirit wolf tested yours.''

Wes looked at Turtle sharply. "Hold on a minute. That's all well and good for you, pal, but don't forget, I'm no shaman.''

"Nor was I, until the shamanic spirit came to me in the form of the tortoise.''

Wes shook his head slowly.

"It was not an ordinary wolf, my friend. He was alone, not in a pack. He didn't fear the fire of your camp. He spoke to you.''

"That doesn't mean..."

"Let me tell you a story, Raven Eyes.''

Wes opened his mouth to object, then bit his lip. Let Turtle talk. Maybe…maybe some of this would make sense if he listened.

"There was an old shaman living alone, with no descendants and no young man with the spirit shining in his eyes. He knew his time in this world would come to an end soon, but he'd vowed to pass his wisdom along to a young shaman before he died. To give the next generation the traditions to cling to, and keep alive."

Wes stared at the coffeepot as it started to bubble, at the condensation hissing on the outside of the tin.

"The old shaman made a fire, and danced around it, and he called on the old gods, and on the spirit of the tortoise, to bring a young man to him. The one they brought would become his student, and he would teach him the old ways, and make of him a fine and worthy shaman to take his place when this life ended."

"Turtle, listen—"

"The old shaman prayed for this all night, and made powerful medicine, and he knew his student would come to him the next day. But as that day burned low, no young man came. And growing restless, the old shaman drove in his truck for some distance along the road, to see if any stranger seemed to be heading his way. The truck's tire went flat. At first the old man thought he'd made a mistake. That now he would be away from home for too long, and might miss the young man's arrival there. But he soon knew it was the work of the gods. Because the young man came to him there on the road, and fixed his tire for him, and followed him back home."

Wes couldn't do much more than sit there shaking his head in disbelief.

"All I have taught you, Raven Eyes, all the stories I have told you and the ways you have learned, all have been to prepare you for this day. The day when your spirit guide came to you, tested you and accepted you by calling you brother.''

Wes rubbed his temples with his forefingers. "I can't believe this.''

Turtle shrugged. "It is not so different. But now you can ask the spirits for advice directly. And if you listen, they will guide your steps.''

Wes nodded. "Good. First thing I'll ask them is the name of the guy you say is Wolf Shadow's descendant, so I can make sure he never gets within a hundred feet of Taylor.''

Turtle smiled. "The spirits might tell you that. Or perhaps they, like me, will decide it is something you must learn for yourself.''

Wes lowered his head, gnawed his lip, couldn't decide whether he felt foolish or skeptical or excited. But what if it were true? What if he could get some kind of direct line to...to some higher power? He could find out what he should do with the last secret he was keeping from Taylor. Whether he should tell her he'd found Little Sparrow's resting place.

He cleared his throat. "How...uh...does one go about...asking?''

A gnarled, warm hand fell on his shoulder. "Come to me tonight, my friend.''

Wes sighed. "Good. It's just as well. I need some time to digest all this.'' Then he eyed the rising sun, burning down, scorching already. "But if you sit out here all day again, I doubt you'll be around when I come back tonight. Turtle, you have to—''

Turtle held up a hand, shook his head. "It's time for me to return home,'' Turtle said. "My stay here has served its purpose.''

Wes blew a sigh of pure relief. "Thank God for that. If I had to make the trek out here one more time, I'd have hogtied you and hauled your butt back there." He softened his words with a smile. "So you aren't about to die after all?" he asked, and if his voice broke just a little with the words, then he supposed it was understandable. He hadn't realized just how afraid he was of losing the old goat, until now, when it seemed he wasn't going to lose him at all.

"Not just yet, at least," Turtle said, and he smiled broadly. "The spirits wouldn't leave so clueless a shaman here to bungle things on his own."

"So you get to stick around and help me bungle things?"

Turtle got to his feet and blinked a couple times, averting his face. "I am as proud as if you were my own blood, Raven Eyes." He made a show of brushing the dirt from his pants legs, but Wes sensed he was just avoiding looking him in the face.

"Makes sense," Wes said. "It's been a long time since I've been as close to a man as I am to you. Since before my father died."

Turtle looked up at him, and their eyes met. Uncomfortable, they both looked away at the same time.

Wes shook his head and turned toward the fire. In another second they'd have been hugging or some ridiculous female thing like that. "Let's have that coffee," he said in his most macho voice. "Then we'll pack up and head back."

A young stranger arrived at the camp around noon, handed a letter to Taylor and then left without a word.

Frowning and battling a creepy sense of foreboding, Taylor opened the envelope, extracted the sheet of expensive notepaper and looked it over. Dennis Hawthorne's name gleamed in gold script across the top. There was no greeting.

> I'd like a progress report soon. Don't forget, my funding for this project stops on Sunday. Unless you've found evidence of this alleged sacred site by then, I fully expect you to inform the tribal elders that it doesn't exist so that my purchase of the property can go ahead on schedule.

It was signed with a nearly illegible scribble she thought was supposed to resemble an *H.*

She crumpled the sheet in her hand. "Damn, why do I get the feeling that man is up to no good?"

Scourge approached then, and narrowed his eyes at her. "Ms. McCoy...I...that is, Kelly and I...were wondering...about you and Mr. Brand, that is, if—"

She lifted her head. "Stop wondering." And she turned to go into her tent. And then she sat slowly on the floor, because she was wondering, too. She'd made love to Wes last night, and it had been an experience like nothing she'd ever known. But a physical one. She still got the feeling he wasn't telling her everything. About himself. About this place. About so many things, including his true feelings for her.

How could she love a man she didn't trust? And how could she prevent herself from doing just that? Her heart ached for him every second they spent apart, but her mind constantly rebelled. He'd lied to her, deceived her, might very well still be doing so.

So why did she want to forget all of that and surrender to her heart? Why was it so hard to keep resisting him?

And what the hell was she going to do when this dig was over, in a few short days?

Wes talked Taylor into joining him at the house for dinner that night. Of course, when he made the invitation, she'd thought he meant the Texas Brand, with the family. And he'd deliberately let her go on thinking it. But as he drove over the roads leading to the ranch he'd finally made his own, he could see the understanding dawning on her pretty face.

"You do like your practical jokes, don't you?" she asked him, and Wes bit his lip. Had he screwed up yet again?

"It's not a joke, Doc. It's a surprise." Then he lowered his head. "I thought..."

"No." She touched his hand. "I'm being oversensitive again. I'm sorry." She looked through the windshield as the tumbledown house came into view. "It's a nice surprise. I love this place—you know that."

"I'm learning, Taylor. I'll try to keep a handle on the urge to surprise you from now on, okay?"

She closed her eyes slowly and nodded. "Just so long as you know I'm the one with the problem, not you."

"You don't like being surprised. I'm filing it away. I won't forget again." He stopped the vehicle, then reached into the back to pull out a picnic basket before getting out.

Taylor got out on her side and stood for a moment, taking in the view. "My mare is going to love it here."

"My brothers and I have been stringing some fence," Wes told her, and he pointed out beyond the barn. "We've got a good hunk of grazing land secured and ready. Once the barn is done, I can start bringing horses in here."

Taylor squinted, shielding her eyes with one hand. "When have you had the time?"

Wes shrugged. "Four men can get a lot done with a couple of hours here and a couple of hours there."

She nodded. "The stream runs right through the section you fenced in. It's perfect, Wes."

"It's progress," he said. "The only perfect thing on this place right now is you."

She smiled and dipped her head.

"So where do you want to eat? Outside under the sky?"

She shook her head. "I've been eating outside every day," she said. "Why don't we dust off a place in the house? That spot with the bay windows in the back would be perfect."

"You don't mind the cobwebs?"

She rolled her eyes. "I live for cobwebs."

Wes grinned at her and took her hand, hefting the basket in the other and heading up the rickety front steps and across the porch. He set the basket down to unlock the door, and then waited for her to precede him inside.

She made a beeline for the big room with the fabulous view, and cautiously opened a couple of the windows there. Wes set the basket down and looked around. "There's an old table here. We could clean it off a bit and—"

"What would we clean it with?"

He reached into the cupboard beneath a very old stainless-steel sink and pulled out a pail brimming with cleaning supplies. "My sister put these together for me and told me to be sure to use them. So far they've just been keeping the cupboard company."

Taylor smiled and drew closer, looking into the big plastic pail, pawing the contents. Sponges and cloths, window cleaner and oil soap and several other cleansers. Taylor nodded and met his eyes. "If she gave you a broom, too, then she thought of everything."

Wes nodded toward the brand-new broom, dustpan and mop leaning in one corner. "Jessi *always* thinks of everything. She's bound and determined I'm going to clean the place up."

Taylor tilted her head. "She does have a point." And she looked around her, and he could see her eyes sparkling. "You know we could really go to town on this mess tonight."

Shaking his head, Wes said, "I didn't bring you here to put you to work, Doc."

"But it would be fun!" She reached to the sink to crank one of the faucets there, but frowned when nothing happened.

"Electricity isn't turned on yet," he explained. "I need to double-check the wiring first."

She shrugged. "There's a hand pump out front, though."

He grimaced. Cleaning wasn't what he'd wanted to spend the night doing with Taylor. But she seemed so animated about it. She snatched the pail right out of his hand and dumped its contents onto one side of the sink. Then she headed outside, leaving him no choice but to follow. "Okay, just the table, then," he said. "We clean the old table and then we eat."

"Whatever you say." She trotted down the steps, around the side of the house, set the pail down and began pumping on the handle. There was gurgling, spitting, and finally water rushing from the spout.

Five hours later Wes's hands were beginning to resemble prunes. The big room, which he was now sure would have to be the living room, was all but sparkling, and

Taylor was standing in the middle of it looking around and beaming.

"It's even more wonderful than I realized," she said.

"Do you know it's ten o'clock?" he asked.

"You know this room really is in great shape."

Wes looked up at the place where the plaster had fallen from the ceiling, leaving ancient lath visible, and the spot where old cloth-coated wires stuck down with no light fixture attached.

"We could patch that hole in no time flat," Taylor said, and he realized she was looking at him, following his doubtful gaze. And then he realized she'd said *We*.

"And can you just see it when we replace the old wiring and put some fabulous chandelier up there? Nothing too fancy. Maybe one of those wagon-wheel types, you know?"

He frowned, picturing the fixture above his head, and then he nodded. "That would work."

"No carpeting, though. These hardwood floors are fabulous. Just need some sanding and a few coats of varnish. Some throw rugs maybe, here and there, but we wouldn't want to cover up these great floors."

He hadn't even known the place *had* hardwood floors until Taylor had shouted out the news as she mopped. But as she went on, talking about valances instead of curtains on those windows to preserve the view, and the banister on the staircase that curved up out of this room to the second floor, and what kind of furniture would look perfect here, he could see it all very clearly. And he liked what he saw. For the first time he was thinking of this place as a home, instead of just a great place to raise Appaloosas.

And then he realized that it was because she was here. When Taylor was here, with him, the house wasn't a ruin;

it was a home. Warm and wonderful, comforting and so serene. Without her, though, it would just be a pile of boards and nails again. A shell. No matter what he did to it, if he rebuilt it to look like a castle, it would still be empty and lifeless.

He needed her.

She looked at him, and he opened his mouth to tell her just that. But before he got a single word out, the front door slammed, and Jessi called, "Wes? You here?"

Smiling, Taylor turned. "In here, Jessi," she called.

Wes sighed and lowered his head, and then Jessi and Ben came in, and Jessi looked around the room and grinned. "Hot damn, this place has some potential after all!"

"Your donation helped," Wes said. Then he nodded to Ben, who was looking around the place and nodding approval. Not smiling, though. Ben rarely smiled anymore. And Wes remembered that desolate feeling that had crept over him when he'd thought about losing Taylor forever, and impulsively hugged his brother.

Ben slapped him on the back, then stood back and blinked at him. "You okay, Wes?"

Feeling foolish, Wes just shook his head, then turned to Jessi. "So what brings you out here this time of night?"

"Lookin' for you, of course," she said. "You weren't at home, so I checked over at the site, and when I didn't find you there, either, I figured you must be here."

"Persistent, aren't you?"

Her brows rose at his tone. Then fell again. "Oh, heck, Wes, we're not…interrupting…anything, are we?"

"Of course not," Taylor said. "We've just been cleaning. It looks great, doesn't it?"

And Jessi tilted her head. "Well…'great' might not be

quite the right word…'' Then she gave her head a shake.
"But I brought you some news that is better than great."
She looked at Wes a little doubtfully. "I just hope I
didn't…overstep."

No one could overstep like Wes's baby sister, and he
groaned inwardly. "What did you do?"

She smiled at him. "First I called the lumberyard to
check on those supplies you ordered for the barn. They
said they couldn't deliver for three days, but I…*discussed*
it with them—"

"You bitched at them," Ben clarified. He glanced at
Taylor. "I could hear her yelling clear out in the stable."

"You're exaggerating," Jessi said. "But anyway,
Wes, they'll be delivering the stuff tomorrow."

Wes couldn't help himself. He chuckled aloud. "Leave
it to Jessi Brand to put the fear of God into a man."
Then he frowned. "Still there was no hurry. I won't have
time to work on the barn much until…"

"Saturday," she said, and she said it firmly.

A little foreboding tiptoed up Wes's spine. "Why Saturday?"

"Because on Saturday, big brother, we are having a
good ol'-fashioned barn raising!" She clapped her hands
together, practically bouncing up and down in excitement.

Wes blinked, then glanced at Ben, who only nodded
in agreement. "A barn raising." Then he shook his head,
and put one hand on his sister's shoulder. "Look, Jess,
it's a fabulous idea and all, but don't go getting your
hopes up. I'm not exactly the most popular guy in town."

"Don't be silly, Wes."

"I'm not," he told her. "Look, I may be a Brand, but
that doesn't mean people like me. Hell, a lot of 'em still
believe that time I did in prison was well deserved."

"Oh, Wes, that's bull. Everyone knows you were set up. Besides, it's ancient history. And I'll tell you, they might not vote you Mr. Congeniality around here, but there's not one person in the county who wouldn't want you on their side if they were in trouble. And most of 'em know you'd be there if they asked you."

"No," Wes said. "You're wrong about that. It'll never work, Jess."

"But it already has worked." She smiled again. "Everyone I've talked to promised to come."

Wes frowned. "They did?"

"Mmm-hmm. The women are bringing food enough for an army, and the men are dusting off their tool belts. It's going to be incredible, Wes. And before the weekend is over, that barn of yours won't be a barn at all. It'll be the Taj Mahal of stables."

Wes looked at Ben, who nodded once more. "It's true," he said. "She's been like a bumblebee on a caffeine high putting this thing together."

He just shook his head. "I can't believe it." Then he looked at Taylor, who was very quiet and wide-eyed. "Hey, Doc, what's wrong?"

She lowered her eyes, shook her head. "I was just thinking...how lucky you are, Wes."

"Heck, they aren't always this nice," he said. But he said it softly, and touched her face so she'd look at him again. Damned if there wasn't moisture in her eyes. "Most of the time they're a royal pain in the backside."

She smiled, but it was shaky. "I'd give an awful lot for a handful of pains like these two."

"Well, now, that's good to know," Wes said softly. And her eyes met his, widened a little, maybe in alarm, he wasn't sure. He'd dropped a pretty heavy-duty hint there. Was it too soon? Would he scare her off?

Jessi cleared her throat, and Taylor looked away. "You know," Jess said, "I've never seen the upstairs. Would you show me, Taylor?"

Taylor nodded and turned toward the stairs. As she led Jessi up, Wes sent his sister a warning glance. She read it, nodded to tell him she wasn't going to push or pry or meddle. But he figured he knew her well enough to know she would anyway.

When they were out of sight, Ben clamped a hand down on Wes's shoulder. "So? You gonna tell me what's going on between you two?"

Wes sighed. "Not much to tell. I'm nuts about her."

"But?"

He looked at his older brother whose shaggy blond mane made him look more rock star than cowboy. Oversize bulk concealing his grace. Unless you caught him at dawn, doing those tai chi moves out on the front lawn, facing the sunrise.

"She doesn't trust me, Ben. I lied to her once and I'm not sure she can get past it now."

Ben pursed his lips in thought. "A person can get past just about anything," he said.

"Not this."

"I know it might seem that way now, but..." His head came up. "Do you trust *her?*"

"Sure, I do."

"No. I mean, really trust her. Implicitly. Wes, the best way to win her trust is to show her that she has yours. All of it. You can't hold anything back, nothing at all, because as wary as she is, she's bound to sense it if you do. And if she senses you're keeping something inside, how's she gonna be able to trust you?"

Wes frowned as he thought about the things he'd shared with Taylor. And then about the things he hadn't told her. The site of Little Sparrow's grave. The things Turtle had told him today. What he planned to do tonight. He blinked at his brother. "Maybe you're right."

Ben nodded.

"What about you, brother?"

"What *about* me?"

Wes sighed. "I've been thinking about you a lot the last couple of days." He lowered his head. "I don't think I knew just how bad you must be hurting until…"

"Until you fell in love," Ben said.

Wes nodded. "Yeah. Before now I was just thinking you ought to be getting over…losing Penny. Now…I have to wonder if it's even possible."

Ben's head tipped upward, and he stared at some spot beyond the windows at Wes's back. "I don't think you ever get over losing the woman you love," he said. "You know, Penny and I knew she was dying when we fell in love. We both knew our time together was going to be short, so we filled it with…joy. Just sheer joy. It was the most incredible time of my life."

"But now?" Wes prompted.

Ben met his eyes. "The joy died with her." He drew a deep breath. "She made me promise that I would find someone else, eventually. She said she wouldn't be at peace if I went through the rest of my life alone, mourning her. So I said I would, but you know, I'm sore afraid that's one promise I won't be able to keep. And it's the only promise I ever made to Penny that I broke." He looked at the floor. "I've never told anyone about that before."

Wes nodded, understanding more than he ever had, how his brother must be feeling. "It's only been two years," he said. "Give yourself time, Ben. Don't feel guilty for loving your wife. She wouldn't have wanted that, either.''

Ben's lips curved very slightly in a sad half smile. ''I hadn't thought of it that way.''

''There's plenty of time to keep that promise. Penny would understand.''

''Yeah,'' Ben said. ''I guess she would.'' Then he seemed to shake the deep sadness from his eyes, though Wes was sure it lingered in his heart. ''Let's take a walk, have a look at that barn. I'm under orders to organize the volunteers into teams and assign each team to a project.''

''Jessi again?''

''You really need to ask?''

''You're good for my brother,'' Jessi said.

Taylor paused in perusing what would have to be the master bedroom, and looked at Jessi quickly.

''He's always been such a loner,'' Jessi said. ''But he's opening up. I can see it in his eyes. And I think it has a lot to do with you.''

''I don't think—'' Taylor began.

''He's in love with you. You know that, right?''

Taylor blinked and averted her face. ''I think you're jumping to conclusions.''

''No way. I know my brother. He's nuts about you. Gosh, Taylor, you mean he hasn't told you yet?''

Taylor licked her lips. ''No.''

''He will. You give him time, and he will.''

''I'm not sure I...want him to.''

Jessi touched Taylor's arm, drawing her gaze again. ''You mean, you aren't sure how you feel about him?''

Taylor nodded. Then bit her lip, not wanting to insult Jessi by implying her brother wasn't up to her standards. ''He's the most incredible man I've ever met,'' she said slowly, thinking her words through. "I mean…my… uncertainty—it has to do with me, not with Wes."

"It's his job to *make* you certain," Jessi said, nodding hard. "Apparently he hasn't done it very well, though." She frowned hard. "If he lets you slip through his fingers, I'll never forgive him."

That made Taylor smile. "I guess that's a compliment."

Jessi grinned at her, and ran a soothing hand over Taylor's hair. "You're beautiful, Taylor. And smart. You've touched Wes's heart when nobody else could…well, nobody besides the kids, at least. He's just mush when it comes to Bubba and little Maria. But with everyone else there's always this wall…I don't even think it's intentional on his part, but it's there."

Taylor nodded, listening intently.

"Besides," Jessi said. "You fit."

"I *fit?*"

"The family," Jessi told her. "You're like a missing puzzle piece. You come to that barn raising on Saturday and you'll see what I mean. You just fit. Trust me, I always know when someone belongs in our family."

Taylor tilted her head. "And you've never been wrong?"

Jessi made an exaggerated pout. "Well…once. About my brother Adam."

"Adam," Taylor said. "I haven't met him, have I?"

"Not yet," Jessi said. "A few years back Adam was engaged to his high-school sweetheart, Kirsten Armstrong. And I was so sure they were perfect for each other…" She shook her head.

"And what happened?"

Jessi sighed. "She didn't show up for the wedding.

Left him standing at the altar and just didn't show. We found out later she'd eloped with the richest jerk in the county, a fellow old enough to be her father."

"God, how horrible for Adam," Taylor said.

"It was. Crushed him. Not long after that he headed to the East Coast. Works for a bank there and says he loves being a big-shot executive city slicker. But I know better. He only left so he'd never have to face her again. If he'd stayed, he might have run into her. Not that it's likely. She's like a hermit now. No one ever sees her."

"Still," Taylor said softly, "you were wrong once. Could be you're wrong this time, too."

"Nah," Jessi said. "I know better. Besides, who says I was wrong about Adam and Kirsten? I still feel like I had the right idea with those two, and I get the feeling there's going to be a sequel to that little episode in my brother's life."

Taylor laughed. "You really don't give up easily, do you?"

"I don't give up *at all*."

Chapter 14

By the time Jessi and Ben finally finished inspecting the place, and—Wes thought—satisfying their curiosity about his relationship with Taylor, it was well after eleven. And he'd promised Turtle he'd come tonight for...

Well, hell, it sounded too far-fetched to think about, so he let the thought die. Taylor sat on the lowest step of the front porch, watching Ben's taillights fade in the darkness. Wes sat down beside her.

"So..."

She stiffened a little. It was awkward as hell. She was probably thinking he expected a little more of what she'd given him last night. But he knew better. He just didn't know how to tell her that.

She glanced at her watch.

"It's getting late," Wes said. "You want me to take you back?"

She blinked up at him. "You want to take me back?"

He smiled and decided to be honest with her. "Hell, no, Doc, I *want* to take you to bed. But it's too soon for that. Last night...last night happened, and I'll never stop bein' grateful it did. But the next time we make love, I'm hoping it will be with no walls still standing between us. No doubt in your pretty eyes."

As he spoke, she stared hard at him, first in confusion and then in some kind of wonder. "You're one special man, you know that? I must be nuts to be dragging my feet this way. Any other woman would—"

"I don't want any other woman," Wes said, and he ran the backs of his fingers down her cheek, as soft as down. "And I don't want you feeling pushed and unsure of me. Take your time, Taylor. Just don't write me off and walk away, okay?"

She lowered her head, swallowed hard. "The funding for this dig runs out on Sunday."

An icy fist gripped Wes's heart. He closed his eyes slowly. Took deep breaths. Counted to ten. Resisted the urge to grab her by the shoulders and tell her not to go. Shake her until she realized that his feelings were real. Beg her to listen to him for once. Instead he grated his teeth. "And you haven't decided what you're going to do about that yet," he said softly, but there was an edge to his words. Patience had never been his strong suit.

"No. I mean...I just don't know, Wes. There's another job waiting. I could call it off...to stay..."

"If you were sure there was something worth staying for," he finished for her.

She met his gaze, saying nothing. And she was feeling the stress; he could see it building in her eyes. Telling herself to make up her mind, to either trust him or not trust him and just get it the hell over with. Scorning her own insecurities, when they were no more than the results of past heartbreak and his own foolish mistakes.

He didn't want her feeling all that pressure because of him. He drew a deep breath, let it out slowly, relaxed his muscles. "Then I guess I'd best work fast to convince you, hadn't I, Doc?"

She blinked up at him. "This isn't your problem, Wes. I keep telling you that."

"I disagree with you there. Hell, any Don Juan worth his salt would have swept you right off your feet by now. I'm obviously not going about this the right way."

She shook her head, but Wes leaned forward and kissed her mouth very gently. "You stop worrying and leave it to me, Doc. I got connections now. I'll figure things out."

Frowning, she tilted her head to one side. "What kind of connections are you talking about?"

He pursed his lips. Remembered what Ben had said about trusting her first. Nodded his decision. "Turtle says that wolf last night was really a spirit guide. He says it came to let me know I'm...er...a shaman."

Her eyes widened.

"He told me," Wes said slowly, "that what that means is up to me, but that above all, it means I can get in touch with..." He shook his head slowly. "I'm trying to be open about all this, but it feels a little silly."

"It's not silly," she said quickly. And she impulsively pushed his hair away from his face. "It's almost...holy."

"Yeah. And almost insane."

She smiled at him. "You're a little bit scared, aren't you?"

"Scared? Of course I'm not scared. For crying out loud, why would I be—?"

She met his eyes, lifting her brows.

Wes licked his lips. "Yeah, I guess I am."

"I would be, too. Actually I already am. I feel…
wrapped up in all of this somehow."

He nodded, understanding why she felt that way. She
was wrapped up in it all. "Turtle wants me to come over
tonight. I told you he buckled and went back to the
trailer, didn't I?"

She nodded. "It's awfully late. Will he still be up?"

"Yeah. Probably already knows exactly when I'll
show." Wes shivered a little. Then started in surprise
when Taylor slid her hand into his and squeezed, moving
herself closer to his side.

"I shouldn't keep you, then. It sounds important."

"Sounds downright creepy."

"I'd offer to come along," she said softly, "but I have
a feeling this is something you need to do alone."

He turned her head up with one hand on her chin.
"You getting to be as perceptive as Turtle is?"

"As long as you don't start thinking *I'm* creepy." He
touched her nose with his, and her eyes fell closed.

"If…if it gets too intense, and you want to talk," she
said.

"I know where to find you, Doc." He kissed her then,
lingeringly, and he thought maybe he was making some
progress after all.

Because he'd told some of his secrets. But not all of
them. There was one secret that simply wasn't his to tell.

When he arrived at Turtle's place, the old man had set
up the tepee in the front lawn, and was sitting patiently
outside it, waiting as if he'd never had any doubt Wes
would show.

"What happened?" Wes asked when he approached

the old man. "You get so attached to that thing you decided to keep sleeping in it?"

Turtle shook his head. "You are late."

"I was with Taylor. Sorry about that."

The old man only shrugged. "The night is good. Clear. There is still time." He got to his feet and looked at Wes as if waiting for him to do something.

Wes looked back, lifted his hands. "What?"

"The sweat lodge is ready for you, Raven Eyes. But you are not ready for it."

"I..."

"Take off your clothing." When Wes gaped, Turtle grinned and shook his head in silent amusement. "If you wish, I will turn my back, Raven Eyes, though if you are that painfully shy, this is the first time you've shown it."

"Very funny," Wes said, and he stripped right there on Turtle's front lawn, thanking his stars the trailer was on a deserted bit of back road. Turtle gave him a towel to anchor around his hips, and then held the tepee's flap open. And Wes felt the heat hit him in the face hard enough to knock him to his knees when he peeked inside. He saw the pit of glowing coals in the center of the tepee. Saw the woven mat where he was to sit, and ducked inside, feeling as if he'd just been shoved into an oven.

Turtle came in behind him, wearing no more than Wes was, and carrying a pail of water. As Wes sat silently, Turtle used a wooden ladle of some sort to spoon water over the red-hot coals, sending wafts of steam into the air. And Turtle kept this up until the steam became too thick to see through.

"This purifies the body," he explained, and he was a voice in the mists now. Invisible. Like a spirit. "You must prepare yourself before attempting to communicate with the spirits. Sit in silence. Empty your mind. Release every thought.''

Wes tried to do that. It was hot as hell, but within a short time he forgot about that. His brain got hazy. He smelled something pungent and sweet, and wondered what sorts of mystical—quite possibly illegal—herbs Turtle had sprinkled over the coals to add their scents to the mix. He felt his hair growing damp, then clinging to him. His skin was soaked in the steam and his own sweat. The temperature was soaring in here, and still getting hotter. And time seemed to stop moving. He could no longer tell if he'd been in the tepee for a half hour or a half a day. And since he couldn't see in the mists, he closed his eyes and opened his mind. And the scent of the herbs got stronger and made him cough.

"Speak to the spirit of the wolf when he shows himself to you, Raven Eyes. Ask him your questions.''

Wes moved his mouth to say he would, but no sound emerged. His head was swimming, and he thought it might be heat exhaustion. How long had he been in here, anyway? He opened his eyes, but couldn't see anything. Not Turtle or the tepee's sides or even those glowing coals. There was only the steam. Thick, swirling clouds of it, encompassing him. And as he strained to see through the stuff, it formed itself into a shape. The shape...of a wolf.

Wes blinked and looked again. Tried to breathe deeply and calmly. But the apparition was still there, a wolf-shaped cloud with glowing red eyes that might have been embers...or might not.

"W-wolf spirit?'' Wes asked slowly, uncertainly. A distant, ghostly howl was his answer. And the eyes glowed a little brighter.

Wes cleared his throat. Okay, he was here, he was

hallucinating, he might as well run with it. "H-how can I win Taylor's trust without betraying the secrets of...of my people?" he asked. Because more than anything else, this was what he wanted to know.

The mist faded and blended into the rest, and the wolf was gone, and for a minute Wes thought he'd failed, and he closed his eyes in misery. But when he did, he saw a vision, just as clear as if he were watching a movie. He saw Wolf Shadow standing a long distance away, facing a woman who had to be Little Sparrow. They were surrounded by rocks and boulders, like that place where she rested. And as he watched, the camera of his mind seemed to zoom in closer and closer, until he could see the loincloth and bear-claw necklace Wolf Shadow wore, and Little Sparrow's beaded white dress of doe hide. And still closer his viewfinder moved, focusing in on Wolf Shadow's hands. They were moving, lifting something. A pendant on a thong, lowering it slowly around Little Sparrow's neck.

The turquoise heart! That was what it was. That was what he was seeing! But why? What did it mean?

Then, as if to answer his question, his point of view backed away from the hands, widening the angle until he could see only the two faces. But instead of those long-dead lovers, he was seeing his own face. And he was seeing Taylor's. And as the view broadened still further, he saw the clothing change to their own modern dress.

And then the vision faded until it was gone. He saw only darkness. He opened his eyes to see the steam thinning. And light coming through the sides and top of the tepee. And Turtle sitting silently on the opposite side of the pit of cooling stones.

He drew a deep breath, let it out and then started to get up, but the kinks in his back and legs almost put him back on the ground again. He stumbled to the flap, pushed it open and stepped outside.

Turtle was right behind him. "The wolf came to you. He spoke to you."

"Yeah," Wes said, eyeing the sun's alarming height in the sky. "I'm just not sure what he was telling me."

"Come. Clarity of mind is what you need now. You'll understand. If you let the understanding come on its own, rather than trying to force it." He clutched Wes's forearm and tugged him around behind the trailer to where the small stream ran shallow and fast.

Wes barely clung to his towel as he hurried along. His bare feet were not used to walking over pebbles and stones. But Turtle was ruthlessly dragging him along, and he stopped only when he reached a spot where the stream's flow had been partially blocked, resulting in a small pool of swirling, deeper water.

"Jump into the pool," Turtle instructed.

Wes slanted him a glance. "You're kidding, right? Turtle, do you have any idea how cold that water must be? It's still morning. And it's a fast-running stream, probably bubbling right out of some underground all but icy spring." Turtle crossed his arms over his chest and stared at him. "Turtle, I just spent half the night in hundred-degree heat. Now you want me to—hey!"

Too late. Turtle shoved Wes with one had, and snatched his towel away with the other. Wes hit the icy water hard, and went under. It felt as if his skin were being flash frozen. When he emerged again, Turtle was laughing out loud, but a second later the old man was splashing down beside him.

Wes shook his head and clambered out, reaching for his towel and wondering what sort of torture the old goat had in store for him next. Turtle came out, too. "Now your mind is clear," he said to Wes.

"Clear as ice water," he snapped. "Are we done with this little sadistic ritual of yours yet, pal?"

Turtle grinned, knotted his towel and nodded once. "For now," he said. "Now you must contemplate your vision. If you listen to the wolf, you will know what to do."

Wes shook his head, rubbed his arms and made his way around to the front lawn again to retrieve his clothes from the ground beside the tepee. "It'll take some thinking," he said.

"Then go and think," Turtle told him. "Time is short, you know."

Wes nodded. It was short, though he hadn't told Turtle that. He pulled on his clothes and headed to his truck. But the ideas were coming to him before he got a mile down the road.

When Taylor claimed to have seen Little Sparrow, she said it was like looking into a mirror. When Wes saw Little Sparrow, her image slowly changed into Taylor's beautiful face. Turtle said that Little Sparrow was Taylor's ancestor.

Now, following the same line of thinking, when Wes had seen what he thought was the ghost of Wolf Shadow, it had been...like looking into a mirror. He shivered, but continued following his train of thought. When he saw Wolf Shadow in the vision, that face had slowly changed into his own. Turtle said Taylor was to marry Wolf Shadow's descendant, and he refused to tell Wes who that man was. He'd even said it was something Wes had to learn for himself.

He jammed the brake pedal and came to a dusty stop in the middle of the dirt road.

For crying out loud. Was it *him?* Was *Wes himself* the last living relative of Wolf Shadow? Was *he* the one Turtle was so determined would marry Taylor?

He blinked in shock.

One way to find out. He gently eased up on the brake and drove, and decided that tomorrow he'd head into the town and the hall of records. They'd have something there. They must have. Why hadn't he ever checked this out sooner? It just hadn't occurred to him.

What if he was Wolf Shadow's descendant? What the hell would it mean?

Wes showed up at the site just as Taylor and the students were cleaning up the breakfast mess. And he looked…haunted. Pale and tired. Dark shadows ringed his eyes.

She stopped what she was doing and just looked at him. He'd stopped walking and stood there looking at her a little oddly. Taylor dropped the tin plate in her hands and went to him, touched his face. "You look exhausted."

"Haven't slept."

She narrowed her eyes, scanning his face. "Something happened last night…with Turtle."

He seemed to blink out of the state he was in then. "I can't…I can't talk about it, Doc. Not yet."

A prickle of suspicion danced up her spine and into her nape, but she shook it away. "Is Turtle all right?"

He nodded.

"Are you?" she asked him, because he really didn't look as if he was.

"Yeah. I just need some rest, is all."

So she nodded. "You should go home."

"I'll tell you all of it, Taylor. As soon as I—" he

shook his head "—figure out what it means." He touched her hair, searched her face and seemed to sense her doubts. "I'm not keeping secrets from you, Taylor. I just…I'm not really sure what the hell happened. I need some time…I have to—"

"It's okay. I understand. You'll tell me when you're ready." She hoped her words carried more conviction than she was feeling. But all she could think was that he was keeping something from her…again.

His eyes blinked slowly closed. He forced them open again.

"Go home," she told him. "Get some sleep."

"I'll get some sleep," he said. "But not at home." His tired eyes roamed her face for a moment. "I need to be near you."

She felt herself smile, and warmth pooled in the pit of her stomach. "My tent, then?"

He nodded, stroked her hair slowly, then turned and walked toward the tents. He ducked into her tent and let the flap fall closed behind him. She stared at the tent after he'd disappeared inside, and then she walked quietly closer and peered in at him.

He'd crawled into her bed, and was hugging her pillow to him with his face nestled in its folds.

I need to be near you.

Taylor backed away in silence, and blinked at the sudden burning in her eyes.

Wes still hadn't talked to her about his late-night ritual with Turtle. That bothered Taylor. And it shouldn't. She told herself that over and over as they drove together to Wes's ranch for the barn raising his sister had arranged. It had been a personal thing; something deep had happened to him. She could sense that. But his reluctance to discuss it still gnawed at her gut. Another secret between them. God, how she hated them.

But why? Why was she letting this come between them this way? He'd been as attentive as ever. Helping out at the site, taking her to dinner at the ranch each night as they worked side by side to put the house in some kind of order. He'd gone out and bought the exact light fixture she'd described to him, and installed it in the living-room ceiling, then took her over there to show her.

She glanced up at the wagon-wheel chandelier and felt herself get soft inside again. So many things he did made her feel that way. She should love this man. She should get past her stupid mistrust and let herself love him. He was almost perfect.

Almost. It was that damned *almost* that kept getting in the way. If only he'd open up, tell her the things he was keeping from her.

And if only he'd do it before she finished up on the site and had to make a decision. One more day. That was all she had left. One more day. And she hadn't found anything at all on that entire chunk of Comanche land that indicated it was some kind of sacred ground. Nor anything that would make the tribe prosperous as the legend had foretold. No reason in the world they shouldn't sell it to Hawthorne and collect the money they so desperately needed. Nothing.

Nothing except a niggling feeling in her gut. And the Comanche elders couldn't take that to the bank, or use it to repair their children's schools or send them to college. Or fix up their homes or…or anything at all.

One more day.

Wes pulled the truck to a stop and killed the engine. Then he just sat there blinking at what he saw. Taylor pulled herself out of her thoughts and looked ahead, and saw people. So many people there didn't seem room for two more. Milling around like ants, each seemingly intent on doing his or her part. Men and women worked with crowbars to pry bad lumber from the barn walls. Two men in hard hats were on a ladder, stringing an electrical cable to the barn. Five or six were way up on that roof replacing the shingles. And a half dozen more were removing boards from inside the barn, carrying in fresh new lumber.

Taylor shook her head in wonder.

"I can't believe..." She looked at Wes when he stopped speaking, and saw his throat move as he swallowed hard.

"You're more well liked than you thought you were, I guess," Taylor told him.

Shaking his head, Wes opened the door and got out, and Taylor did likewise. The noise hit her at once, not unpleasant. But beautiful. The whir of circular saws, the steady thud of hammers, the loud grinding sound of the generator that provided electricity for the power tools, the ebb and flow of voices raised above the ruckus. One raised louder than the rest. One she recognized. She searched the crowd and spotted Jessi, hurrying from one group of workers to another, pointing and shouting directions above the din.

"That sister of yours should have been a drill sergeant."

Wes looked at Taylor, and she nodded toward Jessi. He spotted his sister and smiled. "I'll be..."

Elliot was up on the roof nailing shingles down. Garrett manned a saw, steadily cutting lumber on a pair of sawhorses. Lash took each cut board away, carrying it into the barn, while Ben was on Garrett's other side, hefting new lumber onto the horses to be sawed each time they were empty.

And there were others she recognized. The man from the little general store in town, manning several huge coffee urns on a picnic table. The bartender from that place with the funny name—La Cucaracha, wasn't it?—wielding a hammer. Three young men she thought must be brothers, tying bundles of shingles to a rope to be hauled up to the roof. Chelsea and several other women alternated between watching the children who played a few yards from the hub of activity, and working with the men.

Jessi spotted them standing there, and came rushing over. "Isn't this great?" she shouted above the noise. "Everyone in town is here. Paul Loomis dropped the boys off and headed back home. Said he had a vat of his special chili brewing to bring over later."

She was grinning ear to ear.

Wes just shook his head. Jessi tugged his arm. "Well, come on, brother, don't just stand there. They need you inside. Want to know how many stalls you want and how big the tack room should be and…" She dragged him a few steps, then turned. "You have some say in this, too, Taylor. Shake a leg, willya?"

Taylor met Wes's bemused gaze. And then he smiled at her, and she went to join him.

Trouble lights dangled from every possible appendage inside the barn, and the place smelled of sawdust. One man pulled Wes aside, and they leaned over a makeshift table made up of a stack of lumber, while the man pointed to some drawings on a large sheet of graph paper, and shouted questions.

Wes frowned at the designs, took the pencil, made a few scratches on the sheet, then turned and waved at her to come over. "What do you think?" he asked her. "These stalls could be smaller. We could get more in."

She blinked at him, and then saw in his eyes that he *wanted* her opinion. *Valued* it. That he felt she had a stake in this, just as his sister did. And she closed her eyes slowly, because he was assuming so much. Moving so fast. Acting as if this would be her place, as well as his, when she wasn't even sure...

"C'mon, Doc. I need you with me on this."

She met his eyes, went warm all over. Damn, he had that effect on her every time he glanced her way. Then he pushed the pencil into her hand, and she couldn't refuse him. She'd worry about later—later. She leaned over the drawings, pushing her hair behind her ear. "I think the bigger stalls are better," she said. Then she glanced up at the barn. "We can always add on later. Build a whole new section if we..."

She bit her lip. She'd said *we*. As if...as if...she'd already made up her mind.

But Wes was nodding hard. "She's right," he told the other man. "Forty stalls is plenty to start. It'll be years before we fill 'em all and need more."

Years. We.

She swallowed hard and tried to stop her heart from racing. He hadn't told her so, but Wes was making it pretty obvious he wanted her to be a part of his life...for a long time to come.

And yet...he was still keeping something from her. And she'd sensed he was even before his mysterious night with Turtle, so it had to be more than that. Would it always be this way? Her wondering what he had to hide? Her mistrusting him constantly? God, she couldn't live that way.

He smiled at her, and her heart tripped. "I'm going

outside,'' she said. "The dust..." And she dropped the pencil atop the page and turned to leave him.

Since Wes was everywhere from the roof to the saw-horses, hopping from one project to another like a Mexican jumping bean, Taylor headed over to the area where Chelsea supervised the children. She couldn't be near him, couldn't listen to him asking how she wanted things in the barn, as if it were hers, too. Not yet. She wasn't ready for all this.

Chelsea sat on a blanket spread on the ground, where Jessi's little baby sat propped with pillows, gnawing a toy she held in her chubby hands. Little Ethan—Bubba to the Brands—ran and played with several other children, trying to catch grasshoppers. Chelsea patted a spot on the blanket beside her, and Taylor sat down.

Maria dimpled, crawled closer and climbed right into Taylor's lap.

"You look worried," Chelsea said. "Everything okay?"

Taylor stroked the baby's reddish hair, so like her mother's. It felt like corn silk against her palm. Maria leaned her head on Taylor's chest.

"I don't know," Taylor said. "I just..."

"He's moving too fast," Chelsea said.

Taylor lifted her head in surprise. How could she know...?

"He's my brother-in-law. I know him. He doesn't have a patient bone in his body, Taylor."

Taylor shook her head. "He's trying. Told me to take my time, that he wouldn't rush me. But then he keeps talking about this place in terms of 'we' and 'us' and it—"

"It's just a Freudian slip," Chelsea told her. "It's how he hopes it will be. It's on his mind, so it comes out in what he says, especially when he's not thinking. It's normal. Don't take it as pressure."

Taylor lowered her head. "How can I not? Chelsea, I don't want to hurt him, but—"

"But you're scared. And you're uncertain. And you're not ready to make a commitment to a man you still aren't sure you can trust."

Sighing, relieved to have it said so plainly for her, Taylor nodded. "Exactly."

"Wes is a big boy, Taylor. He can handle being hurt. It's yourself you have to think about now."

"That feels so selfish."

"Then be selfish. Look, you can't love Wes the way he wants you to until you take care of those old hurts you're still nursing inside. So by thinking of yourself, you're doing what's best for both of you."

That made perfect sense. So why did it feel so wrong? "I want to love him," she whispered.

"I have a news flash for you," Chelsea said softly. And Taylor looked up, met her eyes. "You already do."

"I—"

"I've seen the way you look at him, the way you two are together. God, to look at the two of you, I'd think you'd already been together for a hundred years."

Taylor licked her lips. "Sometimes…it feels like we have."

"Take it slow, Taylor. Take your time. Wait until you're sure, and then—"

"But I don't have time." Taylor blurted it, and saw the alarm in Chelsea's eyes. She closed her own. "I have to pack up and leave the site tomorrow. Time's up, Chelsea, and I have to decide what to do. I can't just hang around here waiting for the clouds to part and tell me.

And I can't just leave Wes with the vague promise that I might come back someday. I can't do that to him."

Chelsea's soft hand closed around Taylor's and squeezed. "Then maybe it's time you stopped thinking, and let yourself feel. I think your answer is in your heart, Taylor. Maybe you should listen to what it's telling you."

Trust herself, in other words. And trust Wes.

She bit her lip and wished to God that was as easy to do as it was to think.

Chapter 15

Wes's frustration ate at him all day. Even through the thrill he felt at seeing his barn being converted into the stable of his dreams. And the even bigger rush of seeing nearly everyone in town pitching in to help him the way they were.

There had been nothing to find in the hall of records. And then he'd checked with the tribal elders, but they'd had no information for him, either.

He barely saw Taylor through the morning. The work kept him so busy he couldn't get away to search for her. But at noon, when people started hauling coolers full of food out of their vehicles, and Paul Loomis arrived with a kettle of chili that outdid the sawdust for aroma, he found her.

And she smiled and put on a very nice show for him, but he saw through it. She was thinking about leaving him. And he couldn't lose her. He couldn't lose her now.

He started toward her, when a heavy hand fell on his

shoulder. And he turned to see his brother Ben, looking as worried as Wes felt.

"Did you do what I told you?"

Wes blinked and drew a blank. "What did you tell me?"

"Little brother, you can be dense as solid granite. What did I tell you?" He shook his shaggy head. "That if you want her to trust you, you have to show her that you trust her. Completely. Implicitly. Prove it to her beyond any doubt. Now, dammit, it doesn't look to me like you've done that, have you?"

Wes lowered his head, shook it slowly. "No. I guess I haven't."

"And why the hell not?"

"Look, Ben, if I thought it was that simple, I'd—"

"It *is* that simple. Damn, Wes, you gonna let her walk away? She's the best thing that ever happened to you, and you know it."

Glancing at Taylor again, Wes nodded. "I know it."

"Something's eating at her, Wes. You gotta chase those shadows of doubt out of her eyes once and for all. No matter what it takes, you have to do it."

"But—"

"No buts."

"Ben, it's not that easy. If I tell her—"

"Then you *are* keeping something from her." Ben shook his head. "And here I thought she was wrong about that."

"It's not my secret to tell," Wes said, and he felt his heart breaking with every word.

"Then you're gonna lose her," Ben told him. He sighed heavily. "Wes, I'm telling you, it's not worth it. I lost the only woman I ever loved, so you can take my word on that. Hell, I'd shout government secrets from the rooftops if I thought it could bring Penny back to me.''

His voice broke a little, and Wes's heart broke with it for his brother's pain.

"No stupid secret is worth losing her, Wes. I guarantee it. And I'll tell you something else. If you really did love her, you'd trust her. And if you really trusted her, you'd know your deep dark secret would be safe in her hands.'' He nodded toward where Taylor was standing. "Safe as little Maria is there.''

Wes followed Ben's gaze and saw Taylor snuggling Maria in her arms, sitting down at the picnic table with the baby on her lap, lifting a spoon to eager lips.

"Damn,'' he whispered.

"Looks awful good with the baby in her arms, doesn't she, little brother?''

Wes had to avert his face. Hot moisture burned his eyes, and he blinked it away.

"Don't do it, Wes. Don't lose her. You'll never forgive yourself if you do.'' Ben clapped Wes on the shoulder one last time, then wandered over to the picnic area to join the others.

And Wes knew his brother was right. If he lost Taylor, he'd never forgive himself. Maybe it was time he took Turtle's advice, and listened to the visions. Let his gut or his guide or whatever the hell you wanted to call it, tell him what to do, and stop thinking so much. He'd seen that vision or hallucination or whatever it was. And instead of believing in it, he'd gone out looking for proof of what it had shown him. Well, it was too late for proof, and maybe he didn't need any. Maybe he should just believe. Just trust. Trust the vision.

Trust Taylor.

He swallowed hard. Okay. Then he'd trust her.

*   *   *

Wes sat with her as they ate lunch, but it was all too brief an interlude. Within minutes the men were swarming over that barn like bees on a honeycomb, and the women were collecting the dishes and putting away the food.

Wes got up to leave, but then he leaned down over her, his lips brushing her ear, and he whispered, "You don't have to worry about this anymore, Doc. I think I finally have it figured out."

She turned quickly, frowning up at him. He only planted a kiss on her mouth, and then smiled, and turned to join the workers.

Taylor frowned after him, wondering what on earth he could mean. He'd said he couldn't talk about what had happened that night with Turtle until he'd figured it out. Was that it, then? He was ready to talk to her about it?

And was that going to make the difference? Would she get past this stupid suspicion that he was still hiding things from her then? Would it be enough?

She was a fool. The biggest fool in Texas if it wasn't. But she also knew in her heart that Chelsea was right. She had to be sure. They'd both be miserable unless she was.

By the time the sun went down, the wiring work on the barn was complete, and the men who'd done it had headed into the house to check out the wiring in there. The stalls were in place, the tack room half-finished, the roof brand-new and leak free. People were beginning to pack up and head home.

"Tomorrow we can slap a coat of paint on this baby," one man announced loudly.

"Plumbing still needs doing. An all-day job," someone else said.

The three men came out of the house nodding and talking among themselves, and one called out to Wes. "Wiring in the house isn't bad at all. Couple of places need repairing, but it shouldn't take long. And you need a new pump. It's shot, but once you get one, and a hot-water heater, that place'll be darned near perfect."

Jessi sniffed. "Won't be perfect till we get some paint and wallpaper in there, and patch those holes in the plaster."

Wes made a face at his sister. "Women. I suppose it won't be livable until we hang lace curtains and line the shelves with knickknacks, either."

"That's right, brother." Jessi winked at Taylor. "But I think we girls can handle that end of things, when your budget allows." Then she came closer. "How is the money holding up, Wes? All this lumber and stuff must've cost a fortune."

"There's still enough left for that pump and water heater," he told her. "You saved me a bundle, setting this up. You know what it would have cost me to hire someone to get all this done?"

She smiled and lifted her chin. "That's what baby sisters are for." And she smiled at Taylor. "My brothers hate to admit it, but they couldn't get along without me if their lives depended on it."

Lash came forward and slipped an arm around her shoulders. "Neither could I," he said, and dropped a kiss on top of her head.

But Wes was frowning. "I think we'll be a little short of funds for lace curtains and wallpaper, though. Whatever's left has to go for breeding stock." He smiled softly. "Mares," he said. "Lots of mares."

Taylor opened her mouth...then she snapped it shut again. She'd very nearly blurted that she had savings enough to decorate the entire house. Damn. She was falling into Wes's fantasy again. Thinking as if the place were her home, as well as his.

Instead she said, "You could board a few head, bring in some cash that way. You'll have empty stalls for a while. And you could always give riding lessons on the side."

Garrett came forward then, and the big man was holding Bubba's tiny hand in his, and taking small steps so the little guy could keep up. That toddler looked up at Garrett with sheer worship in his eyes. "Wes, you know you still own a share of the Texas Brand. One-sixth of the place is yours."

"And if you're thinking I'll keep taking one-sixth of the profits when I'm not working full-time on the ranch, you're nuts, big brother."

Garrett shrugged. "You could let me buy your share of the place."

Wes blinked, and Taylor could see he hadn't even considered it before. "I don't know—"

Garrett nodded toward the house. "Place needs paint," he said. "Roofing. And those front steps need replacing, and the porch rail." He met Wes's eyes. "You think it over, and we'll talk, okay?"

Cars were pulling away now, engines purring or growling, headlights flashing over their faces. Only the Brands remained here now. The real Brands. Taylor felt like an outsider.

Then Wes slipped an arm around her shoulders, and she got the overwhelming feeling that she belonged right here, at his side, surrounded by this huge family. "I'll think about it," Wes said. "Thanks, Garrett." Then he squeezed Taylor closer. "We'd best go now, though. I got something needs doing."

He met Ben's eyes. Ben nodded encouragement, told him without a word to do whatever it took. And Wes swallowed hard and prayed his trust in Taylor would be well placed.

Wes took Taylor back to the Texas Brand, instead of the site. As they pulled in beneath the giant arch, she asked him why, but he only shook his head and kept driving.

He pulled the truck to a stop near the stables, and when she got out, he drew her into the musty dimness, flicking on lights as he went. He released her hand and hurried to the back, disappearing into what must be the tack room and returning with two saddles, and a pair of bridles over his arm.

"Feel like a moonlight ride?" he asked her. But the way he said it, the way he looked, she got the feeling he was asking for a lot more. That her answer was vital.

"Wes, what's this about?"

"It's about everything, Doc. Just come with me. Trust me." He dropped the saddles to the floor and came closer, taking one of her hands in both of his. "Trust me, Taylor. Just this once."

And she trembled. But she nodded. "All right."

Wes seemed to sag in relief, but only for a moment. Then he was drawing a horse from a stall, saddling it and moving on to ready a second mount for her. Side by side they led the horses from the stable, and Taylor kept searching Wes's face for some hint of what he was up to. But he showed nothing. So good at hiding things. Damn.

He held her horse while she mounted, and then climbed aboard his own. "This way," he said. And he dug in his heels, setting off at a fast pace. Breaking into a gallop across the fields. Taylor kicked her horse into action, falling into the familiar rhythm of horse and rider, and they raced through the night, her hair flying behind her. It was exhilarating, and for a while she forgot to worry about her feelings for Wes, her inability to trust him, his secrets, and just lost herself in the heady thrill of racing heedlessly through the darkness.

She rode up to his side and together they ran, and she wished they could be like this, this carefree and wonderful together, for always. But then she realized where they were heading, and all the old questions and doubts crept in again. Gnawing at her brain like hungry rodents.

They skirted the site, and ended up in the cool desert, and Wes drew his horse in a bit, slowed to a walk.

"Is it Turtle?" Taylor asked, her horse close beside Wes's. "Is he back out here with that raggedy tepee again?"

"No. Turtle's safe in his trailer. It's just you and me tonight, Doc."

"Wes, this is really throwing me. Can't you tell me what—?"

"I have a present for you." He fumbled with something at his waist for a moment. It was too dark to see what. But seconds later he reached out and handed her a rawhide thong, and she recognized it. He'd taken it from that medicine pouch he always wore tied either to a belt loop or around his neck. As she took it from him, he stuffed the pouch into a pocket.

Taylor held the thong, looked at it and shook her head. "I don't understand."

"You will," he said. And then he fell into silence. There was only the gentle night wind blowing, rippling the horses' manes, and the steady soft sound of hooves on arid ground. And then the rocky hill rose up in the darkness just ahead, and Wes pulled in front of her. Single file was the only way to pick through the boulders. He was moving up higher, not down toward the spot where Turtle had set up his deathwatch such a short time ago. It seemed as if it had been much longer since that night. The night she'd spent wrapped in Wes's strong arms. Making love to him.

His horse's tail twitched, and pebbles clattered underfoot. And then Wes stopped, and he climbed down, twining the reins around the limb of a scraggly tree. He came to her, and helped her down, as well, leading her horse up beside his, tying it there. He took her hand.

"I figured something out today," he said. "Took a lot of help. Turtle's been trying to tell me, I think, but he wanted me to see it for myself. Ben...well, Ben's a little more blunt about these things."

Taylor drew a breath. Let it out slowly. Waited. He was going to tell her something. Something important. Please, she thought, let me be right. Let him open up to me, finally.

Wes turned, drawing her close to his side, and walked a few steps farther. "You told me once, Doc, that your career means everything to you."

"It has," she said. *Until now.* But she didn't say that last part aloud.

"The sacred ground on this site isn't meant to be invaded," he told her. "If it is, its magic will die. But if it's treated with the respect it should be...then The People will prosper because of it. That's the way the legend goes, anyway."

She nodded. "I know all that, Wes. But there is no sacred ground. I haven't found anything to indicate—"

"There is."

She frowned and tilted her head, searching his face.

"There are only two people alive who know where, Doc, but there is a magical place here. Turtle knows. But as shaman he was sworn to keep the secret, to keep the ground from being desecrated by outsiders. But he was torn, because unless the spot was discovered, the elders were determined to sell this property. That was why he wanted me to play the Wolf Shadow game with you. To convince you there was magic here without letting you get close enough to actually find it. But I'm taking that decision out of his hands, because...because I can't lose you now."

The breath was knocked from her lungs. She didn't know what to say. And then something occurred to her that hadn't before. "I'm Comanche," she said softly. "Why would it desecrate the ground if I discovered the site?"

"Because your career is your life. And a find like this one could make your career more than it ever was. You could get backing, dig it all up, put the artifacts on display in some white man's museum."

She lowered her head very slowly. Did Turtle really believe she would do that? And then she blinked. Maybe he was right. Because maybe she would have, a few short weeks ago. But she wasn't the same person she had been. She was Comanche now.

Her head came up quickly as she replayed all Wes had said. "You said there were two people who knew where this sacred place was." And Wes nodded. She licked her lips. "Are you the other one?"

He stared hard into her eyes, and she knew he was opening his soul to her at this moment. "I found it that night Turtle was out here. I was looking for firewood, and..."

"And that's what you've been keeping from me." And

why did it hurt so much? Why did it sting to know he didn't trust her any more than Turtle did?

"Give me the thong," he said softly. And she did, not looking up or meeting his eyes.

But then he knelt on the ground and pulled some stones away from the base of a boulder. And he reached inside. Taylor stood riveted as he fumbled in the darkness. Then he rose and turned to face her. And he lifted the thong, and she saw the turquoise heart, roughly hewn, but all the more beautiful for its crudeness. As she sucked in a breath, Wes draped the pendant around her neck.

"Wes...?"

"That night I spent with Turtle, I had a vision, Taylor. And this is what I saw. I'm not keeping anything from you anymore. Because I trust you. And everything inside me is telling me that this is the only way to make you see that. I trust you, Taylor. This is the site you've been looking for. It can make you famous, if you want it to."

"My God," she whispered. "Then it's all true. This is...this is where Little Sparrow is buried. This is her necklace."

"It's your necklace. I think...I think that's what the vision was trying to tell me."

"But...but this...this ground...the legend..."

Wes shrugged. "What you choose to do with this spot is up to you now, Taylor. The elders gave you permission to dig here, and you can excavate most of this spot before your time runs out tomorrow. Or you can leave it, as the legend says it should be left."

Taylor looked at the ground, shook her head slowly.

"I can only tell you one thing for sure," Wes said, and he reached out to trace the shape of the heart where it rested on her chest with a forefinger. "No matter which choice you make, right or wrong, Doc, I'm gonna be right here. Because I'm in love with you." He paused, touched her face and shook his head in wonder. "I love you, Sky Dancer." He bent closer, kissed her gently and then he straightened and turned, began walking back toward the horses.

"Wes."

He stopped, his back to her, and stood motionless, waiting.

"I feel like I know her," she said softly. "It's like she's with me, like she's been with me all my life. I just...never let myself feel it. Didn't even know how to let myself feel it."

Wes turned, and she knew he could probably see the tears in her eyes. But she didn't care. She could trust Wes with her tears.

"No one is going to be digging on this site. I'll make the elders understand that they can't sell it to Hawthorne. But I won't betray Little Sparrow for the sake of my career." She touched the necklace, felt it warming in her palm. "And I won't betray you."

As he stood, maybe shocked motionless, maybe unsure, she sniffed. She hadn't told him how she felt for him. Not yet. But first...

She lifted the necklace over her head, and bent to lovingly tuck it back into the place where it had been. Bracing one hand on the boulder to steady herself, she looked for the hole. But then she paused, because something slick and wet was coating her palm. She straightened fast, turning her hand, trying to see what it was.

"Taylor?" Wes came to her. "What is it?"

Taylor drew her hand to her face and sniffed at the substance. She shook her head, and took Wes's hand in her clean one, drawing it forward until his fingertip touched the wetness on the stone.

"What the...?"

Wes rubbed his forefinger with his thumb, and then he sniffed, as well.

And then his eyes widened. "It...it smells like..."

"Oil." They said it together. And then they turned, bending nearly double to trace the trickle of black gold back to its source. And they found it, uphill, nearly three hundred yards from the site of Little Sparrow's grave, a tiny chasm between the boulders where the small stream of liquid seemed to disappear into the earth.

Taylor looked up at Wes. "Thank God it's not too late," she said, beaming. "The People still own this land. If this is what we think it is, they..." She shook her head slowly.

"Hawthorne must have known about this," Wes said slowly. "It's bugged me all along that he'd make such a generous offer on this hunk of ground." He looked at Taylor and smiled. "Do you know what this is going to mean to the Comanche people here?"

And a voice came from behind Wes, an aged, wise voice. "It means, Raven Eyes, that the prophecy is being fulfilled."

Wes turned fast, and Taylor went forward to stand close beside him. His arm came around her shoulders as Turtle stood smiling at them.

"How the heck did you get up here, Turtle?" Wes asked. "What are you doing here?"

"By preserving Little Sparrow's resting place, you two have ensured the fulfillment of Wolf Shadow's promise. The People will know prosperity now." He nodded slowly. "You did well to listen to the visions, Raven Eyes. I knew you would."

"I'm glad someone did," Wes said. "But, Turtle, you

could have saved us all a lot of grief if you'd just told us about this from the start.''

Turtle blinked slowly. "That I could not do. Sky Dancer had to come here. She had to find herself in the spirits of her ancestors, and to know who she is. And you, Raven Eyes, you needed to find your own way. To tell you would have accomplished nothing. And now there is only one part of the prophecy left unfulfilled. The spirits of Wolf Shadow and Little Sparrow are still not at peace. Not until they are united. And, Sky Dancer, this part of the prophecy, only you can fulfill.''

Taylor's stomach clenched. She closed her eyes, lowered her head. "You mean, you want me to marry this man you have chosen for me...the last descendant of Wolf Shadow. That's what you're saying, isn't it, Turtle?''

When she dared open her eyes and look at him, Turtle was nodding slowly.

"I'm so sorry," she whispered. "But I can't.''

Wes started to say something, but Turtle held up a hand. "Tell me why," Turtle said.

Taylor drew a deep breath. She turned and looked into Wes's eyes, and whispered, "Because I'm in love with someone else. There's only one man I want, Turtle. Only one man...and for the life of me I can't imagine why it's taken me so long to realize that.''

Wes's hands came to rest in her hair, stroking it slowly as he searched her face, unashamed tears brimming in his eyes. "Taylor?''

"I love you, Wes," she whispered. "Tell me I didn't wait too long. Tell me it's not too late.''

His lips trembled as he lowered his head to kiss her. And when he lifted his head again, he whispered, "I'd have waited a lifetime, if that's what it took.''

Turtle came closer. She hadn't heard him approach, so it startled her when his powder-soft hand closed on hers, and gently took the pendant away. Holding her to his side, Wes turned to face Turtle.

The old man held the pendant up before him, looking at it, eyes gleaming. "There is no need to put the pendant back into the ground, Sky Dancer. Because it is yours to wear. As your ancestor, Little Sparrow, wore it before you."

But he didn't hand it to her. Instead he pushed the heart into Wes's hands. "And yours to give to the woman you love, Raven Eyes. Just as your ancestor, Wolf Shadow, gave it before you."

Taylor blinked twice, and then sucked in a breath. "You mean...?"

Turtle nodded in a very turtlelike way. And then he simply vanished. Before her eyes. She emitted a startled cry, and scanned the place where he'd been standing only a second ago. But he was gone. And when she met Wes's eyes, she saw that they were wide...but accepting.

He put the pendant to his lips, kissed it reverently and then lowered it over her head as he had before. "Marry me, Sky Dancer," he whispered. "Share that ranch with me. Share everything with me—our lives, our children...*everything.*"

"Yes," she told him. "Yes."

Epilogue

Wes stood on a rocky hilltop, holding Taylor's hands in his. Beyond them a wrought-iron-filigree rail surrounded the sacred resting place of Little Sparrow. And in the distance the beginnings of an oil rig loomed like a shadow. But the work on that had stopped for today.

His family surrounded him, smiling, crying some. He'd cried once or twice himself today, and maybe would again before it was over. He'd never dreamed he could be this happy, love this deeply, feel this much.

Taylor wore a doeskin dress, bleached white and lined with fringe and beads. And the turquoise heart hung around her neck. And Turtle recited words in his native tongue above them, and they both answered in the same language, which he'd been teaching to them, along with so many other things.

And then Wes held Taylor close in his arms, and he kissed her as if he would never stop. And she kissed him back just as deeply. And when Wes lifted his head away, he saw something, far off in the distance. And he touched her face and pointed, and she looked and saw it, too.

The two lovers, twined in one another's arms, as thin and transparent as mist, and as real as the ground under their feet. From somewhere beyond them a wolf yipped and then howled in a long, joyous wail. And then the phantom shapes vanished, and a warmth like nothing he'd ever known settled over Wes's heart.

"They're together," Taylor whispered. "They've finally found each other."

"And so have we, Sky Dancer," Wes whispered. "So have we."

* * * * *

COMING THIS OCTOBER 1997 FROM

THREE NEW LOVE STORIES IN ONE VOLUME BY
ONE OF AMERICA'S MOST BELOVED WRITERS

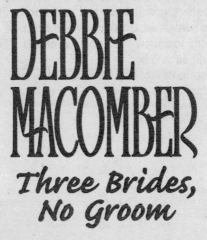

DEBBIE MACOMBER
Three Brides, No Groom

Gretchen, Maddie and Carol—they were three college
friends with plans to become blushing brides. But
even though the caterers were booked, the bouquets
bought and the bridal gowns were ready to wear...the
grooms suddenly got cold feet. And that's when these
three women decided they weren't going to get mad...
they were going to get even!

DON'T MISS THE WARMTH, THE HUMOR...THE
ROMANCE AS ONLY DEBBIE MACOMBER CAN DO!

AVAILABLE WHEREVER SILHOUETTE BOOKS
ARE SOLD.   TBNG-S

Take 4 bestselling love stories FREE

Plus get a FREE surprise gift!

Special Limited-time Offer

Mail to Silhouette Reader Service™

3010 Walden Avenue
P.O. Box 1867
Buffalo, N.Y. 14240-1867

YES! Please send me 4 free Silhouette Intimate Moments® novels and my free surprise gift. Then send me 6 brand-new novels every month, which I will receive months before they appear in bookstores. Bill me at the low price of $3.34 each plus 25¢ delivery and applicable sales tax, if any.* That's the complete price and a savings of over 10% off the cover prices—quite a bargain! I understand that accepting the books and gift places me under no obligation ever to buy any books. I can always return a shipment and cancel at any time. Even if I never buy another book from Silhouette, the 4 free books and the surprise gift are mine to keep forever.

245 BPA A3UW

Name	(PLEASE PRINT)	
Address	Apt. No.	
City	State	Zip

This offer is limited to one order per household and not valid to present Silhouette Intimate Moments® subscribers. *Terms and prices are subject to change without notice. Sales tax applicable in N.Y.

UMOM-696   ©1990 Harlequin Enterprises Limited

DIANA WHITNEY

Continues the twelve-book series 36 HOURS in September 1997 with Book Three

OOH BABY, BABY

In the back of a cab, in the midst of a disastrous storm, Travis Stockwell delivered Peggy Saxon's two precious babies and, for a moment, they felt like a family. But Travis was a wandering cowboy, and a fine woman like Peggy was better off without him. Still, she and her adorable twins had tugged on his heartstrings, until now he wasn't so sure that *he* was better off without *her.*

For Travis and Peggy and *all* the residents of Grand Springs, Colorado, the storm-induced blackout was just the beginning of 36 Hours that changed *everything!* You won't want to miss a single book.

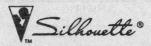

Look us up on-line at: http://www.romance.net   36HRS3

SILHOUETTE WOMEN KNOW ROMANCE WHEN THEY SEE IT.

And they'll see it on **ROMANCE CLASSICS**, the new 24-hour TV channel devoted to romantic movies and original programs like the special **Romantically Speaking-Harlequin® Goes Prime Time.**

Romantically Speaking-Harlequin® Goes Prime Time introduces you to many of your favorite romance authors in a program developed exclusively for Harlequin® and Silhouette® readers.

Watch for **Romantically Speaking-Harlequin® Goes Prime Time** beginning in the summer of 1997.

If you're not receiving ROMANCE CLASSICS, call your local cable operator or satellite provider and ask for it today!

ROMANCE CLASSICS

Escape to the network of your dreams.

©1997 American Movie Classics Co. "Romance Classics" is a service mark of American Movie Classics Co.
® is a reg'd trademark of Harlequin Enterprises Ltd.   RMCLS-S-R

1998

SUNDAY   MONDAY   TUESDAY   WEDNESDAY   THURSDAY   FRIDAY   SATURDAY

Keep track of important dates

Three beautiful and colorful calendars that celebrate some of the most popular trends in America today.

Look for:

Just Babies—a 16 month calendar that features a full year of absolutely adorable babies!

1998 CALENDAR
Just Babies
16 months of adorable bundles of joy!

Hometown Quilts
1998 *Calendar*
A 16 month quilting extravaganza!

Hometown Quilts—a 16 month calendar featuring quilted art squares, plus a short history on twelve different quilt patterns.

Inspirations—a 16 month calendar with inspiring pictures and quotations.

Inspirations

A 16 month calendar that will lift your spirits and gladden your heart

Steeple Hill™

 HARLEQUIN®

Value priced at $9.99 U.S./$11.99 CAN., these calendars make a perfect gift!

Available in retail outlets in August 1997.   CAL98

Daniel MacGregor is at it again...

New York Times bestselling author

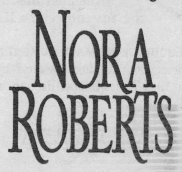

NORA ROBERTS

introduces us to a new generation of MacGregors
as the lovable patriarch of the illustrious MacGregor
clan plays matchmaker again, this time to his three
gorgeous granddaughters in

THE MACGREGOR BRIDES

From Silhouette Books

Don't miss this brand-new continuation of Nora Roberts's
enormously popular *MacGregor* miniseries.

Available November 1997 at your favorite retail outlet.

Silhouette®

Look us up on-line at: http://www.romance.net

NRMB-S

The Stars of Mithra

Three gems, three beauties, three passions... the adventure of a lifetime

SILHOUETTE·INTIMATE·MOMENTS®
brings you a thrilling new series by
New York Times bestselling author

Nora Roberts

Three mystical blue diamonds place three close friends in jeopardy...and lead them to romance.

In October
HIDDEN STAR (IM#811)
Bailey James can't remember a thing, but she knows she's in big trouble. And she desperately needs private investigator Cade Parris to help her live long enough to find out just what kind.

In December
CAPTIVE STAR (IM#823)
Cynical bounty hunter Jack Dakota and spitfire M. J. O'Leary are handcuffed together and on the run from a pair of hired killers. And Jack wants to know why—but M.J.'s not talking.

In February
SECRET STAR (IM#835)
Lieutenant Seth Buchanan's murder investigation takes a strange turn when Grace Fontaine turns up alive. But as the mystery unfolds, he soon discovers the notorious heiress is the biggest mystery of all.

Available at your favorite retail outlet.

Look us up on-line at: http://www.romance.net   MITHRA